THE SHATTERED RITE

BOOK ONE OF THE SIGHTLESS PROPHECY TRILOGY

JAIMIE L. VERMETTE

BLACKTOP PUBLISHING

Cover design by GetCovers.
Chapter art and illustrations by Jaimie L. Vermette.

Published by Blacktop Publishing

First Edition: 2025

ISBNs:

Hardcover: 979-8-9996385-0-2

Paperback: 979-8-9996385-1-9

eBook: 979-8-9996385-2-6

Gloss Edition (Paperback): 979-8-9996385-3-3

Printed in The United States of America

To the only one who's ever brought stillness to the endless movement of my mind.

THE SIGHTLESS PROPHECY

WHEN FLAME WITHDRAWS ITS HALLOWED SPARK,
AND SILENT SKIES NO LONGER MOURN,
THE BLOOD OF WYRM, LONG CAST TO DARK,
SHALL WAKEN CREATURES ONCE FORLORN.
WITH SMOLDERING GAZE THAT SEES NO LIGHT,
AND ASH-BOUND BREATH BENEATH HER TREAD,
SHE BEARS THE WEIGHT OF OATHLESS FLIGHT—
OF BONDS BETRAYED, OF DRAGONS BLED.
FROM SHATTERED LINE AND FIRE'S DISGRACE,
THE FLAME SHALL STIR, THE THRONE UNMAKE.
HER SHADOW LOOMS WHERE SILENCE ACHES—
AND RUIN WALKS, OR HOPE SHALL WAKE.

Prologue

The Flame That Chooses

Before the first crown was forged, before sky-bound beasts darkened the sun, there was only the Flame.

And when the Flame dims, the land must choose.

For the Flame is no mere fire, but the gods' will made flesh of light—an ancient, sentient force, watching and waiting.

When the realm's magic wanes, when thrones fracture and kingdoms rot from within, the gods do not send saviors. They summon trials.

The Trials of Sovereignty are not the work of kings or councils, but the decree of silent gods—speaking only in fire and ruin, never in mercy. When corruption festers in the bones of a kingdom and unrest poisons its crown, the gods awaken, and the trials stir in the dark beneath the citadel.

Each era's trials are different:

Oaths carved into flesh with blades of obsidian.

Duels fought blindfolded atop bridges of bone swaying over molten rivers.

Hunts through labyrinths built from the ribcages of dead titans, where the walls still breathe.

They come like a storm at the end of an age—merciless, inevitable, and always demanding blood.

Whatever form they take, they end the same way: with a crown of flame, and the bearer of it.

Mercy has no place in the god's design; only survival and the ruin it demands.

Once—two centuries past—a warrior rose among the chosen.

He bore no noble name. No prophecy favored him.

But he knew one truth: if the trials tested the worthy, then to win them, he had only to make sure he stood alone.

And so he carved a path of blood, not glory.

One by one, he murdered the others.

He fed lies to the kind and steel blades to the strong.

He did not win the trials—he erased all others who might.

When the last fire was lit and the last soul slain, the Flame had no choice.

It crowned him Sovereign.

Now, his magic flickers like a dying torch. His breath rattles with unseen rot. And he knows the trials will rise.

But again, he is ready with a plan.

He sends a shadow.

Not a competitor. Not a name drawn from flame.

A phantom. A blade hidden in the folds of fate.

An assassin with no past and no cause but the Sovereign's will.

He will walk beside the contenders.

He will befriend.

He will remove.

One by one, quietly, until the field is cleared once again.

All but one.

The Sovereign leans forward on his throne, bones aching beneath opulent threads.

Below, the assassin kneels in silence—a ghost in the shape of a man.

"You know of the prophecy," the Sovereign murmurs.

His voice rasps but carries the weight of a tested blade. "The Flame whispers of a Dragonrider. A child of ash. A name without sight. One who will rise not through bloodshed, but through something older. Something forgotten."

He spits.

"Blindness dressed as vision. Mercy dressed as power. Fool's fire."

He stands with effort, towering over the silent killer.

"I want her alive long enough for the world to see her rise."

He steps down from the dais, takes the assassin's face in one withered, calloused hand.

"Then I want her broken."

A smile, cruel and thin.

"Let her fall screaming from the back of the last dragon if she dares to take flight. Let her bones teach the people what comes of hope."

The assassin gives no reply.

He turns. Disappears into the shadows.

Far from the dying throne, in a vale beaten hollow by unending winds, a girl marked by prophecy dreams of wings to carry her beyond ruin, and of flames that whisper her name as they rise to swallow the sky.

And the ancient gods watch.

Chapter 1: Called by Flame

"The Flame answers not to time, but to thread. What has been woven must one day burn." —Spoken Legend, Dragonrider Chronicles

Long before Eliryn drew her first breath, the prophecy had already claimed her. By the time she was old enough to feel its pull, magic was dying—and so was her sight.

The scent of wild herbs and fresh earth filled the cottage, wrapping around Eliryn like a memory she didn't want to forget. The aroma carried more than comfort—it carried history. These were the same herbs her mother had crushed into poultices when

Eliryn scraped her knees as a child, the same bundles that once hung in her cradle to "keep the dark dreams out." Her mother had said that in the old days, dragonriders carried these herbs in their saddlebags, a charm against the cold above the clouds.

She sat by the window—though "seeing" was a word she used loosely now. What vision she had left was dimmed, more suggestion than sight. The outlines of the world slipped through her grasp like smoke. She could make out the light shifting against the wall, the shadow of a branch moving in the wind, but never enough to feel certain of anything she saw.

Her fingers traced the smooth curve of a salve jar. The cool clay steadied her, grounding her in the moment, even as the rest of her began to unravel. Her mother had made this jar years ago, clay pulled from the riverbank in a spring flood. "It will last longer than I will," she had said with a smile at the time. Eliryn hadn't understood the weight of those words back then.

Outside, the village stirred with tension. Voices rose in anxious clusters, feet shuffled along the packed-dirt paths. The trials were nearly upon them, and the air buzzed with fear thinly disguised as preparation. Somewhere, a cartwheel rattled over cobblestones, and she imagined faces tight with suspicion, eyes quick to slide away from the cottage if they happened to glance this direction.

"Why me?" she whispered, not to be answered. It wasn't the first time she'd asked. It never felt any less hollow.

A wooden board creaked behind her, the familiar weight of her mother's step. "They believe it's a death sentence," her voice cracked gently, "but I see more than they ever could."

Eliryn didn't turn, but her shoulders lowered, just slightly. The words were familiar—too familiar. Her mother had been telling her she was "meant for more" since she was old enough to sit at the table and listen to bedtime stories. But they had never felt real enough to hold on to.

"You've said that before," Eliryn murmured. "I used to think it was just... comfort."

Her mother crossed the room, the scent of lavender and pine drifting with her. She settled beside Eliryn, one hand finding hers. "It's more than comfort, Eliryn. I've seen it. The prophecy has been waiting for its thread to be pulled. I knew before you even drew your first breath."

Eliryn said nothing. Her thumb rubbed slow circles against the back of her mother's knuckles.

"Our line carries gifts," her mother continued softly. "You know that. Dragonrider blood did not vanish just because the dragons did. But sometimes, gifts bloom in strange ways."

A tired smile tugged at Eliryn's lips. "You get visions of the future, and I get blindness. Honestly? I feel robbed."

Her mother chuckled—dry but warm. Eliryn hated that it still comforted her. "The blood always balances itself. Your sight is fading, yes. But that only means you're meant to see in other ways."

"Is that one of your visions?" Eliryn asked, only half-teasing.

"No," her mother said, more quietly now. "That's a mother's knowing. The prophecy came to me long before you were born. I saw a girl with a pendant of black stone and a name spoken in fire. A rider without sight. The last hope for the realm's magic."

That stopped Eliryn. She turned her head slightly, as if it helped her see her mother more clearly.

"I've always known you were meant for more than this village," her mother went on, voice barely above a whisper now. "Even when the dragons fell silent and magic began to wither, I knew. The night you were born, the stars paused in their dance. Even the moon leaned closer, like she wanted to see you for herself. The air smelled of rain though the skies were clear—that's how the old ones said destiny announced itself."

A long silence stretched between them, soft and heavy like snowfall. Eliryn thought of the old tales her mother used to tell—of skies lit with fire as great wings blotted out the sun, of magic flowing in every river and root, and of the day that magic began to die. She remembered believing those stories as a child, before the first hints of darkness clouded her vision, before she learned that her bloodline's name was spoken with suspicion.

"When the Flame chose me," Eliryn said at last, "I didn't doubt it. Not even for a breath."

She paused, the weight of memory pressing against her ribs.

"I felt it... like something ancient stirring in my bones. At that moment, I knew you'd been telling the truth. About all of it."

Her mother didn't speak, but her silence said enough. It always had.

"I didn't want to believe you before," Eliryn continued, voice cracking. "Because if the prophecy was real... then so was the ending. Your ending."

She finally turned her face toward her mother fully, searching the blurry edges for something solid to hold onto. "I think part of me kept pretending you'd be wrong, just this once."

Her mother's hand slid to her cheek, warm and certain. "I hoped I would be. But the gods don't let us choose the path. Only how we walk it."

Eliryn closed her eyes, pressing her face into her mother's palm like a child again.

And for a moment, there was no prophecy, no trials, no fading sight—just the space between two heartbeats, shared.

"I'll grieve you forever," she whispered.

"No," her mother said. "You'll carry me forward. That's different."

———◦◦◦———

The wind had teeth that night.

It howled through the cracks in the cottage walls, rattling the shelves and shaking the herb bundles strung above the hearth. Sprigs of sage, thyme, and dried starflower quivered in the draft like they were shivering, shedding tiny flakes of brittle petals. The chimney whispered in a voice too old to remember its own words, a low, steady hum that seemed to carry secrets.

Eliryn couldn't sit still. She paced the length of the hearth like a trapped bird—short, quick steps, fingers flexing at her sides. The fire crackled low, casting restless shadows across the stone floor that leapt and fell like they were trying to escape.

Her mother sat in her chair, silent. Watching—not with her eyes, which had long since turned inward, but with that strange, weighty awareness she'd carried for as long as Eliryn could remember.

"I should go instead," Eliryn said for the third time. Her voice felt sharp against the quiet. "I can handle the forge. I can—"

"No," her mother said, gently but with finality. "They spit on our doorstep yesterday. You think they'd stop at words if they caught you out alone?"

"They won't help you either," Eliryn snapped. "Not gladly. Not without cruelty."

A silence stretched between them. Heavy. Familiar.

It reminded Eliryn of countless evenings before this one—her mother staring into the fire after a vision, her lips pressed thin, her gaze somewhere far beyond the walls.

"They won't have to help," her mother said at last. "I've bartered what I need. The forge is old, but the armor is sound. Dented, maybe. But strong."

Eliryn turned sharply toward her. "Ma—"

"We both know," her mother cut in, voice steady, quiet. "This is how it's meant to go."

That silenced her. Because they did both know.

Her mother had been preparing for this night long before Eliryn realized it. Little things, hidden in plain sight: keeping the black pendant polished, showing Eliryn how to braid dragonrider knots into her hair, and the stories—always the stories. Tales of the Flame's choosing, of sovereigns forged in trial, of the Sightless Prophecy whispered in ages past.

It happened often—her mother waking in the middle of the night, sweat-soaked and shaking, whispering truths she could scarcely bear to speak aloud. Her own death, painted in fractured glimpses: blood, cold iron, and Eliryn's arms catching her as the world slipped away.

And after the vision of her death came the other vision, the one that tied it all together: the prophecy. Eliryn's future braided with fire and ash. A rider without sight. A name spoken by the Flame.

Eliryn had tried not to believe. She had told herself that her mother's visions were only dreams, or else mistakes in the reading. Because if the prophecy was real, then so was the ending.

But the moment her name had burned in light above the square, something in her had settled. A gravity, as if a door she hadn't realized was closed had swung wide—and locked behind her.

So now here they were. On the edge of that ending.

"You could run," Eliryn whispered. "We could both run. Take the pendant. Leave the trials behind."

Her mother smiled, tired and sad and a little proud. "The Flame would find you again. And you'd go anyway. Because it's in you, Eliryn. The blood. The call. You've already started to hear it."

Eliryn thought of the quiet moments in recent months—how the wind sometimes carried voices she couldn't quite make out, how the hum in her pendant deepened when she stood near the ridge. She had chalked it up to imagination. But maybe... maybe not.

She sank into the seat beside her mother, pressing her temple to her shoulder.

"Maybe I would have," she murmured. "But not without you."

Her mother's hand came to rest over her own. Thin. Weathered. Steady.

"You won't be without me," she said softly. "Not ever. When the dragons flew, riders carried the spirits of those who came before them. You'll carry me the same way."

The wind outside moaned against the door like a warning.

Her mother stood slowly, joints stiff, wincing as she pressed her hands to her lower back. "It's time."

Eliryn rose too, trembling. "Stay until dawn," she said. "You don't have to leave just yet."

"I wish I could."

They looked at each other for a long moment.

Then her mother reached out and clasped the pendant around Eliryn's neck—fingers lingering on the stone.

"This will burn, before the end," she said. "Don't be afraid of where it leads you."

Eliryn huffed—just barely. "That's not ominous at all, thanks."

The door creaked open. The wind swept in—biting and wild.

Neither of them said goodbye.

Because they had already mourned what was coming.

The house was too quiet.

The hearth had burned down to coals, their glow a faint, uneven heartbeat in the dark. Shadows pooled in the corners, thick and unmoving, as if the air itself had forgotten how to stir. Outside, the wind carried the brittle hush of pre-dawn—a silence not born of peace, but of waiting.

Eliryn sat alone at the wooden table, her legs curled beneath her, spine pressed against the chair back as though holding herself upright took too much effort. Her skin prickled despite the fire's warmth, like even her body knew her mother wasn't coming back.

Sleep hadn't even tried to find her. Each moment felt like a thread pulling taut, drawing tighter and tighter toward a knot she could not untangle.

Her mother had walked out into the dark nearly four hours ago. She should've been back by now. But Eliryn knew—they both knew—that she wouldn't return whole.

Their village, Lirin's Edge, was small, poor, and bitter. The kind of place where the wind always smelled of woodsmoke and damp stone, where joy came hard-won and never without cost. The healers lived on the outskirts, past the cobbled square and down the slope of the ridge—close enough to be summoned, but far enough to be forgotten.

People whispered about them. It was said their blood was touched by something old. That their ancestors had once called dragons from the clouds and spoke in tongues older than the Flame. That when the dragons vanished, so too did the dragonriders' purpose.

Now, the villagers said the legacy had curdled. That the bloodline had soured.

Half-souled. Strange.

And Eliryn? She was the worst of them. At least, that's what they said. She'd stopped caring—mostly.

Magic itself was dying, and the world had started to turn on it. Powers once praised as gifts were now called curses. Creatures of legend had become nothing more than fading sketches in old books. In Lirin's Edge, the change could be seen in small, cruel ways: the fireflies that no longer glowed in midsummer, the orchard's frostward charms failing so fruit spoiled early, the village well losing its taste of mineral-sweet water. Even the herb bundles above their hearth didn't hold their strength as they once had; remedies her mother swore would heal now only dulled the pain.

Sometimes, Eliryn wondered if her own failing sight was part of it—another symptom of magic's slow death. If her vision and whatever power ran in her veins were bound together like twins, both snuffed out by the same wind. No one could tell her for certain, and no one tried.

Her blindness had begun before she was sixteen.

A girl whose eyes dimmed too soon, who drifted into thoughts too deep, who asked questions no one wanted to answer. A decade of whispers and turned backs had followed. She'd learned to live in the margins, to keep her head down when the stares lingered too long, to let their pity and suspicion slide off her skin like raindrops. The world had decided she was meant to fade quietly.

And then came the Flame.

Not just in Lirin's Edge, but everywhere. At dawn, without warning, a pillar of flame erupted in the village square. No smoke. No heat. Just light—tall and golden, rising as if summoned by nothing but silence.

In its center, a name began to form.

Eliryn's name.

In the square, beneath the gaze of every skeptic and stranger, her fate had been spoken—not as a request, not as a question, but as a command written in fire.

She'd stood there like a statue, her heart pounding loud enough to drown out the world. "Maybe they spelled it wrong," she'd almost whispered, absurdly, as her name blazed in gold.

The villagers had stared. Not in awe. Not in pride. In fear.

No one spoke. Not even a breath.

Because when the Flame chose, it did not ask permission. It reached through time and blood, through myth and marrow. It saw things people no longer remembered how to see.

In other villages, the chosen were lifted on shoulders—warriors, scholars, wardens of noble houses.

But in Lirin's Edge, they looked away.

As if by not meeting her eyes, they could pretend the fire had spoken someone else's name.

Now, Eliryn traced the edge of the black pendant at her throat.

Smooth as river stone. Cold once, but now warm against her skin. She had worn it since childhood—a relic, she'd thought, from a line of women too proud to admit their legacy had crumbled into myth. But lately, it had begun to hum.

Not with sound. Not even magic, not exactly.

More like a weight. A rhythm.

As if it were waiting.

Her mother said it was one of the old gifts—passed down the bloodline, awakening only when the soul was ready. "When the stone burns in your hand, the path will open," she'd told her once.

She said it would show her the truth, when the time came.

Eliryn wasn't sure if that sounded like a promise or a threat.

"The Flame doesn't just choose power," her mother had said. "It chooses those bound to a thread. And yours is wrapped around something vast. Something old. We were dragonriders once, Eliryn. Our blood remembers. And one day, the world will remember with it."

Eliryn hadn't believed her—not fully. But the moment the Flame carved her name in gold, something inside her had stirred. A gravity she couldn't shake.

She remembered the look in her mother's eyes that morning, a quiet sorrow resting just behind the pride.

And now, in the flickering hush of this house, with the fire gutted low and dawn pressing at the windows, all that knowing sat like a stone in her throat.

She'd thought grief came after. Apparently, it liked arriving early.

She felt it now—slow and raw—gnawing at the edges of her resolve. She kept listening for the door, for footsteps, for her mother's voice calling out in the dark.

But the only sound was the wind.

And in it, somewhere far off, she thought she heard a whisper.

Not words. Never words.

Just the sense that something was watching. Something vast. Ancient. Waiting.

Eliryn closed her fingers tighter around the pendant.

And she waited, too.

Chapter 2: By Blood and Bond

"To mourn is to tether the living to the dead, weaving bonds that neither time nor death can sever." —Spoken legend of the Flamebound

A noise at the door finally came, much later than it should have.

Eliryn ran, already knowing.

She flung the door open—and the world tipped sideways.

Her mother collapsed into her arms, dead weight and the stink of blood flooding the air. Crimson streaked down her face and arms in thick, uneven rivulets, dark as spilled ink. The battered silver armor—etched with curling, half-forgotten sigils—slid from her shoulders and hit the floor with a sound that was almost human.

"I got it," her mother rasped, breath hitching in jagged bursts. "They said... we should be grateful. Grateful to give you... a chance at greatness."

"No. No, no, no." Eliryn eased her down onto the floorboards, her hands moving on instinct, healer's training overriding the panic clawing at her ribs. Fingers swept along limbs, pressing for breaks, for heat. Her brow was split, shallow. The left arm hung wrong—fractured. But that wasn't what froze her blood.

It was the sound in her chest.

A wet, rattling inhale. A bubbling exhale.

Lungs filling with blood.

She dragged her closer to the hearth, desperate for light, for warmth that might anchor her to the living. "Stay with me, Ma. Tell me what happened. Did they—?"

Her mother's mouth twitched into something that might've been a smile if it hadn't been smeared with blood. "Didn't like that I haggled too well. Thought a cursed healer should pay in more than coin."

Eliryn's hands shook so badly she could barely grind the goldenroot and frostblossom between her fingers. "I can fix this. I can slow the bleeding, bind your chest, draw the fluid—"

"Shh," her mother whispered, her voice fraying like old cloth. "You know it's past saving."

"Stop." The word came out sharper than she meant. "Just let me try."

Her mother's eyes softened, shining with something that wasn't just pain. Peace. Resignation. "This was always the way it would go."

Eliryn's throat closed. "You saw it. Before the nightmares came."

Her mother didn't deny it. "You think I didn't try to change it? That I didn't beg the vision to shift?"

Eliryn's laugh came out cracked and empty. "Then beg harder. There's still time."

"Some truths," her mother murmured, "stay fixed."

"I didn't want to believe it," Eliryn whispered. "Not until the Flame chose me. And then I knew. I felt it in my bones, in my blood. I just didn't want it to be real because... because if it was—"

Her voice splintered.

Her mother cupped her cheek with blood-slick fingers. "Then I would die. Yes. I know, my firefly. I've known for years."

The world narrowed to heat and her mother's pulse under her palm—slowing, slipping. Eliryn tried to speak but nothing came.

"You have her spirit," her mother said, voice paper-thin. "Your grandmother's. Stubborn as stormlight. Gentle as smoke."

"I don't want her spirit," Eliryn choked. "I want you."

"There's more waiting for you," her mother breathed. "He waits for you. The bond. You'll know it when it comes. You'll feel it like a second heartbeat."

"He—?" Eliryn's brow furrowed, but her mother's eyes were already drifting, glassing over, seeing something beyond the rafters and firelight.

"Trust the bond when it comes," she murmured. "And never mistake kindness... for love."

Her chest stilled. Her fingers slipped from Eliryn's cheek.

Silence.

Eliryn pressed her ear to her mother's ribs, straining for even the faintest whisper of breath.

Nothing.

"No," she whispered, shaking her. "No, no, no—"

The hearth spat a spark. Somewhere outside, the wind rattled the shutters. But in here, the world had gone still.

And Eliryn knew—whatever came next, she would never be the same.

The world didn't end with her mother's last breath. But it did pause—like the moment between thunder and its echo, stretched so thin it hummed in her bones.

Eliryn knelt in that hush for what felt like hours, her forehead pressed to her mother's shoulder, her palms sticky with blood cooling too fast. The armor lay beside them, dim and waiting, a silent witness to the final chapter of a woman who should have worn it in her prime.

Not a warrior in the eyes of the village. But in her daughter's eyes?

A legend.

When at last Eliryn rose, the pendant at her throat burned with quiet heat, the warmth of a presence that had not left with her mother's breath. Not comfort. But... *awareness*. As if something now stirred fully awake, no longer dormant.

She almost tore it off. Almost. But instead, she clenched her fist around it until her palm stung.

She moved through the house in silence, each step guided by memory and the press of grief. She cleaned her mother's wounds with gentle hands, as she had done for countless others.

"I'm sorry," she whispered, over and over. She wasn't sure what she was apologizing for.

Eliryn dressed her in a linen shift, simple but clean. She chose the cloak her grandmother once wore—the one her mother kept folded at the back of the trunk, always too sacred for use, too heavy with stories.

She braided her mother's graying hair with careful fingers, weaving in the sacred threads:

Gold, for strength handed down.

Red, for sacrifice given freely.

Green, for truths no tongue can tell.

She bound the braid with a worn strip of leather, torn from the very satchel her grandmother once carried into war. Three generations of hands had touched that leather. Three generations of women who bore fire in their blood and stayed silent through their grief.

She placed ember nests with care—one near the window, one beneath the hearth, and one at the door. Each one a promise: this home would not be left for strangers to tear apart.

The rites for the honored dead required more than mourning.

They required *remembrance*.

They required *fire*.

She built a pyre from stormwood logs her mother had saved for a midwinter feast.

Stormwood logs. Her mother's "no point hoarding good fire" stacked neatly for a feast that would never happen. Eliryn thought it fitting. If death had to come, let it come cloaked in warmth and old laughter.

She made the pyre on the small altar they had inside their cabin, set with wild herbs—*lavender, juniper, dragonspine root*—and laid the family crest etched in soft wood atop her mother's chest.

And when all was ready, she stood beside the pyre and tilted her head back.

Then she sang.

Her throat caught halfway through, but she forced the sound out anyway. The song wasn't meant to sound pretty. It was meant to hurt. It was a song for the fallen—the warriors and dreamers who died with purpose in their mouths and fire in their lungs. Her people's song. Her mother's.

It tore through her like a storm, untamed and unbound, casting echoes that rang like warnings across the silence.

When the final note broke apart in her chest, from somewhere far beyond the trees, beyond the veil between what was and what would be—

Something breathed her name.

Eliryn opened her eyes.

The pendant at her neck pulsed once. Then twice.

It was almost time.

The world was still gray—not the blind kind of gray that clouded her eyes now, but the kind that came just before the sun crested the world. The kind that promised nothing, but left room for everything.

She moved through the house like a ghost, touching every surface. The basin by the door. The crack in the windowsill. The hearth where the last of the embers slept in silence. She didn't need to see clearly in the dim light to know they were there.

She washed quickly, in silence. Her hands stung in the cold water. She didn't notice at first; grief numbed more than just her fingers. She took her hair roughly in hand and braided it tightly. A warrior's braid. Her mother's braid.

The armor came next.

Piece by piece, she dressed. Bracers. Greaves. Chestplate. The sigil over her heart—a dragon's eye shadowed by a starburst—was nearly worn smooth. Her mother had fought for this. Bled for this. Died so Eliryn could wear it not in shame, but in *truth*.

The pendant she did not remove.

She tucked it under the armor, against her skin.

It beat now in rhythm with her heart.

When she reached the door, her hand paused on the carving in the frame. The old family words, carved long before Eliryn was born:

By Blood and Bond, We Prevail.

She bowed her head to it. Then opened the door.

The wind met her, cold and impersonal. Behind her, the house was full of ghosts and ash. Ahead of her, the road.

Her mother's voice echoed in her mind: *"Your eyes may fail you. But your soul will always know the way."*

With a deep breath, she stepped into the light with clouded eyes and steady feet.

Her vision made it harder to grasp. Shadows blended. Colors warped. Still, the center of her gaze held some clarity—fleeting, like water slipping through her fingers.

The steady fog that once hovered at the corners of her sight had begun to encroach. Faces blurred. Landmarks softened. Even voices sometimes felt sharper than what her eyes could give her.

But she had learned to move through uncertainty.

She lifted her chin and steadied her breath.

Then came the hoofbeats.

Not rushed. Not loud. Just steady—four beats pressing into the earth like a summons.

Three riders appeared at the edge of the village, cloaked in ash-colored wool, their armor dulled with wear. Their sigils were visible even in the distance: a crown cracked clean through, encircled by tongues of fire.

Guards for the Trials of Sovereignty.

She turned on her heel, with a speed born of certainty, and rushed back into the house one final time.

She lit the first ember nest beneath the window. The second near the hearth. The third at the threshold.

The fire caught fast.

As the smoke thickened and the beams began to groan, Eliryn stepped outside, closing the door behind her with quiet finality. The blooming heat pulsed against her back, swelling with each breath.

It felt wrong, leaving her mother behind.

But Eliryn couldn't afford to be sentimental. Not anymore. That part of her burned too.

She stepped down from the doorway and stood tall, her hands clenched tight behind her back. Every muscle was a taut string. Every breath, measured.

She had no intention of breaking—no matter how they looked at her. Weak. Quiet. The healer's daughter. The one too frail to carry the weight of her family's lost legacy.

The villagers gathered, but not for her. They lined the dirt path like ghosts, speaking in hushed voices. No farewells. No blessings. No offerings.

Their silence said enough.

Eliryn kept her chin high anyway. Let them think what they wanted.

Her throat tightened with unease, but she swallowed it down.

She turned toward the waiting riders. They hadn't moved. Still as stone, as though they had always been there.

She took a breath.

One step.

Then another.

Ashes curled into the morning air. Behind her, the roof collapsed with a hiss of sparks.

Each step took her farther from the only home she'd ever known.

Closer to the ancient purpose that had waited lifetimes to claim her.

Chapter 3: The Weight of Smoke

"Fate doesn't knock. It drags you by the bones." —Caelen Vorr, last rider of the Hollow Watch

Eliryn didn't speak. Not when the guards arrived, not when the villagers watched from alongside the dirt path, afraid to meet her eyes. Her breath fogged in the morning chill, shallow and controlled.

One of the riders dismounted as she neared—boots sinking slightly into the frost-hardened earth. His movements were smooth and practiced, like someone who had collected many things in his life: taxes, criminals, unwilling trial chosen. His armor was scuffed but polished, marked by long travel but worn with obvious pride.

His face was stark against the pale morning—sharp cheekbones, a dark braid looped over one shoulder, and a narrow scar splitting his bottom lip. He looked at her the way someone might study the edge of a blade—curious, not yet impressed.

His eyes lingered on hers. Not with sympathy. But recognition. Noticing the strange, blind fog that coated her irises—and the distaste she did not try to hide behind them.

"So," he said. His voice was rough but even, like gravel under snow. "This is what the Flame has chosen."

She said nothing.

Another rider, still mounted, gave a laugh—dry and cruel. "She'll last just long enough to die in the depths of the citadel. The only mark she'll ever leave."

Eliryn didn't flinch. Her jaw tightened, just enough to ache, but she'd heard worse from her own village.

"Lead the way," she said.

That caught them. Both of them, for just a beat. The first rider's brows lifted slightly, as if measuring her again with new information. The second gave a snort but didn't answer otherwise.

The third rider didn't speak at all.

He remained still, hood drawn low, horse perfectly motionless beneath him. His presence was unnerving—not just silent, but *absent*. As though he took up space without belonging to it. Eliryn couldn't sense his attention outright, yet she felt watched.

Without a word, the first rider turned and gestured toward a fourth horse—tethered quietly behind the others. A compact, dark-coated mare with intelligent eyes. Her breath curled into the cold air like smoke, and she stood completely still as Eliryn approached.

No blessing. No words. Just the mare, waiting like a sentence handed down. Eliryn swung onto the saddle anyway.

Her fingers closed over the reins like memory—tight, but certain. Her mother had taught her well, even if her body had never left the village. She could feel the strength of the mare beneath her, the low hum of anticipation in its bones.

Behind them, her house was already burning.

The ember nests she'd laid—dried root-cloth, oil-soaked bark, birdflame twigs—caught fast. Smoke billowed upward in thick gray tendrils. The thatch had fallen in. She could hear the last groans of the beams as they collapsed.

The first rider paused to glance back. "What kind of girl burns her house down before she leaves?" he muttered—not to her. Not to anyone.

The second rider sneered. "The kind who doesn't come back."

She let the silence answer for her.

What kind of girl burns her house down?

The kind who can't afford to look back.

The road out of Lirin's Edge passed quiet, shuttered homes. Smoke coiled into the sky, dark against the pale dawn. Silence accompanied the riders as they traveled forward.

They made no conversation.

By the time they stopped near a bend in the forest road, night had fallen in earnest. A fire was lit before Eliryn had the chance to dismount from her mare. The others gathered close to the heat, muttering in clipped phrases, inspecting weapons and saddles. Eliryn stood at the edge of the firelight, unsure if she was meant to join them, if that would even be allowed.

The silent rider approached.

He moved without sound. Not even his armor gave him away. He extended a blanket toward her, and she took it, their fingers brushing.

A chill went up her spine.

"Thank you," she said quietly.

His voice came so softly, it could have been mistaken for wind through leaves.

"You don't ask questions," he said.

Eliryn blinked. "Would you answer them?"

A long pause.

"No," he admitted, but without cruelty.

She almost smiled. Almost. But that felt like too much, tonight. "Then we understand each other."

He didn't reply with words, but the smallest shift in his expression suggested amusement. He moved away like a shadow drawn back toward the trees.

Later, when two of the guards murmured among themselves, Eliryn sat alone. She kept her ears open. Not just to what they said, but to what they didn't. No names. Not even once.

The woods whispered behind her. Something cracked softly underfoot.

She hated how her voice cracked. Hated that she asked at all. "Someone there?"

Silence. *Of course there's no answer. That would make things easy.*

He was there again. The third rider. Watching. Always watching.

When a venomous crawler darted toward her, she flinched at the sudden thud of a stone. She never saw it die—she only heard the crack of bone, smelled the metallic tang of something broken. Her stomach flipped. She hated that, too.

That night, she dreamed—of wind and voice and presence too large for shape. She woke gasping, the pendant branding heat into her sternum. She tore it out from under her armor, clutching it in her fists until her knuckles turned white. A perfect ring of melted frost had formed around her bedroll.

The others said nothing. But their eyes lingered too long.

By the next afternoon, the towers of the capital broke across the horizon. The road beneath them seemed to pulse, as if something ancient stirred far beneath its stone spine.

They passed a black-liveried wagon going the other way.

"Royal physician's crest," the scarred rider muttered.

"Strange time to run," said the cruel one.

"Strange time for everything. First the call. Next the culling."

Eliryn stayed silent. But the words coiled somewhere low in her stomach, heavy as stone.

By nightfall, the city swallowed them in stone and shadow.

And somewhere far below it all, something old stirred.

Waiting.

And whispering her name.

Eliryn clenched her jaw and told herself it was the wind.

CHAPTER 4: THE CITADEL

"Trust no throne whose walls were built by silence."
—Sayings of the Wandering Flame

The gates of Vireth opened with a sound like a sigh—old wood groaning against iron, heavy with the weight of forgotten oaths. No herald greeted them, no fanfare. Only the measured clatter of hooves on worn stone, and the silent watch of sentries tucked into shadowed battlements above.

Eliryn sat straighter in the saddle as they passed beneath the arch. The cold hadn't lessened, though the sun now hung high and weak behind gauzy clouds. She blinked hard, trying to focus. Light and shadow flickered oddly across her vision—no longer distinct shapes, only drifting impressions. Smears of color. Echoes of what should be. The road below pulsed like wet ink; the sky above was a smear of ash-white.

Her knuckles whitened. She tried to loosen her grip. Failed. Her body wasn't listening anymore.

Her body knew how to feel the road's slope, the shift of terrain, the tremor of danger near. But here, inside the city walls, that knowing faltered. The ground was too even. The air too still. It felt... muted.

The streets were empty. Swept clean as bone. No merchants. No children. No curious eyes peeking from behind curtains. The shutters were nailed shut. Flags hung limp, colorless in the dim air. Even the wind passed carefully here, as though afraid of waking something.

None of the guards spoke. Even the second rider had long since run out of jeers. The city itself seemed to smother speech. Eliryn told herself it was just fear. Old stone didn't smother people. It didn't watch.

Then again, she'd just learned that pretending something wasn't real didn't make it less dangerous.

They passed under archways that grew older and taller with each bend in the path. Statues watched them from above—winged things, faceless kings, cloaked warriors without names. She couldn't see their expressions. She didn't need to. The weight of their gaze was enough.

The first rider led them forward with a seasoned calm, drawing them toward the citadel perched at the city's heart. Eliryn couldn't see its full shape—only slanted walls and the glint of spires like spears against the pale sky. Her mare shifted nervously beneath her, hooves tapping a faster rhythm. She placed a hand to the horse's neck, steadying it with a whisper.

Her stomach twisted. The saddle felt safer than standing.

The road behind had become *familiar*. The wary watch of the first rider. The venomous barbs from the second. And the third, always present just beyond sight, moving like a thought half-swallowed. She didn't know them—but she knew their rhythm.

What waited inside was *unknown*.

When her boots finally met stone, she felt it: the break. The shift. The world rethreaded itself the moment her feet touched ground.

The horses were led away without ceremony, the citadel seemingly swallowing them without a sound.

Inside, sconces of cold witchlight lined the walls, casting pale blue fire that made depth vanish. No echoes. No warmth. Even her footsteps felt like an intrusion.

A woman emerged from the shadows—tall, robed, unmoved. Her hair pale, her mouth thinner than judgment. Eliryn couldn't see her clearly, but the shape of her attention was razor-sharp.

"So," the woman said, her tone bored, "the final chosen. Late, but not lost."

A low snort behind her. The second rider, no doubt. The woman silenced it with a flick of her fingers.

"There were no problems," the first rider said, voice clipped.

The woman gave a single nod and turned her gaze back to Eliryn. "I imagine not."

"I'm ready," Eliryn said, trying not to sound too small.

"Not quite yet," the woman replied, almost gently. "There's an order to these things; a written way of progression."

Eliryn frowned. But before she could ask about what the written way was, a guard approached. Silent. With cuffs.

"What are those for?" she asked, voice low.

"Formality," the woman said. "Even our chosen guests must be... *contained*."

The first rider did not speak.

The second looked *too* pleased.

Her stomach dropped so fast she almost swayed. Then, before she could think too long, she extended her wrists. Slowly. Quietly.

Pretending she had a choice was easier than admitting she didn't.

The cuffs clicked closed. Cold and deceptively light. Not tight, not painful—but the moment the metal kissed her skin, something shifted inside her. A pressure formed behind her eyes.

She gasped—and hated herself for allowing the sound.

The woman's expression didn't change. But her eyes lingered on Eliryn's face just a second too long.

"You'll be taken to the Hall of Holding. The others have arrived. You'll meet them soon."

The *others*.

The word fell hard.

A new guard took her by the arm. No words. Just pressure and motion. They moved through quiet corridors where even the glass windows glowed faintly with enchantment—colored panes casting blurred light across the stone. Beneath her boots, the floor vibrated faintly. A heartbeat. A *pulse*. The citadel was alive in ways that had nothing to do with people's presence.

She didn't look back until the corridor curved. Then, just once, she turned.

The guards still stood in the archway. Not watching her. Speaking fervently, heads ducked together, they were unconcerned with her departure.

The hallway narrowed. The air cooled further. Her skin itched where the cuffs had been, but the sense of presence lingered—not the guard beside her, and not anyone near. Somewhere else. Above, perhaps. Behind. The crown must have eyes within the stone.

At last, the corridor opened.

The Hall of Holding.

The emptiness felt heavier than walls, like standing inside a throat about to swallow. The floor was a mirror of black stone. The ceiling stretched up and away into darkness, too high for torches, too tall for echoes. Moonlight—or its illusion—poured down in ribbons, washing everything in silver and blue.

At its center stood a ring of carved pillars, each one etched with symbols that stirred something in her bones. Things half-remembered. Shapes from firelit stories. Impressions from dreams she couldn't name.

Figures lingered at the chamber's edges. Shadowy. Unfamiliar. Some seated, some pacing, some whispering beneath their breath like coiled serpents.

The guard gestured her toward a stone bench. She sat straighter than she felt. If they wanted to watch her, let them. She wouldn't curl in on herself. Not here. She let her wrists rest lightly on her knees, and let her head tilt ever so slightly. Not bowed. Not submissive. Just... *listening*.

No one came near.

Snatches of conversation drifted through the quiet.

"...from the coast, I think. The Virean lilt."

"Doesn't matter. The trials will break her."

"...one of us is twin-born. If that's true..."

Names were more than just scarce, no one used them at all. Not even in gossip. That absence unsettled her more than any spell. An old warning from her mother returned: "*Never speak your name into strange air, Eliryn. You don't know who's listening—or what.*"

She shifted. Tuned her hearing to footfalls. One paced with a limp. Another had the clipped step of someone used to command. One wore silk—rich and whispering. And one—*someone*—breathed with her. Matched her every move.

Not hostile. Not friendly. Just... *aware.*

The cuffs had ceased their glow, but their influence remained. Eliryn now knew how false her mother's description of magic had been—magic didn't feel like fire or light.

It felt like pressure. Like being *held down.* And Eliryn hated being held down.

A sound broke the stillness—a deep, resonant *boom* as a door opened far across the chamber. No one raised their voice. No one moved.

A figure entered.

Robes of silver and dusk, layered like smoke. No crown. No medals. Only a pendant of twisted crystal and rings of bone and obsidian. His eyes were the color of old storms and his presence instantly filled the room.

"The Steward of Trials," someone whispered.

The steward walked to the center. Turned. Looked at each of them in turn. When his eyes reached Eliryn, they *stayed*—just long enough to register her, just short of giving her meaning. She couldn't help feeling small under his gaze.

"You stand in the Hall of Holding," he said. His voice was soft, but it carried. "You were chosen. Not for what you are—but for what you may yet become."

A pause.

"But do not mistake the trials for a game."

Another pause. Longer.

"No spellwork. No names. No way out other than death."

That final word echoed when he spoke it, more so than the others. *Death.*

"You will remain here until dawn. No food will be given. No comfort offered. Let your hunger teach you discipline. Let your fear sharpen your mind."

He raised his hand. The cuffs shimmered and then unlatched—one by one. They fell like harsh whispers, clattering in heaps on the hard floor. She should have felt relief. Instead, she felt an even heavier weight.

"You are free... for now."

He turned, and the chamber grew colder with his departure.

No one spoke.

Eliryn flexed her wrists. The weight of the cuffs had vanished at once, but the magic had lingered, brushing over her skin like it knew her, before fading away.

She was free for the moment.

But not safe.

And tomorrow, the real trial would begin.

Chapter 5: The First Trial

"It is not the beasts that kill you. It is the moment you believe you will die." —Recorded in the journal of a trial survivor

Eliryn didn't sleep.

Not truly.

She tried to steady her breathing. Failed. This space was too cold, the silence too taut—thick with the tension of so many held breaths and unseen thoughts. Even without her full sight, she could feel the weight of the others nearby. Shifting. Whispering. Dreaming. Dreading.

She had backed into a corner, spine to the wall, one hand curled around the pendant beneath her armor. Its warmth pulsed faintly, like a buried ember. Steady. Alive.

In the village, her mother had told stories of magic—rare and strange, born of old blood and older promises. But Eliryn had never touched it. Never seen a spell cast, or a relic glow with purpose. The cuffs, the way they'd released with a whisper of power, had shaken something in her. A reminder that she was in a world she'd only heard about in fireside tales—a world she was no longer just observing.

Now she was part of it.

And still... apart from it.

She kept her head down, listening instead of watching. She heard the scrape of boots, the rustle of wool, the clink of someone's hidden blade. Someone else whispered prayers in a tongue older than the capital's stones.

Snatches of strategy drifted like smoke—boasts wrapped in nerves, fear lacquered with bravado. It was hard to tell how many chosen were in the hall with her; there were too many overlapping breaths and unsteady heartbeats.

Eliryn listened until voices blurred into shadow. Her mind floated at the edge of sleep but never fell in. Her body was exhausted. Her senses strained. But rest wouldn't come. Not here. Not now.

When a horn sounded—low and mournful, like the cry of some ancient thing waking—she was already on her feet.

The doors of the hall swung open—one side heralding the return of the steward's guards, the other revealing... something unknown.

A breath of air met them. Not cold, not warm—but dense with the scent of the earth. Deep earth. Eliryn inhaled deeply without meaning to. The smell was strange and grounding all at once: damp stone, mineral-rich dust, a trace of something old.

Not decay. Not quite. More like the promise of things that lived beneath.

No one spoke.

The guards urged them forward in silence, and one by one, the chosen descended. The stairwell twisted downward, carved directly into the bedrock, its edges worn smooth by time or magic—or both. Eliryn's fingers brushed the wall as she moved, the stone humming faintly beneath her skin.

She walked carefully, leaning on sound more than sight. Her fading vision flickered like a sputtering lantern. She focused on the rhythm of boots ahead, the pattern of breath around her—some shallow and panicked, others held like practiced weapons.

At the base of the stairs, the passage widened into a stone hall lit by braziers sunk low into the floor. Shadows clung to the walls in long, flickering arcs.

The silence did not last.

The same official who had greeted them previously, The Steward of Trials, now stood before a massive archway, cloaked in rich robes, a scroll unspooling from his gloved hands.

"The First Trial begins now," the steward intoned, his voice echoing like ritual. "You stand at the threshold of the Undermire, a chamber older than the throne itself. It was carved to test the untested. To separate those who can endure... from those who can not."

A hush swept the group, brittle as frost.

"You are not meant to face this alone," the steward continued. "You are meant to bond."

A ripple of tension stirred the air.

"Form an allegiance. Old practice, nearly forgotten. But necessary. In this place, the creatures cannot be bested by steel or fire alone. You must anchor yourself to another. By choice. By instinct. A bond that can only be broken in death."

"What sort of bond?" someone demanded—a tall boy with copper-threaded hair.

"It's called the Vow of the Undermire," the steward answered. "A binding willingly sworn within the Undermire. Once taken, the Vow threads your life to another's—until death or unraveling claims you both."

A moment of stunned silence—then it fractured.

"That's madness," someone muttered.

"We were told this was a competition. Not a wedding."

"What if no one chooses you?"

"So we die... or give away our soul?"

The steward's expression didn't flicker as he faced the onslaught of questioning.

"Those who remain unbound," he said flatly, "rarely see morning. If you survive, the Undermire itself will sever your tether. Fail, and your soul rots beside your counterpart's corpse."

He stepped aside.

The archway yawned open, revealing nothing but shadow and flickering torchlight.

"You will have one full day. One full night. Survive, or do not. When the bells toll, your time is over."

The group hesitated.

Then it broke.

Pairs formed with ruthless speed. Whispers flared and vanished like sparks in kindling. By the time Eliryn registered what was happening, most had already vanished into the corridor.

Of course no one picked her. She wouldn't have picked herself, either. That didn't stop the sting of finding herself standing alone.

The weight of the stone ceiling pressed low. The torchlight dimmed. She moved forward anyway, her boots scuffing against the stone as she crossed the threshold.

The Undermire swallowed her whole as the air around her thickened.

The passage opened into a cavernous chamber strung with ruin—pillars eaten by moss, forgotten shrines, broken archways leading into deeper dark. Bioluminescent vines curled along the ceiling in pale green arcs, casting a faint, otherworldly glow.

Far off, something shrieked.

Too distant to name. Too close to ignore.

Eliryn veered toward a narrow path where no one else had gone. Her boots made no sound. Her hands traced the damp walls for balance, skimming over runes she couldn't see well enough to read.

Anxiety clawed at her lungs, each breath shallow and sharp. Beneath the fear, doubt bloomed darker—an aching certainty that she was too small for this fight.

It wasn't just loneliness. It was being measured. And discarded.

Not *with* them.

Not even *against* them.

Lesser.

It seemed apparent that they had noticed her eyes and had passed judgement accordingly.

She crouched beneath a crumbled overhang, pressing her forehead to her knees. Her pendant beat steadily beneath her hand. She remembered her mother's voice then. Not words—just the sound of it. Gone now. She curled her grip tighter.

How will I survive the night?

Her throat tightened.

"Ma..." she whispered. Not a call for help. Just... needing to say the word.

Her mother's stories had never included anything like this. Only dragons. Sorcerers. Chosen champions with sight like starlight and fate like mirrors.

But her mirror had always been cloudy.

Her sight, fading.

She was no champion.

She was a mistake the Flame hadn't noticed yet. And somehow, that hurt worse.

And here she was, alone, given one chance to prove she could outlast whatever the Undermire held.

Eliryn snorted softly, though her throat was too dry to make it sound anything like a laugh.

"Outlast what, exactly?" she whispered. "The crippling anxiety?"

Her voice fell flat. The stone ate the sound.

She was starting to regret skipping breakfast.

Somewhere ahead, water dripped. Slow. Steady. Like the ticking of some cruel clock.

She forced herself forward.

One more step.

Another.

And then—

Her boot caught on something.

She stumbled forward, arms flailing, and hit the ground hard. Her knee slammed into stone. Her palms scraped open. She lay there for a moment, gasping.

Flat on her stomach, bruised and breathless, she stared at the ground in disbelief.

"Oh, perfect," she rasped, her voice cracking. "Brilliant work, Eliryn. Stalked by monsters, and you manage to injure yourself before they even show up."

She turned her face against the cold, wet stone, breathing shallowly.

"This is going so well."

For just a heartbeat, she considered staying there.

Let whatever hunted her find her like this. Broken. Pathetic. Easy.

But she didn't.

Because even if she wasn't brave, she was still too stubborn to die lying down.

She pushed herself up slowly, every scraped muscle protesting. Her knee burned. Her palms bled. She tasted copper.

Her pendant hung heavy against her skin.

Mocking her.

She wiped her bloodied hands down the front of her already-dented armor and staggered forward.

One step.

Then another.

Every movement hurt.

Every shadow felt closer.

Then—something shifted.

Not a sound. Not a breeze.

Just a ripple in the air. Vast. Heavy. Like something breathing in before it hunted.

Eliryn froze.

Her pendant thrummed once beneath her collarbone. Not a warning.

A summons.

She pressed a blood-slick palm against the stone and whispered to herself, "Brilliant. Absolutely brilliant. What part of 'lost in an underground crypt' screams go deeper?"

She moved anyway. Because there wasn't a choice. Not anymore.

Her boots slid on moss-slick stone as she followed the faint sound of water ahead. Not a roar. Not even a stream.

Just a steady trickle.

Because of course death would come in a dramatic fashion.

Her breath grated her throat.

Gods, she was out of shape.

"Mother always said I wasn't built for running," she muttered.

The Undermire didn't care.

Its walls pressed closer as she moved. The faint bioluminescent glow of lichen lit the carvings ahead: stretched figures, their faces bound in stone blindfolds, mouths sewn shut.

Their hands weren't held in offering.

They were reaching.

Clawing.

She told herself they were just carvings.

Just stone.

But they looked like they'd been waiting.

And Eliryn, panting, bleeding, choking down fear, whispered, "Get in line."

Then—breathing.

Not hers.

Heavy. Wet. Just behind her.

She spun.

Nothing.

Only the soft, deliberate exhale of something large enough to swallow her whole.

At the next bend, she dropped to one knee, lungs wheezing.

"Gods, I'm dying because I'm winded and scaring myself. That's ironic."

Then—a shape unfolded from the dark.

At first, she thought it was broken stone.

Then it moved.

Limbs. Too many. Long and thin like spider legs, but bending wrong, shuddering at every joint.

Skin like wet obsidian stretched thin over something twitching, something too fast.

A face—no. Not a face.

A split where a face should've been. Jawless. Rows of teeth spiraling inside the split. No eyes. Just raw, glistening black skin pulling tight as it inhaled.

It tasted the air.

Eliryn's throat closed.

Behind it, another one unfolded. Taller. Bones piercing through its flesh like spines.

She stepped back.

Her heel caught a stone.

A crack.

So soft.

But they heard.

Heads snapped toward her. If those were heads.

She whispered, "Of course you heard that."

Then they charged.

She ran.

Fast.

Sloppy.

Not like a hero. Not like a warrior.

Like a girl who wanted to live.

She bolted through an archway, lungs heaving, boots skidding on stone. Her shoulder slammed into a wall hard enough to make her teeth rattle.

Behind her, claws shrieked against stone.

Not footsteps. Too many limbs. The sound was faster than any running beast.

She dove beneath a collapsed altar, arms scraped raw, ribs grinding, heart battering her ribs.

The hiss followed.

She didn't breathe.

Didn't blink.

She tasted her own blood in her mouth.

Then—pressure.

Not air.

Not sound.

Just weight. Pressing against her skin like invisible hands.

The creatures froze.

Quivered.

Then—turned.

Dragged their claws back into the dark.

Silent.

Drawn elsewhere.

She stayed frozen long after they vanished.

"I'm going to die down here. And worse, my body might get eaten."

When she finally crawled out, her legs shook so badly she nearly fell.

Her pendant pulsed again.

Warm. Urgent.

She followed.

Her mind was swimming with all the possibilities of her impending death when the next one found her.

She didn't hear it.

She felt it.

Claws hooked her shoulder from behind—dug deep, dragged.

She screamed.

Spun. Slashed blindly with a rock.

It wasn't enough.

Her blood splattered stone.

She ran.

Faster.

Didn't matter how much it hurt.

Didn't matter how much her body screamed to stop.

She ran until her vision blurred, until breath was something she didn't have anymore, until every footstep felt like a countdown.

And the thing followed.

A nightmare given flesh.

Jaws split sideways down its face, spiraling teeth grinding.

Limbs bending over walls, over ceilings. Crawling like something built to move anywhere it wanted.

Claws raked across her ribs.

She screamed again.

"This is it," she gasped aloud. "Prophecy, destiny, and I'm going to bleed out in a pit because I'm slow."

Her body didn't listen.

Her legs kept moving.

Instinct and terror did what pride couldn't.

Then—light.

She stumbled.

Fell.

Into a cavern.

She hit stone hard enough to lose her breath.

Behind her, the thing shrieked.

But didn't follow.

She turned.

It crouched in the threshold.

Its spiral jaws quivered.

But it didn't enter.

It couldn't.

And then it retreated.

Vanished.

Eliryn's mind spun. She couldn't understand.

Couldn't think.

Until the air shifted behind her.

Warm.

Heavy.

Ancient.

She turned and rose to her feet at once.

And saw him.

Golden eyes cracked open in the dark like molten suns.

The cavern pulsed—not with fire.

With breath.

A shape larger than nightmare stirred. Scales black as midnight glass, veins of molten light coiling beneath like magma.

And when he rose?

Stone shuddered.

The nightmare creatures had fled from *him*.

Eliryn, bruised and broken, took one step forward.

She didn't choose to.

Her soul remembered him before her mind could.

A memory burned into her blood.

"Oh," she whispered, voice raw. "There you are."

She collapsed to her knees.

The dragon didn't move.

Didn't roar. Didn't reach for her.

Just watched.

Silent. Endless.

Not a savior.

Not a god.

Just a question.

And somehow, impossibly, she was its answer.

She wasn't chosen.

She'd simply... arrived.

Bruised. Bleeding. Lost.

And the dragon—who had waited lifetimes—was no longer alone.

Not prophecy.

Not destiny.

Just inevitability.

Her breath shuddered once. And in the hush that followed, she whispered, broken but alive:

"...Well. Shit."

And the dragon finally blinked.

Chapter 6: The Flame of the Last Bond

"When a soul answers the call of Flame, even the void trembles." —Unknown

The obsidian pool shimmered in the dark like starlight caught beneath glass.

Eliryn's heart pounded—not from fear, not exactly, but from the deep, nauseating certainty that something was about to change. Something final. Something big.

She really hated "final."

The air thickened. She felt it shift, like the whole cavern was holding its breath.

From somewhere deep beneath the stone, something ancient stirred.

Bound by blood and bound by soul. In silence I burned, awaiting your call.

Her throat closed. She didn't think the voice was inside her mind so much as around it, like the air itself had decided to speak.

She stepped back. Probably the least heroic move she could've made, but reasonable.

Then the surface of the pool cracked open—like glass spiderwebbing—and from that impossible shimmer, something rose.

Wings folded like waiting blades. Scales of black and bronze glimmered as if the earth itself had melted and re-formed him. His horns curved like a crown. His eyes—

Oh gods. His eyes.

Twin suns—molten and endless—locked onto her.

Her lungs forgot their purpose. The air between them was a living thing, thick and trembling, as if even the wind feared to move in his presence.

And Eliryn, practical to the last, nearly whimpered.

"Okay," she rasped, heart hammering so hard it shook her vision. "That's... that's a dragon."

He stepped forward, each movement rippling through the earth like distant thunder. The ground trembled beneath her boots; dust shivered in the air.

When you call, I rise.

The voice didn't pass through her ears—it struck straight into her bones, rattling the air from her chest.

"I didn't know I was calling," she whispered.

You have been calling since the day you first drew breath.

Her throat worked, but nothing useful came out. "...Cool," she managed. "That's not alarming at all."

Heat rolled over her in a slow, suffocating wave. His breath was warm and metallic, edged with the sharp tang of scorched rain and stone cracked by lightning.

I am Vaeronth... the Endbringer.

The name landed like a warhammer against the silence—final, unyielding, carved in the language of endings.

It didn't just settle in her ears—it pressed into her bones, etched itself into the space between her heartbeats.

She laughed. Not because it was funny, but because if she didn't, she was going to start crying, and once she started, she wasn't sure she'd stop.

"I'm not ready," she whispered, half to herself. "I'm really not."

You are. His voice rumbled like a storm clawing its way over mountains. *While I have been waiting, you were becoming.*

"Gods, that's intense," she said, her laugh breaking into something breathless.

Behind Vaeronth, the pool flared with sudden light, igniting from within until it glowed like a second sun. Golden fire rippled across its surface, not burning, but alive—patterns spiraling outward in runes older than the first kings. The light caught his wings as they spread, vast enough to blot out the pool entirely, and the shadows they cast rippled and bent as though they too were alive. Shapes formed in them—dragons, battles, crowns, storms—prophecy given form.

Speak the words.

Her stomach dropped. "I... I don't know them."

You do.

And gods help her, she did.

They rose from somewhere hollowed out inside her—a space she hadn't known was waiting. The syllables were not hers, yet they belonged to her. They tasted of copper and rain, of smoke from a long-dead fire.

Her lips parted, and the first word escaped like a thread pulled from the world itself.

"I offer not just breath," her voice cracked, "but all that I am..."

The vow came in fragments and floods, each syllable dragging up memories she had never lived, pain she had never felt, triumphs she had never claimed. Images burst behind her eyes: a sky full of wings, a world blazing with magic, the roar of dragons as they wheeled above armies.

Her voice trembled. Her body shook. Tears she refused to name burned down her cheeks as the weight of each word branded itself into her very marrow.

At the final line, her voice broke entirely, shattering like glass struck by lightning:

"My soul is yours... as yours is mine."

Silence fell, but it was not still. The air was thick, humming with the raw current of something ancient recognizing itself.

Then Vaeronth roared.

It was not a sound.

It was an event.

Not a voice, but a verdict.

The ground split in hairline cracks at her feet. The water in the pool surged upward, caught in an invisible spiral toward the sky. Her bones vibrated with the force of it; her heart stuttered, then raced to keep up.

And in that sound—in that impossible, all-consuming roar—she felt the bond settle.

Not chains, but roots, threading through every part of her, anchoring her to him, and him to her.

There was no going back.

The cavern shook. The mountain shook. Her bones shook.

Magic broke over her like a tidal wave, crashing into her with incredible force.

Her last fully formed thought before the world drowned was half-terrified, half-horrified, and wholly herself:

Oh, gods. What have I done?

Magic ruptured the air.

It wasn't wind. It wasn't sound.

It was pressure—crushing and total. The light didn't fade. It collapsed.

The cave folded in on itself, reality bending like molten glass. Shadows burned. It was as if the stars had been dragged down to watch.

And then it hit her.

It didn't seize her skin first. It gripped her bones.

The scream tore from Eliryn's throat before she knew she was screaming. She tried to move, to think, to flee—but her body betrayed her. Liquid fire surged through her veins, gold and iron threading up her arms, down her spine, curling through her lungs like molten wire. She wasn't just burning.

She was being rewritten.

"Stop," she gasped, voice breaking as she fell to her knees. "Stop—oh gods—"

No one listened.

Because this wasn't punishment.

This was her destiny.

Tendons snapped and rewove. Muscles tore and reknit. Symbols she could not name burned themselves into her marrow. Her skin seared from the inside out, covered not in ash, but in light.

"Vaeronth—Vaeronth!" she screamed. "Make it stop!"

I cannot, he said softly. *This is yours.*

She convulsed, fingers clawing at blood-slick stone, her breath stuttering like something broken.

"I'm dying," she rasped.

No. You are becoming.

Her body betrayed her last. Her vision split with silver, her skull cracked open by a pain not even nerves were built to carry.

She heard herself beg, though she didn't know who to.

"Please. Please, no more."

Then everything went silent.

The pain wasn't gone. It simply... ceased to matter.

She tasted it on her tongue—not blood. Not ash.

Starlight.

She collapsed to the stone, trembling, hollow, her heart barely beating.

Her next breath was like dragging air into a body that wasn't hers anymore.

Symbols burned beneath her skin.

Not ink. Not scars.

Living script.

She turned her hands numbly, watching lines of molten silver coil around her fingers—talon-shaped runes flexing as she moved. Spirals of sacred geometry looped her ribs and throat. Her collarbones glimmered beneath skin stretched too thin, veins lit from within.

Her voice came raw. Quiet.

"What... what did you do to me?"

Vaeronth's shadow loomed, vast and certain.

I did nothing.

"You're joking."

The runes along her forearms pulsed—answering her anger.

You called. I answered.

"I didn't call for this."

You did.

Her knees buckled.

Her ruined armor cracked, splintered, then fell away in glittering fragments. She looked down as the plates disintegrated at her feet like a serpent shedding its skin.

And beneath it...

A second skin. Scaled sigils. Glimmering script. A body no longer entirely human.

She pressed her palm to her own arm, then drew it back like she'd touched flame.

"I'm a monster."

You are mine.

His voice wasn't comforting.

It was absolute.

Vaeronth lowered his head. She could barely think when she reached out and rested her shaking hand against the bridge of his snout. His scales burned like stone left too long in the sun. But she didn't flinch.

"I should hate you for this."

You will not.

"Bold assumption."

I know you.

And somehow... he did.

His warmth pressed around her, wings folding, foreclaws cradling her like she was something precious and breakable.

Eliryn let herself collapse inside the cage of his limbs. She could hear his heartbeat now, deeper than thunder, older than the mountains.

"I didn't ask for this," she whispered.

No one does.

"I'm not strong enough."

You are.

"Vaeronth..."

She hesitated.

Thought about what to say, changed her mind, and settled on:

"My name is Eliryn."

Vaeronth paused.

And then, reverently, like naming a star:

I know, Eliryn. I have known you in the silence between heartbeats.

Her throat caught. Her eyes burned—not from pain this time, but from something deeper. Something older. Something terrifyingly close to hope.

"I'm not alone anymore," she whispered.

No. Never again.

She closed her eyes. The stone floor wasn't cold now. Not within the vault of his wings. Not with his breath steady beside her.

"You're mine," she murmured.

And you are mine, Vaeronth answered. *Now and always. Until death, and beyond death's reach.*

At the depths of the Undermire, dragon and rider weren't just reborn.

They were forged.

Chapter 7: Marked for More

"The bond is not salvation. It is surrender." —Inscription found at the Shrine of the Bound

When she woke, the silence felt wrong.

It wasn't a quiet peace, it was a stillness that spoke of a draconian aftermath.

Her heartbeat pulsed in her ears. Slow. Heavy. Her body ached—not from wounds, but from something deeper. Change.

She sat up stiffly, her breath tight as she touched her throat.

Her fingers traced strange patterns along her skin. Lines of smooth, raised symbols curled over her collarbone, spiraled her wrists, and looped down her ribs. The marks weren't scars. They shifted faintly beneath her fingertips, alive. Her skin caught the low light, runes glimmering black and gold, scales rippling faintly at her sides like the breath of something sleeping.

"I... don't recognize myself."

No, Vaeronth answered, his voice rich as iron and old as ruin. *Because you are no longer the girl who entered the dark.*

Her throat caught.

"I don't know if that's reassuring."

It is truth.

She smiled faintly, brittle and fragile. "You know that that's not comforting, right?"

I have waited for three hundred years. Comfort might take some building up to.

That silenced her.

The hush stretched long. The weight of his words settled against her skin, heavier than the runes.

"You've been... waiting? That long?" She pause. "For me?"

His presence pulsed. Not warmth, not pride. Something deeper. Endurance.

I waited for you before your mother's mother took her first breath.

Vaeronth's voice filled the cavern like smoke. Not cruel. Not cold. Just... absolute.

"Great," Eliryn muttered, pressing a trembling hand to the wall as her knees wobbled. "No pressure, then."

His scales shifted in the dark—too large, too real for her mind to process clearly. Her blurred sight caught only fragments: molten veins of gold, ridges like black iron, wings that seemed to shudder the air itself. Her brain tried to fill in the blanks, but the image her mind painted was too vast.

"I can't even see you properly," she admitted, voice catching. "After all that waiting, you get stuck with the blind girl."

There was a pause.

And then Vaeronth's voice rumbled low and quiet.

Your eyes are not your weakness.

"At least you're not pretending I don't have any weaknesses. But, I thought dragons chose their riders." She swallowed. "Wasn't that the whole... legend?"

Once, we chose.

A pause thick with something heavier.

And once, we burned.

Eliryn gripped the stone, her humor faltering. "I'm guessing those two are connected."

A long silence.

Yes.

Her throat worked, but no words came. Not until her voice cracked small and hopeless:

"So why are you here in the Undermire?"

Because I am the last.

That silenced even her sarcasm.

I watched the world forget my name. Watched my kin die one by one. And still I remained. Not for glory. Not for revenge.

"For me," she whispered, the realization slicing clean through her. "You waited for me."

I've been awaiting the start of the prophecy. Waiting for fate. And when you were born, I felt you. The beginnings of a bond ignited. From your first breath, I knew.

Eliryn sagged. "Gods."

You were not what I expected.

She almost laughed. "That makes two of us."

Vaeronth's exhale stirred her hair, carrying the scent of old fire and dust.

I was meant to find a warrior. A leader. Not a girl who trips over her own feet.

"I do not trip."

Silence.

She huffed. "I don't trip that often."

Another silence.

"Try flying without your vision and come talk to me after you hit a couple trees."

A sound like distant stone cracking... not quite laughter, but close.

"Okay. Fine." She rubbed a hand over her face, exhaustion gnawing at her. "So you're stuck with me. A half-blind, slightly-cursed, vaguely traumatized healer who can't tell her left from her right some mornings."

You are my bonded.

"I don't know how to be that."

You will learn.

Her voice broke, her self-deprecation cracking into something raw.

"I don't know how to be what you need," she whispered, her voice crumbling. "I'm not... enough."

A long pause. Then Vaeronth's voice, low and certain as mountain stone:

It isn't about what we need.

She frowned faintly, her hands tightening into fists.

It was never about choice. Or readiness. Or want.

"What, then?"

We are two halves of one flame. I carry what you lack. Together, we fulfill the shape the world cannot name yet.

She swallowed. "Because of the prophecy."

Because of fate.

He shifted closer, the ground vibrating softly beneath her boots.

Neither of us chose our destiny, he said. *Neither of us wants to be the last of our kind. But the gods named us to mend what has been left to rot. To tear the sickness from the kingdom's heart before it kills all that remains.*

Her breath hitched. "Well... how are we supposed to do all that?"

By becoming what they fear most, Vaeronth rumbled. *By being exactly what the prophecy promised—and more.*

His voice softened, but it was no less absolute.

Whatever comes, we face it as one. Dragon and rider, bound to heal a realm dying by the Sovereign's hand.

Her throat cinched. "I'm scared."

At last, something in his voice shifted. Gentler. Like thunder made soft.

You seem it.

She laughed, cracked and wet. "Oh, you've got jokes."

I assure you, I do not.

She blinked. "I'm not sure if that's comforting or depressing."

Neither am I.

Her laugh came easier this time. Small. Fragile. But real.

"I don't know how to do this," she admitted softly, curling her arms around herself. "My mother used to tell me about the prophecy... about how it would be me in the end. Like I was meant to win the trials and wear the crown. To fix everything." Her voice thinned. "But standing here, it all feels... impossible."

You are the last Dragonrider.

She let out a short, almost bitter laugh. "Yeah, and according to her, that title is supposed to change the world."

She saw what I see, Vaeronth rumbled. *The shape of what you will become. The magic that you will unlock. She knew it as surely as I do.*

Her breath hitched again, but no tears came now. Only the steady, quiet ache of a heart too tired to break.

"Alright," she whispered. "We'll do it together."

In the silence that followed, she felt him—a constant immovable presence.

Not her savior.

Her tether.

And for the first time since leaving her village, Eliryn didn't feel lost.

She felt... found.

And Vaeronth, ancient as the mountains themselves, shifted closer, lowering his head until she could lean—slow, clumsy, shaking—against his snout.

She whispered into the warm iron of his scales:

"I'm sorry you had to wait so long."

He rumbled softly.

The prophecy is worth waiting for.

And Vaeronth added, quieter now:

So were you.

She pretended not to hear him.

"And what happens when we reach the surface?"

His tone shifted—grimmer, resigned.

I cannot walk with you in the world above.

"Why?"

Because my true form is too large. My wings cannot stretch beneath the ceilings of the castle. My shoulders are broader than their gates. I am shaped for sky and stone... not for corridors and courts.

Eliryn blinked slowly, almost dazed. "Oh."

I will shelter within the vessel at your throat, the pendant forged to bind me. You will carry me. But know this: I am not diminished. I am waiting.

"For...?"

For whatever we may face.

She sat in silence for a moment, the runes faintly pulsing down her arms like they were trying to keep her heart beating.

"You know," she said at last, "you really do sound ancient."

I am.

She huffed a faint laugh. "And here I thought I was bonded to a mysterious young rogue."

If you wish for flattery, you have chosen poorly.

Her mouth twitched. "Gods, Vaeronth, you could at least pretend to lighten up."

I cannot. There is too much at stake.

She rolled her eyes toward the ceiling. "Figures."

A pause.

"You sound tired too," she said more quietly.

I am that, as well.

Her throat tightened. She tried to swallow it down. Failed. "Great. Ancient, tired, and now you're stuck babysitting me."

I am not a babysitter, he said, and when she opened her mouth, he added, *and you are not a child. You are the rider the gods named. If you cannot believe in yourself, then believe in what they saw—the future they set in motion. It will not matter if you doubt, so long as you move toward it.*

Her breath caught. "That's... a lot of faith to ask for."

Faith is not given. It is built. And I will build it with you.

She managed a small smile. "Guardian, then. Mentor. Overly dramatic, scaly life coach."

A long silence. Then: *I accept guardian.*

She blinked, then barked a laugh. "Oh. So you do have a sense of humor."

No.

"Liar."

Another pause. His voice shifted, lower. Closer.

You really are afraid.

"I—" Her breath caught. "Yeah."

Good.

She froze. "Excuse me?"

Fear will keep you alive.

She stared at nothing, then let out a broken sound halfway between a laugh and a sob. "Oh, you're a joy."

I am honest.

"Sure. Honest. Terrifying. A little judgy."

You walk into walls.

"That was one time."

It was four times.

She laughed again. It cracked this time. "Have we established that I'm going blind? You don't have to rub it in."

Well, now you are bonded. His voice softened, like stone crumbling. So at least *you are not alone.*

Her breath hitched.

"Even if I trip over my own feet?"

Especially then.

She wiped her cheek with the back of her hand, managing a whisper. "Guess you're stuck with me."

She rose to her feet, body aching but steadier than she expected. Her sight blurred, light bleeding where it shouldn't. She reached out instinctively, finding the curve of his snout.

He bent to her touch. His breath washed warm across her face.

We walk to the surface now.

She hesitated. "And after that?"

Then... you continue with the trials.

She huffed once. "That's vague."

Prophecies often are.

She smiled, cracked and tired.

They moved as one. Vaeronth led her from the edge of the ancient pool, its surface still burning faintly with the afterglow of their bond—ripples catching the light like liquid fire before melting back into shadow.

The air grew colder as they left it behind, each step echoing in a silence so deep it felt alive. The stone beneath her boots was damp and smooth, worn down by centuries of tides she could not hear. High above, unseen in the dark, something shifted in the cavern roof—a sound like the groan of a sleeping god turning in its dreams.

They passed through narrow fissures and chambers vast enough to swallow cities, the walls glistening with mineral veins that pulsed faintly in the dark. Her blurred vision caught flashes of movement in them—light that seemed to breathe, as if the rock itself remembered the birth of magic.

Deeper still they went, until even her own breathing sounded foreign. Somewhere in the distance, water dripped in a slow, patient rhythm. Her fingers brushed the stone as she walked, and the runes along her skin answered with a faint pulse, as if the Undermire knew her now.

Then—light. Faint at first, a pale shimmer far ahead.

It was not sunlight. It was the ghost of sunlight, fractured and cold, seeping through cracks in the world above. It painted the jagged walls silver, and for a moment she thought she saw shapes moving in it—winged, crowned, robed in flame—but the images were gone when she blinked.

Vaeronth moved unerringly toward it.

"You know the way back," she murmured.

I have always known, he said, voice echoing low through the stone. *The Undermire keeps its paths for those it remembers.*

They wound upward through a tunnel that spiraled like the inside of a shell. The air grew warmer, sharper. A breath of wind ghosted over her cheek—wind, real wind, touched by the scent of pine and rain.

At last, the stone path opened into the shattered ruin where the trial had begun. The air here felt older, heavier—like the space itself had been waiting for her return. Moss clung to the broken pillars in thick green shrouds, and silver lichen crawled over the stone in patterns like half-forgotten constellations. It looked as though centuries had passed, though it had been only a single day.

Vaeronth halted at the base of the final stair, his shadow stretching up the steps like the memory of a storm.

Beyond this, I cannot go.

"I know."

Her throat burned. "You're too vast for the world above."

My form would crush the castle.

Her fingers curled around the pendant, feeling the low, steady pulse within—not heat, but the measured rhythm of something vast and watchful.

"Will it hurt?"

I do not believe so, Vaeronth said, his voice shifting to something quieter, heavier. *But you will feel me settle.*

She rolled her shoulders back, trying to anchor herself against the echoing dark. "Comforting. Nothing like walking into the unknown with instructions that vague."

You will live. Probably.

Her mouth twitched. "Love that you slipped a 'probably' in there."

I am not in the habit of offering false assurances.

"Ancient and dramatic. What a combination."

I prefer the term timeless.

A small laugh escaped her despite the knot in her chest. "Of course you do."

And then the light began.

It did not burst so much as *unmake* the darkness. Vaeronth's form unraveled deliberately, like a tapestry coming loose thread by thread. Strands of molten gold unwound from his scales, drifting upward in slow arcs. They curled through the air like smoke and spun around her in long ribbons of light, catching in her hair, tracing her skin in lines warm as breath.

The storm of embers didn't burn. It enfolded her, weightless and patient, carrying with it the scent of ancient skies and scorched stone. She felt him thinning, not vanishing, but folding himself into something smaller—into her.

When the last threads streamed into the pendant, it pulsed once—warm, steady—as if it had borrowed the rhythm of his heart.

And for the space of a single breath, she saw.

Not with her failing eyes, but with his.

A sky the color of hammered iron. Riders wreathed in golden armor astride dragons vast as cities. Wings cutting through storms of ash. Battlefields lit by rivers of flame. A black citadel shattering into nothing beneath a roar that could tear the heavens apart. And far beyond it all, a single name—unknown to her—etched into the horizon in letters made of living fire.

Then it was gone.

She stumbled, her knees threatening to fold. Her voice cracked before she could stop it. "What... what was that?"

Memories, Vaeronth murmured in her mind. *Not all are mine. Some belong to the bond all dragons share. And now, they belong to you.*

She blinked, breathless. "Oh, well, thanks. Just what I wanted. More trauma."

He rumbled laughter deep in her thoughts, a sound like mountains grinding under molten stone.

I am with you, Eliryn. Always.

Her throat tightened. "That... is not making this less weird."

Would you prefer I leave?

Her lips twitched. "Nah. It's much too late. All these new tattoos I've got wouldn't make sense without you."

Correct.

Somehow, that made the silence that followed feel less like absence and more like anchor.

Together, they climbed.

Each step up the long, spiraling corridor was heavier than the last, the air growing sharper, brighter, more *alive.* The stone thrummed faintly underfoot, as if remembering the touch of dragon talons from ages past. Her muscles burned, but her legs remembered their strength. Her mind hummed with the weight of him inside it—both comforting and strange, like carrying a sword that had not yet learned how to be balanced.

You will find your stride, Vaeronth assured.

"I'm struggling just climbing stairs out of this haunted crypt. You might be overestimating me."

Your sarcasm is becoming tiresome.

She smiled faintly. "Then I'm doing it right."

At last, the great stone doors loomed ahead, carved with runes that no longer looked like mystery to her. Her fingers brushed them.

When they opened, silence crashed down like a blow.

The Hall of Holding stretched ahead: a cathedral of dust and defeat.

Survivors crouched in exhaustion, their faces hollow-eyed. Some bore burns. Others bled from wounds too deep for quick healing. One girl was sobbing quietly into her hands.

But it was the empty spaces that stole Eliryn's breath.

Not everyone had survived the night.

She stepped forward, steady now. Her shredded clothes, her bare skin streaked in blood—none of it mattered.

What mattered were the marks that curled up her arms, coiled across her collarbone, symbols alive with faint light even in the shadows.

She moved like a queen.

She walked like she believed it.

And in her mind, Vaeronth whispered softly, almost like a benediction:

You have been graced with more dragonmarks than the old riders of legend. You should stand proud.

The pendant at her chest burned gold, casting restless light over the bare skin of her collarbone. The tattoos—no, not tattoos, not really—flickered faintly. Living scripture, curling beneath her skin like someone had branded fire into her bones and dared her to survive it.

Dragon-scale patterns shimmered when she turned her head, crawling up her throat like flame-shaped vines. They didn't feel like a gift.

They felt like a warning.

She just wasn't sure if the warning was meant for others... or herself.

Every step she took echoed like something older than fear. Older than pain. Older than her.

The hall fell silent. Heads turned. One figure gasped. Another crossed himself like she was a nightmare clawing free of a hellscape. A third just stared, wide-eyed, lips moving silently around a single word:

"Impossible."

Eliryn met their gazes, steady and unblinking.

She was no longer the half-blind girl tripping over moss in the dark.

She was bound.

Flame-marked.

Changed.

And she was going to do her damnedest to act like it.

Behind her, a voice cut the quiet. Calm. Sharp.

"They say the dragonbond changes you." A pause. The scrape of boots against stone.

She turned.

A broad-shouldered man, eyes narrowed with suspicion or maybe fear, met her gaze like it was a duel. His voice was like a steel blade drawn slow. "They say the bond makes you less. Hollow. So what are you now?"

Eliryn stopped.

She turned.

And smiled. Slow. Lethal.

"I was reborn in the fire of a dragon," she said softly, voice like silk drawn over a blade. "So whatever you're trying to be right now? A threat, a judge, a man worth fearing?"

She stepped toward him.

"You're just a bug underfoot."

He flinched. Only slightly. But she saw it.

And then, dismissively, she turned her back to him.

Vaeronth's voice curled into her mind, satisfied. *You speak like a Queen.*

"I speak like I'm hoping no one notices I have no idea what I'm doing."

Convincing, nonetheless.

She drifted toward one of the stone benches, letting herself move like she belonged here, like nothing could touch her—not the blood drying on her skin, not the molten script crawling along her arms. She settled down carefully, ignoring the way her ribs still ached.

Then... she noticed the others.

Slumped figures scattered across the hall. Not warriors anymore. Survivors. One clutched at a ragged stump of a leg, makeshift tourniquet soaked through. Another's face was pale as snow, blood seeping from between cracked fingers pressed to his ribs. A girl in the corner whimpered softly as she tried to bind a wound on her arm without help.

Her gut clenched.

She should move. Help. Do something. Her healer's instincts screamed for it.

Her fingers twitched against her knees.

Vaeronth's voice cut through, low and firm: *No.*

She stiffened. "They're dying."

You are not a healer anymore, Eliryn.

"Yes, I am."

No. You are not.

She swallowed hard. "But I could—"

You are a dragonrider.

She closed her eyes, her throat tight. The words felt like a stone laid on her chest.

His voice was an ember that refused to go out. *You walk among them, and they see what you are becoming. They see the bond.*

She hesitated. Then, quietly, in her mind: *My mother would have given anything to see this.*

Heck, Eliryn thought, *she might have even seen it in one of her visions.*

There was a pause. Then: *Tell me of her.*

Eliryn blinked. The burn in her throat had nothing to do with fire. She nearly said no. But then the words clawed up anyway. *She was...*

She swallowed.

She was small, but unshakable. Not a soldier, but not ungifted—she had visions that always came true. She told me all the old stories, everything she'd learned: dragons, bonds, the First Flame. Everyone laughed. She didn't care. She used to say... Eliryn's eyes watered.

"The world might forget, but the gods never do."

Wise words, Vaeronth said gently.

She died before I could prove her right.

The words fractured in her chest. *I carry her blood,* she thought. *And now her ghost.*

No, he replied, voice curling warmly through her thoughts. *She knew. In her bones, she knew. The fire in you was never hidden from her.*

She exhaled shakily and lifted her chin.

Above her, she felt unseen eyes—watching, measuring—though when she looked up, nothing was there. All around her was pressure from unknown sources, pressure she wouldn't give in to.

She no longer wanted their approval—no longer needed it.

Not now.

The fire in her veins rose like a tide, and she let it.

Let them watch the prophecy take shape.

Interlude 1: Malric

"You are not a man, Malric. You are a blade I keep sheathed until it's time to bleed the world." —The Sovereign of Vireth

Malric crouched in the stonework high above the Hall of Holding, swallowed by a sliver of shadow between two forgotten arches where the air stank faintly of stone dust and old blood.

The silence here was absolute. Heavy.

Perfect.

No one ever looked up.

That was their first mistake.

He was the patient sickness in the mortar, the quiet in the corner before the knife slid home. From here, he had already watched four die—two by monster, two by his hand—and not a single whisper had followed them into the dark. The trials were cruel by design. He simply made them efficient.

The order had been clear enough:

"Cull the strong. Let the monsters take the credit. Make it look like the trials are working."

Easy. Predictable.

Until *she* walked in.

She came through the yawning stairwell like a ghost dredged from ash and flame. Armor gone, burned to ruin. Only shreds of cloth remained, curling at the edges from heat, sliding against skin marked with something alive. The black shapes weren't ink—they moved, glinting like molten glass beneath her skin, shifting when she breathed. They coiled over her throat, kissed her collarbones, and dove beneath the pendant that glowed at her sternum with the slow, steady pulse of another heartbeat.

His hands itched. Not to kill her. To *touch*.

To find where that strange heat began.

She was built of tension and survival, her red hair wild as if the fire hadn't wanted to let go. Soot crowned her like something ceremonial. And her eyes—sightless in one sense, yet burning with an awareness that made his skin crawl—sought not what was there, but what was hidden.

He remembered those eyes.

The village.

The night she'd stepped out of her cabin in ill-fitting armor, grief sharp as the smell of iron on her skin. She'd looked right at him—not with challenge, but with... acceptance. As if she'd already measured the weight of danger and decided to carry it anyway.

Now she carried something else, too.

The bond.

It didn't just cling to her—it claimed her. And gods help him, it made her *worse*.

Sharper. More dangerous. More *herself*.

She didn't move like the others, bowed by fear or exhaustion. She moved like judgment—unhurried, unrelenting, as though the ground should be grateful she walked on it.

The king wanted her broken last. Wanted her to suffer.

Malric... wasn't sure what he wanted.

Around her, the others reacted like she was a storm crawling into human skin. One man whispered a prayer. Another stared as though she was a god that had noticed him.

And then her chin lifted.

Just enough.

Enough to make every muscle in him go still.

He was hidden—silent, masked by charm and stone. No one ever sensed him unless he allowed it. But she... she tilted her head like a hound catching a scent.

Her fingers brushed the pendant, the glow flaring just enough to make him feel watched. Not by her eyes. By something else.

Malric eased further back into the shadow, though his pulse did not slow.

This was the girl he'd been ordered to kill.

The Dragonrider.

The ruler's words hissed in his mind:

"Let her be the last. Let her watch the others fall. Let her heart burn before her body does."

His blade was steady in its sheath.

But the thought of driving it into her made something in him recoil.

Worse—he realized he didn't want her dead at all.

And that meant one thing.

He wasn't here to hunt her anymore.

He was here to see what she would do next.

To learn how she burned.

And when the fire finally came, he didn't know if he'd be the one to stop it—

Or feed it until it consumed them both.

His gaze tracked her as she crossed the Hall, the pendulum swing of her shadow stretching across the flagstones like a blade being drawn.

Every step she took echoed in his bones.

He'd been sent here to be her ending.

And yet—watching her now—he could not tell if he wanted to be her executioner...

Or the knife she chose to wield.

Somewhere deep in his chest, something shifted. Dangerously.

The others in the Hall looked away from her; he did not.

He followed her every move, storing each detail like a thief cataloging stolen treasure. The faint tilt of her chin. The way the air seemed to thin in her wake. The ghost of heat that brushed his skin though she never came near him.

When she disappeared into the stairwell's shadow, he stayed crouched among the stone ribs above, unmoving.

It wasn't until long after her footsteps faded that he realized his hands had curled into fists—tight enough to ache.

This was the woman the prophecy spoke about. The one he had been ordered to break.

To burn.

To leave hollow.

He licked his teeth, the taste of iron sharp in his mouth.

If he was the fire, she was the storm.

And storms... were not so easily tamed.

Chapter 8: The Living and the Leashed

"Sometimes the castle changes its halls to protect what it fears." —Anonymous guard of the North Wing

The silence in the Hall of Holding was brittle as glass.

Eliryn's ragged clothes clung to her frame—where steel had once protected her, only the script of flame now remained, etched into her skin like holy writ. She willed her eyes to cooperate with her, wanting to see the others who had survived.

She figured she was younger than most here, though she was nearing her twenty-seventh year. There was a boy with copper hair, who seemed impossibly young, far less blemished by what was un-doubtedly a lavish life.

Across the room, someone shifted—a grizzled warrior whose frame looked carved from granite. He was perhaps twenty years older than her, with a beard dusted in gray and arms thick with old scars; undoubtedly a veteran of countless battles. His eyes were dark, unreadable, set in a face that had seen siege and slaughter, and likely caused both. He watched her like one might watch a weapon being forged—equal parts interest and caution.

Eliryn started scanning the room now, taking note of the other survivors. There was another woman, tall and wiry, perhaps just past thirty, hunched over someone's leg, trying to stabilize a broken bone with a length of belt. Nearby, others lay on the ground in a messy heap of bloodied bodies, their asynchronous breaths making it hard to guess exactly how many were left.

She could *feel* their pain. The healer in her flinched with every shallow breath, every shudder from broken ribs or unseen wounds. Her fingers twitched. Memories of poultices, of pressure, of whispered words meant to pull the dying back from the brink.

The healer in her still fought for control.

But she did not move. She wasn't allowed to.

Do not reach for them.

The voice of her dragon came from low in her mind, coiled like smoke in her ribs.

They do not see a healer anymore. They see power. Keep it.

She swallowed the instinct. It hurt more than she expected. But he was right. Any show of softness now would only confuse them—or worse, make her seem *mortal* again.

Then—footsteps.

The hush of the hall deepened into tension as the door at the far end of the chamber groaned open. The steward entered, flanked by two silent wardens. His robes were pristine, untouched by the night's horrors, but when his gaze found Eliryn—he faltered.

Just for a moment.

But she noticed it.

His breath caught. His expression cracked, paling like wax under heat. His eyes widened, and in them she saw not curiosity but *recognition.* Maybe a flash of fear.

And from within his obsidian vessel, Vaeronth purred.

Good. Let them fear.

The steward gathered himself with effort, clearing his throat.

"Of the twenty who entered the first trial," he said, his voice echoing around the high stone walls, "ten remain."

A beat.

He did not name the dead. He didn't have to. Their absence was already a wound stitched into the room.

"They were found... shredded. Torn limb from limb. One body was barely recovered." A pause. "The Undermine was not kind."

The tall boy with copper hair clutched his ribs, wincing. The older warrior merely nodded, stone-faced. The other woman looked down at her bloodied hands, expression unreadable.

The steward's voice cut through again, less steady now.

"The second trial will begin in two days. You will be given a place to rest until then. Rebuild what you can."

She almost laughed. Almost.

Rebuild what? A soul? A sense of purpose?

He hesitated—just a second too long—before adding, "Survival is not victory. It is only permission to continue."

And with that, he turned and fled.

Smart man, Vaeronth murmured.

When the heavy doors closed behind him, the hush did not lift. It only thickened. The steward had barely vanished into the shadows beyond the hall when a wave of guards arrived.

Steel echoed against stone—guards entering in tight formation, armor dull with soot and ash, each carrying a set of glowing manacles etched with faint runes. They were not weapons, not chains of brute force—they were bindings of obedience, pulsing with soft blue magic that shimmered like captured breath.

The room tensed.

The guards stepped forward one at a time, each saying a name heavy with expectancy.

"Stormthresh."

The tall woman with blood on her hands rose to her feet, stepping forward from the injured body on the ground. The guard locked the cuffs around her wrists without a word. She flinched as they clicked into place, a small shudder running through her.

"Tarn's Hill." The copper boy.

"Stonefell." The older warrior stepped forward without hesitation.

"Whitvale." A slender figure slipped past her, not a speck of blood marring his expensive-looking tunic.

One after another, the names were spoken—village names, not personal ones—and the chosen moved toward the guards. None resisted, though several struggled to stand and walk. The bindings glowed brighter once affixed, sealing themselves with magic finality.

The air in the hall grew tighter with every set.

The final guard approached Eliryn slowly, gaze hidden behind his helm. His steps were careful- measured in a way none of the others had been.

Then, loudly, for all to hear:

"Dragonrider."

The title dropped like a guillotine.

Every head turned.

Every breath caught.

She closed the distance to the guard with measured steps, as if her pulse weren't pounding hard enough to shake her ribs. The silence that followed her title wasn't absence—it pressed in on her, dense and waiting, like the moment before a storm breaks.

Her rags clung to her ribs, streaked with dried blood and soot. Her dragonmarks shimmered faintly under the hall's dim light. She lifted her arms automatically, presenting her wrists.

Oh, lovely. Coordinated restraints. Every girl's dream, she thought dryly.

She braced herself for the chill of magic.

It didn't come.

The guard stood before her, but he didn't move. His helm shadowed his face, but his stillness conveyed plenty.

He was hesitating.

Eliryn frowned. "If you're trying to build suspense, congratulations. It's working."

No response.

Her hands hovered in the air awkwardly. She shifted slightly. "It's not polite to keep a lady waiting."

Still nothing.

Vaeronth stirred in her mind, his voice like cool stone brushing molten steel.

He is afraid.

She almost said something. But her throat locked.

Afraid... of me?

Yes.

Her gut twisted.

She forced a crooked smile. "I promise I won't kill you unless you try something with those cuffs."

It was a joke. Mostly.

He didn't take it that way.

The manacles in his hands shook slightly.

"Oh," she muttered under her breath, "I wasn't serious."

Vaeronth's presence curled warmer, steady, a flicker of amusement brushing her thoughts like a tail-swipe of smoke.

He believes your threat.

She blinked up at the guard, feeling awkward now. "Look, I was joking."

No response.

The guard did not move.

She looked up, trying to see the expression in his gaze but her eyes struggled to cooperate.

The hall had fallen completely still. One of the oldest contestants—a sharp-eyed man with sallow cheeks and a suspicious bend to his spine—broke the silence.

"Why isn't she being bound like the rest of us?" he asked, voice low and bitter.

The guard hesitated. His gloved hand hovered near the cuffs at his belt... but he didn't reach for them.

Instead, his voice came out quiet, unsure—meant to sound certain but *wasn't*.

"The cuffs wouldn't hold her anymore," he said, voice low. "She's... beyond them."

A ripple moved through the room like a dropped stone in water.

Her smile faltered. She glanced around as unease slithered across the chamber, the survivors watching her now not like a threat... but like something worse.

Eliryn's throat went dry.

She lowered her hands slowly. "Right. That's... interesting."

Vaeronth stirred, molten gold in the back of her mind.

Dragonblood cannot be leashed.

"Oh, that's comforting."

It should be.

She barely held back a snort. "For you, maybe."

One of the chosen near the wall spat. "Dragonblood."

Eliryn flinched harder at that than she should have.

Vaeronth's voice coiled gentle and cold.

Let them wonder what you are. Let them wonder what it means.

"Fantastic," she muttered. "I'm reaching a whole new level of outcast."

She felt the shift, the unspoken verdict settling into the air like dust after collapse; she was different and now there was no denying it.

One by one, the guards motioned for the contestants to follow them—no words, only sharp gestures and the occasional grunt of command. Heavy doors at the far end of the Hall of Holding creaked open, revealing a dim corridor lined with tall torches and iron sconces.

"Come. Your rooms are ready," said a captain from the front.

The group was herded forward, the clink of enchanted cuffs echoing like dull chimes in the dark.

The guard hesitated beside her as the others were led away. For a moment, Eliryn stood awkwardly, unsure whether to follow.

She glanced up at him, nerves tightening her throat.

"So..." she said softly. "Do I... go with you? Or am I just supposed to... stand here and radiate menace?"

The guard near her startled slightly. She could hear the shift of his armor.

"I—uh... right. No. You're supposed to come with me." His voice cracked at first, then steadied, and he cleared his throat. "If... you want."

She huffed, trying to mask her exhaustion. "If I want? Is it optional? Honestly, even if there was a choice, a nap sounds pretty good right now."

That earned a small, surprised sound from him. Not quite a laugh. But close.

He gestured toward the side hall. "Rooms are this way."

She cleared her throat. "So... what happens now?"

The guard didn't answer at first. Then, "One room per survivor. Hot water, clean clothes. Food."

She raised a brow. "There's food?"

That actually pulled a dry laugh from him—a huff of amusement that surprised them both.

"That's your question? Not *'Where is your med-wing?'* Not *'What's the next trial?'* But *'There's food?'*"

Eliryn shrugged, smiling faintly. "Seems relevant. I nearly died yesterday. And the day before. I could eat a mountain. Though, it would be nice to know where things are located here."

He shook his head, still chuckling, though wariness lingered in his voice. "You're in the North Wing of Castle Othren. Built before the last Sundering. The wings shift sometimes—by design. You shouldn't leave the castle grounds until the last test is complete."

She tilted her head slightly. "And the cuffs? Why won't they work on me?"

That erased his grin. His voice lowered. "They're soul-forged. Meant to suppress will. Control breath. Anyone who resists is slowly drained of their magic. They've worked on kings. Mages. Even bloodborn."

"But not me."

"No." He looked at her again. "They don't work on dragonblood."

She touched her wrist absently, where the cuffs *should* have been, where they had rested just before the start of the trial.

Vaeronth whispered, *Because you are not theirs. We belong only to ourselves. And we do not kneel for any other power.*

She shrugged, wrestling with the idea of being bonded to something so powerful. "Well... I am sorry I scared you before with my word vomit."

"I wasn't scared," he said too quickly, then winced. "Okay. Maybe a little."

She gave him a crooked smile, softer now. "I'm... not going to hurt you."

"I know that." His tone was gentle now. Honest.

A beat.

"I think."

She laughed once, short and real.

"So, Dragonrider?" he asked softly, glancing at her again. "Is that what you... are?"

Eliryn hesitated. "I guess so."

She rubbed at the marks on her arms, fidgeting.

"I didn't... mean for it to happen."

He was silent for a moment. Then, quieter:

"I think most important things happen that way."

She blinked, glancing at him in surprise.

His expression was open, earnest despite the fact that she definitely still terrified him.

"Thanks," she said softly.

"For what?"

"For... that."

They turned down another corridor, warmer than the others, with faint orange light bleeding through the seams of heavy wooden doors lining either side.

"Room eleven," he said, pausing near the door and stepping aside. "You'll find everything you need inside. You'll be summoned when it's time for the next trial."

She stepped past him but paused just inside the frame. "Thank you," she said again, sincerely.

He blinked. "For what?"

"For speaking with me." She had noticed that the other guards did not entertain conversation with their chosen.

The guard hesitated... then offered a short, respectful nod.

Eliryn disappeared into the room beyond.

The door clicked shut behind her.

For the first time in what felt like forever, Eliryn stood still.

No screaming. No blood. No watching eyes.

Just warmth. Quiet. Breath.

Her own.

And Vaeronth, steady and impossible in the back of her mind like an old song she'd somehow always known.

The room felt wrong. Luxurious, yes, but like it belonged to someone else. A stranger. Carpet swallowed her footsteps. A porcelain tub steamed in the corner, water laced with lavender. A feast sat waiting on polished wood: bread, cheese, spiced roots, and meat pink at the center. Beside it, a pitcher of water glinted like treasure.

She just... stood there.

For three whole heartbeats.

Then: "Okay. Either this is real, or I've actually died."

Vaeronth, dry as sun-scorched stone: *You are alive.*

She huffed. "Right. Says the dragon inside my mind."

Don't sass me when you can't even work up the courage to walk across the room.

"Gods, no need to call me out on it."

Her knees gave out the moment she neared the food, and she dropped straight onto the carpet like a stone.

A second later, she was tearing into bread, then root vegetables, cheese, anything her shaking hands could grab. It wasn't graceful. She ate like survival was still a question mark.

Not alone anymore, but still not safe.

Not yet.

Vaeronth watched from within—silent, but present. She could feel him, his vast presence coiled in the bond they shared.

"I'm fine," she muttered mid-bite. "Completely fine. Normal night. Got chased by monsters, fell through a mountain, found out dragons aren't extinct after all, bonded to said dragon, got a magical tattoo that may or may not be alive, and now I'm sitting in a room fit for royalty eating more food than I have in an entire season."

She paused. Swallowed.

"You know, when you say it out loud, it doesn't sound that weird."

A pause.

It sounds absurd.

She laughed, exhausted. "See? I knew you'd get it."

Silence. Then, his voice, quieter: *You do not need to understand all at once. You know what the prophecy proclaims; the rest will come with time.*

She slowed, resting her forehead against the edge of the table, breath shaking out of her like smoke. "I'm trying, Vaeronth. I really am."

I know.

She hadn't expected that to help. But it did. Enough that the trembling in her hands began to still.

When she lifted her head, she studied her fingers—the runes curling across them like vines that refused to stop growing. They shifted when she flexed, restless, alive.

"I wasn't supposed to be this," she murmured. "I was supposed to be... just a healer. I had a garden, once. Red roses." She swallowed hard. "My mother planted the first bush with me. Said one day, I'd grow into something far more dangerous than thorns."

And you have.

Her lips curved, humorless. "All that's left of it now is ash."

Ash feeds new roots.

She huffed a laugh, jagged but real.

Her marks glimmered faintly, catching the lamplight like embers stitched beneath her skin. She wouldn't recognize the woman she had become. And yet... she wasn't afraid of her, either.

"My mother warned me," she whispered, almost to herself. "She said I would be more than I wanted to be. More than I was ready for." Her fingers brushed the runes. "And here I am. No garden. No roses. Just fire."

Not fire. Power. And you were never meant to be less.

Silence settled, deep as a heartbeat. Then Vaeronth added, low and certain:

Stop mourning the girl you were. And stop apologizing for the woman you are now.

She swallowed.

"Okay," she whispered.

Rising slowly, she crossed to the tub. The tattered remains of her shirt and trousers fell away easily, dropping in clumps of bloodstained fabric. Her skin looked... wrong, and right. Dragon marks shimmered in the soft steam, curling down her arms, her back, over her ribs. Patterns meant for battle, not bathing.

She slipped into the water, hissing as heat licked over bruised skin. It wasn't just warmth. It was *cleans-*

ing. Like her body had been holding on for far too long, and only now could begin to let go.

"I thought of my mother," she whispered into the steam, her arms resting on the sides of the tub. "When I walked into the hall. When they looked at me."

Vaeronth didn't interrupt.

"She would have been proud." A pause. "I think."

The silence that followed felt heavy, so she filled it. "She used to talk about the old ways, the old powers, like they were more than history. And I laughed. I didn't believe her. I just thought... she needed something to believe in because we had so little."

She believed in you, Vaeronth said.

Eliryn smiled faintly. Her eyes stung, but she didn't cry.

She slid deeper into the water until it kissed her chin. "I'm still scared, Vaeronth," she admitted quietly. "I don't know if I can carry all of this."

A long pause. Then:

We will carry it together.

The room held her silence, warm and quiet and *whole*. For the first time in days, there was no fear.

Just steam.

And the quiet, burning promise of what she had become.

Interlude 2: Malric

"Tools don't need purpose. They need edge." —The Sovereign of Vireth

Malric was still crouched in the stonework high above the Hall of Holding, wedged into a slit of shadow where the stone was cold and dust hung like breath.

No one ever looked up.

They should have.

He had orders, so he waited. Watched.

Below, the chosen shifted, armor rasping, eyes hollowed out by the trials. Torches spit resin and smoke. Iron rings sank into the flagstones like old teeth. The room remembered what it had been built to do.

He counted breaths, not faces. The loud ones die early. The quiet ones live longer. The useful learn to forget to breathe at all.

He'd already taken four. Two the beasts could keep. Two were his. No one had asked where they'd gone. That was the point: when cruelty fits the pattern, it goes unseen.

His attention kept returning to the rider.

He didn't know her name. He didn't need it. Names made graves in a man's head. Better to call her what she was: the girl, the rider, the myth the court was already pretending not to whisper about.

She moved like judgment. Calm. Lethal. Unbound.

The marks on her skin hooked him. Not because they were magic—he'd seen magic seared into flesh before—but because they *answered* her. The lines shifted when she flexed. The script even brightened when the pendant at her throat pulsed. Not power pressed on from the outside; power that was waking up from within her very being.

She was becoming a waking legend.

And the sovereign had no room left in his kingdom for legends.

Orders were clear. If she still breathes at the end, she dies. His blade. His hand.

His knuckles pressed into grit until skin complained. He let the ache sit. He'd had worse teachers.

The dragonrider moved wrong. Not broken-wrong. Unpredictable-wrong. She wore death like a second skin and called it a change of clothes.

He should have looked away.

He didn't.

He told himself it was strategy. Necessary observation.

He didn't believe it.

He remembered her before the marks. The village. His borrowed uniform. Her braid too tight, armor that didn't fit, dried blood under her nails. She'd looked straight at him. Not with challenge. With clarity. As if she already knew what it meant when silence paid attention.

Even then, she'd been intriguing.

"Dragonrider," the guard called.

The word hit the room like hot iron dropped in water. The young guard didn't even reach for the magical cuffs. He didn't bother pretending.

Heat moved across Malric's mind—not warmth. Presence. A weight that tested the air and tapped one claw against glass.

The dragon.

Malric drew deeper into the stone. Something older than the castle was taking his measure and filing him under watch.

He thought about the dragonrider, and about the unrest that bubbled up from the deep wells of the citadel. The two things happening at once were not coincidence.

Her survival wasn't just dangerous. It was instructive.

The sovereign's voice slid back into his ear, silk over a blade:

"Let her be the last. Let her watch the others fall. Let her heart burn before her body does. That is how you end rebellion."

Malric filed the words and refocused.

The rider moved. Each step was chosen, as if she expected the floor to argue and intended to win.

He slipped from his niche. Invisibility slid over him like a habit. Even without it, he knew how not to be seen. The charm only taught the world to forget where to look.

He followed closer than most would dare.

Torchlight wrote broken lines along rune-cut pillars. The enchantments below the flagstones hummed like old blood. Some halls smelled of oil and iron; this one breathed lichen and stone after rain. He kept to the seam between light and dark. Boots quiet. Breath quieter.

Ahead, he watched as his fixation cradled the pendant at her throat. Her touch was answered with a small pulse. She tilted her head a fraction, not enough for anyone else to notice.

She must feel me.

Not with her eyes. With whatever listens when the eyes begin to fail.

They reached a door heavy with wards. Glyphs cut deep, inlaid with metal that refused to shine. Privacy. Protection. Sovereign claim. And something threaded throughout that felt like comfort.

The trial guard stood aside and tried not to ponder. The rider paused—a heartbeat too long—reading the cuts and seams of her surroundings with her face turned just enough to make Malric's pulse change. Then she stepped forward and the door took her in without a sound.

The air tightened. Light sharpened to a thinner edge. His invisibility wrinkled along its margin as the room's ward tasted him and decided he was not to its liking.

Living chambers set into the castle's spine. No key. No window. No posted guard. The room learned its occupant and gave back what it decided they needed. Warmth, light, food, safety.

She had one now.

He hovered a hand near the door's seam. The air there had a clean bite, the sort of heat that doesn't make smoke. A ward for melting. Quiet. Efficient. He approved of the craftsmanship. He did not approve of what it did to his hand when he imagined pushing through.

He pictured what the room might give her. Not sentiment. Utility. Heat that didn't scorch. Water that ran clear. A bed that let the body unclench without turning soft. The fantasy offended him. It also did something else he didn't want to name.

He'd killed kings on their thrones. Priests at their altars. Heirs before their voices changed. He knew how to end a problem before it learned to breathe properly. He had no room in him for wanting.

And yet.

He wanted to see her again.

Not the spectacle—the title, the flinch of guards, the way the air thinned around her. He wanted the unguarded. How she slept. Whether the marks dulled in rest or burned brighter when she laughed.

The dragon brushed him again. A low note. A weight shifting somewhere inside the walls and inside his skull at the same time. Not quite warning. Maybe amusement. Predators recognize each other.

You don't own her, he thought toward the weight. He didn't decide whether he was speaking to beast or king.

He let his hand fall. His palm tingled as if he'd offered it to a forge and changed his mind at the last sane moment.

He moved back into the corridor. The castle adjusted around him, the way old buildings do when they decide you're a piece of furniture that won't leave. He passed two guards who pretended they weren't afraid and a steward with a new scar that hadn't been there yesterday. Three banners had been replaced since last night; the stitching showed temper. The kingdom was rearranging itself without the courtesy of a warning.

He liked patterns when they held. He liked them better when they broke in ways he could use.

He found a slit window, and leaned till the night put cold fingers on his eyes. The city lay quiet in the way of places that have learned to lower their voices. Beyond the walls, campfires studded the dark. Pilgrims, profiteers, the devout, the curious, the wolves in cloaks. The trials would end when everyone gathered; the sovereign meant to give them a show to watch. He meant that show to be *her*.

The thought didn't sit right.

He went back to the door. He didn't mean to, but he found himself there all the same.

The corridor wasn't the same corridor anymore. Torches had moved by an inch. The air had the fit of a room that sits with its hands in its lap and pretends not to listen. He stood before the seam again and let his palm hover to the edge of burning. He could die here without sound. The knowledge didn't scare him. It made something else turn over in his chest.

"Later," he breathed. The ward made a sound too small for ears, like glass deciding not to crack.

He pictured her again, the way thieves catalog what they mean to take. The tilt of her chin when she pretended she wasn't afraid. The cadence of her walk. The cut on her forearm she held closed by force of will, not cloth. The heat that lifted from her skin when the pendant throbbed. The way people looked at her, away, and then back as if wanting to be punished by their own curiosity.

Malric wasn't one to pray. He did, however, for the first time in a long time, *hope*. For clarity.

The dragon's presence feathered through him one last time.

He flexed his hand, shook the ward out of his bones, and let the castle swallow him.

By the time he reached an outer hall where wind found arrow slits and hunted his face, the night had thinned to bruise-blue. Somewhere a bell tried for the hour and quit. He leaned his head to the stone.

He hadn't planned for her. He had planned for beasts, for fools, for royals with brave mouths and cowards with brave clothes. For trials that let men pretend they earned what gods assigned. Not for a girl who refused to be ordinary when the world demanded she be useful and quiet.

He did not know her name. He did not want it.

But he would learn it anyway.

From a guard's careless mouth.

From a steward's ledger.

From a man begging for his life who thought gossip could buy him breath.

If he had to, he'd take it from the air itself.

He would decide how long she lived. How close she came to breaking. How much the sovereign would get of what he wanted. How much Malric would keep for himself.

He'd been sent to be her ending.

Watching the dark bleed toward morning, Malric accepted something he shouldn't: he didn't want to be her ending. He wanted to be the knife she chose. Or the hand that taught her how to sharpen.

He pushed off the wall and moved into the hour when men sleep poorly and lies sound most like truths. The sovereign would ask for a report. Malric would give him one—with all the pieces, except the ones that mattered.

He had time now. Time to watch. Time to decide.

He wasn't used to wanting things.

But he wanted to see her again.

He wanted to know what came next.

Even if it was her death.

Especially if it was by his hand.

Because someone like her... couldn't belong to anyone else.

Not even herself.

And as he melted back into the shadows of the castle's spine, Malric finally understood:

She wasn't a threat.

She was a temptation.

And that was far deadlier.

CHAPTER 9: A NAME WORTH REMEMBERING

"To name something is to honor it. To remember it is to resist forgetting who we are." —The Book of Binding, Vol. II

She woke slowly.

Water held her like a pair of steady hands. It hadn't cooled; if anything, it was warmer now—thick and attentive, clinging to her skin as if it were listening for her breath. When she shifted, the surface gathered itself and rose with her, as though the bath had learned the shape of her body while she slept and refused to forget.

Light pooled green-gold along the carved stone rim, moving like sunlight at the bottom of a deep lake. Steam feathered the air and carried a faint scent that shouldn't have existed down here—crushed red rose and rain on hot stone. The room's magic, remembering what she had loved and what she had lost, making a ritual of it.

She pushed damp hair from her face and sat up with a low sound. Her muscles answered late. Not pain, exactly—more the slow, dragging heaviness of a body that had been taken apart and put back together by hands that didn't ask permission. Fair. She wasn't convinced it belonged to her, either.

Runes lay muted beneath the water, silvered and soft, then brightened when the air kissed them. Droplets beaded along her forearms and slid in deliberate paths, sketching thin, temporary sigils before falling away. The pendant at her throat warmed, a quiet, steady thrum against her sternum.

Sound was strange—the world muffled and close, her heartbeat too loud in her ears, the small lap of water against stone measuring out the room's patience. When she flexed her fingers, the markings moved with her: not ink, not scars. Living script that stretched and settled as if it had joints of its own.

She tested her breath. In. Out. The tub answered with a soft ripple that steadied, like it was syncing to her pulse.

"Okay," she murmured to no one and the room at once. "We're still here."

From somewhere warm and vast inside her: *I am, too.*

"Good," she said, closing her eyes for one last heartbeat. "Because I'm going to need a minute."

Her skin pulsed faintly in the lavender light, the tattoos alive beneath the surface. She didn't like calling them tattoos. Tattoos were choices. These... weren't.

Her fingers brushed the marks at her collarbone. They were still warm. Still breathing.

At least the scent of tea still lingered in the air—sweet, spiced, grounding.

"Small mercies," she muttered, standing carefully.

The floor softened under her bare feet. Of course it did. This whole room responded to her now; she wasn't sure if that made her cared for or smothered.

She found the robe waiting by the hearth. Rich indigo, lined with silk.

Too soft.

Too fine.

She hesitated. Then pulled it on anyway, the fabric sliding over her skin like a promise she hadn't made.

Vaeronth stirred at the edge of her mind.

You dislike comfort.

"I distrust it."

You shouldn't.

She ignored him.

The light in the room had shifted to soft lavender, like even the walls understood she couldn't handle daylight yet. She appreciated that, though she'd never admit it aloud.

At the hearth, a small table waited. Ceramic jars. Glass vials. She didn't need to open them to know what they were.

Healing balms.

She sat, automatically uncorking the nearest jar. The scent hit her first: mint, pine, jasmine. She dipped two fingers in without thinking and pressed the balm gently to the skin just above her wrist.

Her body remembered what her mind couldn't yet process.

Pressure. Slow circles. Even breath.

A healer's instinct. Still hers, apparently.

The marks pulsed faintly beneath her skin, humming under her fingers. She worked methodically: over her shoulders, along her collarbones, down the lattice of lines etched into her arms. Like armor waiting beneath the surface.

They are your first shell, Vaeronth murmured, warm and steady in her thoughts. *You are no longer just flesh.*

She didn't answer. She wasn't sure what to say to that.

Instead, she traced the largest sigil over her ribs, feeling the pulse there. Not pain. Not anymore. Just... something else.

"I'm losing what's left of my sight."

It wasn't a question.

Sight is only one way of knowing, came Vaeronth's reply.

"I suppose I won't develop the same gift that my mother had..."

A long pause. He let her sit with her bitterness.

What rises in you is not her gift. It will be your own.

"I don't want any more changes."

No answer.

She pressed both hands to her face and breathed slowly, willing herself to stop shaking.

"Will the changes... change who I am?"

Another pause, as if the great ancient dragon was searching for the right words.

Power does not leave a soul untouched, Vaeronth said softly. *But you are not alone in carrying it.*

She let that be enough for now. Let it smooth the ragged edge of her thoughts, though she wasn't sure she'd earned even a breath of peace.

The pulse beneath her skin slowed, syncing to her breathing.

Eventually, she opened her eyes. "The room changed again."

Old magic, Vaeronth replied. *It shapes itself to you. Your needs. Your fears.*

"Explains the lavender."

You needed softness.

She huffed something between a laugh and a sob. "I don't even remember what softness feels like."

As she grew, there had simply been... less. They learned to fold their wants small. If she and her mother didn't grow it, brew it, stitch it, or carve it, they went without. Winters of thin broth stretched with water; summers of the same dress re-hemmed and turned inside out so the seams could pretend to be new. Boots patched until the leather remembered every old stitch, like the ones she had kicked off her feet after the trial. Eliryn remembered how they counted roots daily and saved the good salve for other people's pain. They traded tinctures for flour, poultices for lamp oil, and when there was nothing left to barter, they went to bed early and called it prudence.

Lavender had been a luxury you made by hand: tiny sachets sewn from scrap, bundles drying above the hearth to sweeten the smoke. Not perfumed oil. Not baths. Not *this*.

You do, Vaeronth said, gentler. *You just stopped letting yourself ask for it.*

She swallowed. "Asking made my mother look tired."

Surviving taught you to be quiet with your wanting, he countered.

Her eyes burned. She stood abruptly, the robe trailing behind her.

The canopied bed waited at the far side of the room.

She glared at it.

"Don't you dare be comfortable."

The bed said nothing, smug in its silence.

Grumbling under her breath, Eliryn climbed into it anyway.

And, against her better judgment, let herself rest.

Sleep didn't come easily.

The bed was too soft.

Everything smelled like lavender and warmth. It should've felt safe.

Instead, it felt... wrong.

She drifted, half-caught between memory and whatever the bond was becoming.

Fire filled her dreams.

Not destruction—language.

Symbols, coiling through the air like smoke, written in a tongue her mind knew but her waking self couldn't grasp. Vaeronth stood in the center of it all: wings vast, casting no shadow. The sky above him burned red, as if the world had been lit from the inside out.

In his chest, a second sun flickered.

You must carry it now, he said, voice not a voice.

The realm's magic is fading.

But it cannot be extinguished.

You are its champion.

Then the world cracked.

Glass underfoot.

Sky splintering.

She fell through.

And woke gasping, tangled in silk.

Her chest heaved. Her skin burned cold.

No light.

No sound.

Only the lingering memory of fire.

Eliryn sat on the edge of the bed, head in her hands, heart racing.

"I can't do this."

Vaeronth brushed a wing against her mind in comfort.

It is your fate. Your destiny. Your responsibility.

She stood.

She needed... something. Air. Distance. Control.

The room didn't stop her.

The door unlatched the moment her palm pressed to it. The stone didn't care whether it was morning or midnight. It only cared about what she needed.

So she walked.

Barefoot.

The sconces burned low. Shadows stretched long and spindly down the corridors, twisting in ways shadows shouldn't.

She followed them anyway.

Not because she wanted to.

Because it was easier than standing still.

Down she went.

Lower.

Stone underfoot shifted from polished to worn, from curated to forgotten. The air changed too—thicker, carrying the scent of char and salt, of woodsmoke and... bread.

Of course.

Of course she would gravitate towards the smell of bread.

She followed the scent like a thread, rounding corners and slipping past doorways half-closed. Her robe whispered at her ankles. She didn't know if she looked like a lost noblewoman or a ghost.

Light spilled from a cracked door.

Voices.

Quiet. Careful.

Laughter, too—not the brittle kind.

She stepped inside.

And the world froze.

The kitchens weren't grand. They weren't meant to be.

They were real.

Stone walls. Fires banked low. Flour dusted over every surface. A pot of something thick and spiced simmered over coals.

And every pair of eyes snapped toward her the moment she entered.

Two guards near the back reached for their weapons.

She understood why.

She would've done the same.

Her hair hung in damp curls over her shoulders. Her robe shimmered faintly, too fine for anyone from the lower wings. The marks on her skin glowed softly, tracing her throat, her collarbones, her wrists.

And her eyes…

Gods.

Her eyes probably weren't human anymore.

Palms open, peace offered. "Forgive me. The bread called, and I lack the will to refuse."

A pause. "I used to be better at not frightening people."

That earned a beat of stillness.

Then—slowly—an older woman resumed kneading dough.

"You're one of them," the woman said. Not a question.

"I am."

"The Dragonrider?"

"I suppose."

Another pause.

Eliryn hesitated, then added quietly, "Though right now, I feel more like a starving woman who woke up in enemy territory."

Silence cracked.

A soft, cautious clearing throat from the corner.

A boy—sixteen, maybe—stared at her with wide, frightened eyes.

"But you're… polite."

Eliryn's lips curved. "Should I not be?"

The boy shrugged helplessly.

Someone whispered, "Her eyes glow."

"Of course they do," muttered a cook.

"But it's not... bad," the boy said, glancing around as if waiting for someone to argue. "It's just... bright."

Another voice: "The tattoos move."

"Like fire."

"Do they hurt?" asked a girl, flour smudged on her cheek.

Eliryn blinked.

"Not anymore."

She let that settle.

"At first, yes."

The older woman looked her over like she was sizing up a loaf. "You speak kindly for someone so marked."

Eliryn met her gaze without flinching. "I was a healer."

Silence swallowed the room whole.

Then, after a moment:

"Sit."

Eliryn hesitated.

"You look too thin for someone so powerful."

"I already ate."

"There's always room for honeycakes," the boy said, hopeful.

Without thought, she smiled.

Eliryn stepped further in. "May I ask your names?"

They exchanged uncertain glances. The boy shifted his weight, rubbing at a bruise on his arm.

"People like us... we don't usually get asked that," he said, voice low.

She softened her tone. "I'm sorry. I didn't mean any offense. I forgot—names are held close here, aren't they?"

"Among the highborn, maybe," said the man who was stirring the pot of soup. His mouth twisted in something that wasn't quite a smile. "But not for the likes of us."

"I'm not so different from you," Eliryn said gently.

Can I share my name? she asked Vaeronth silently.

Yes, his reply was instant.

She turned. "I'm Eliryn of Lirin's Edge. My dragon is Vaeronth, the Endbringer."

The older woman exhaled. "Well. Those are names worth remembering."

One by one, they told her theirs.

The boy: Nim. Sixteen. Kitchen apprentice.

The older woman: Marta, third-generation palace baker.

The soup-stirrer: Reven, quiet, scar splitting his lip.

The guards didn't speak, but one gave her a respectful nod.

Another stool was brought forth seemingly from nowhere, and Eliryn was seated with a plate of food in front of her before she could blink.

Nim hovered beside her, eyes bright.

"You really bonded with a *real* dragon?"

Eliryn nodded, mouth too full to answer.

"What's it like?"

She swallowed. Then smiled.

"Like having a second heartbeat."

She let that settle.

"Only... it argues with me."

Marta huffed. "Never heard of such nonsense."

Eliryn laughed softly. "He's listening now, actually."

She glanced down at the pendant resting warm against her skin.

"He says he can't wait to try your bread."

Nim beamed.

And the kitchen... softened.

Quiet. Calm.

For a little while, the kitchen felt like a sanctuary of her own.

But curiosity stirred.

She looked to Marta. "Are you happy here? Do you feel safe?"

Marta physically paused at her words.

Reven raised an eyebrow. Nim turned fully, as if anticipating the response.

"It's work," Marta said. "More than many have. We've food. Beds. But safety?"

She looked over her shoulder at the space the guards had vacated moments ago.

"That depends on which eyes are watching. And how much they fear what you might say."

"The castle itself," Eliryn said. "Does it feel... dangerous?"

Reven's voice was low. "There's always an air of unease here. But lately it's thicker. Sharper. The king watches everything. He has spies no one ever sees."

"Do you think the trials are making it worse?"

Nim hesitated. "I think...people go missing. Nameless bodies carried to the morgue. Everyone's on edge."

"The trials change people," Marta said quietly. "There are rumors—"

Reven cut her off with a sharp hiss. His eyes darted to the archway that led back into the main hall, as if expecting shadows to peel free and listen.

"Rumors can get you hanged," he muttered.

Eliryn studied his face. "If I'm going to survive this place, I need to know what I'm up against."

Marta shifted her weight, rubbing her palms against her apron. "Some say the trials are not meant to test you. Not truly. They're meant to break you down until you're easy to shape."

Nim's voice was barely a whisper. "Or until there's nothing left."

Silence settled over the kitchen. A pot bubbled behind them, the only sound.

Eliryn felt the press of unseen eyes again, that prickling awareness crawling up her spine.

"What happens to the ones who survive?" she asked.

No one answered her right away.

Finally, Reven looked up. His expression was something between pity and resignation.

"They don't come back the same," he said. "If they come back at all."

Eliryn nodded solemnly, sensing that her time here in the kitchens tonight was coming to an end. "Thank you. For your honesty. And your company."

"You're welcome anytime," said Reven.

As she turned to go, Nim called out, "Eliryn?"

She turned.

"You'll come back and tell us more about your dragon?"

She smiled. "I would like that very much."

She walked back toward her chambers, the pendant at her chest humming with warmth, and Vaeronth's voice in her mind was soft with approval.

Well done, Dragonrider. Connection is a quieter power—but no less fierce.

Interlude 3: Malric

"The castle keeps the shapes of those it favors. So do men."
—Mason's Notes from the Spine of Vireth

Something vast shifted in the castle's spine, and he knew she'd left the safety of her room.

Not sound. Not sight. A pressure change—the way air thins before a storm. The wards that had been curled tight around her eased; the weight he'd come to recognize—dragon, bond, inevitability—moved.

He went after it.

Height by habit: lintel, beam, the narrow seam where chimney met wall. Invisibility slid over him like a second posture. The world forgot to notice he existed.

The kitchens were warm and ordinary. Banked fires. Stone damp with steam. Knives asleep in their racks. He'd slit throats in rooms with better stories. Bread, and the quiet barter of people counting coins one by one—none of it mattered.

He almost left.

Then she spoke her name.

"I'm Eliryn of Lirin's Edge. My dragon is Vaeronth, the Endbringer."

The rafter under his hand stopped being wood. It became a grip.

Names make graves in the mind. This one made purchase.

Eliryn. The syllables cut clean. More important was the way the room breathed when she said it. People lean toward a fire before they remember to be afraid of it. The staff did that—leaned, then blinked like they'd caught themselves. He did not care to share the first speaking of her name with flour-stained hands and boys with soft bones. But he took what was given.

The dragon brushed him—lazy, confident, a claw across glass.

He tasted the old impulse to dismiss all of it—the boy with the bruise, the baker's hands, the man who watched the doorway whenever anyone said too much. None of them were his problem. None of them were the mandate.

But Eliryn laughed, low and unguarded, and the laugh moved the marks along her throat like embers waking. She added to the room—heat, ease, the kind of attention that leaves people standing taller than when they arrived. He had spent his life subtracting. The arithmetic offended him. It fascinated him more.

He couldn't hear every word from the rafters; he didn't need to. Hunger met with kindness. Questions met with caution. The small miracle of names exchanged in a place that punished names. And beneath it—her steadiness under scrutiny, the way she let the room study her and refused to be reduced by it.

He waited until she left.

Only then did he allow the thought he'd been refusing since the hall: the distance had become intolerable. Watching was a kind of starvation.

He descended the way shadows do—by not being where light expects. He walked the corridors, letting the castle align its inches around him, learning which torches drifted from their hooks, which stones warmed when she passed. The place had begun to keep her shape. He would, too.

He turned her name once, silent. *Eliryn.* Currency. Tool. Key.

He could spend it with the sovereign and buy approval. He could spend it on the staff and buy loyalty. He could spend it on himself and buy nothing—except the thing he wanted.

He wanted to speak to her.

Not as a voice from a height. Not as a pressure she felt and couldn't place. Face to face. The kind of speaking that plants a stake and makes ground admit it's been claimed.

He would choose the time: a corridor with no witnesses; a stair-turn where sound goes soft; a place the dragon could feel him and decide to wait. He pictured her turning toward his voice—the precise angle of chin that means calculation instead of fear. He pictured the moment her eyes—whatever they were now—fixed where he stood and *saw*. The thought uncoiled in him like a patient animal made to sit too long.

He had thought himself content to be the ending. He was not. He intended to be the interruption. The constant. The problem she learned to account for the way men learn the weight of a weapon they mean to carry every day.

He would give her no choice but to look up. And when she did, he would give her a name to use back.

Malric set his route: kitchens to the service stair that bled into the living wing, then the blind corner before the warded hall where footsteps betray their owners. He adjusted his breath, loosed his shoulders, let the castle's hum climb into his bones until his pulse matched it.

He had a name now. He had a direction. The rest was work.

The castle has learned her shape.

He'll teach her his.

Chapter 10: Shadows That Know Your Name

"Knowledge does not protect you. But it might prepare you." —Unknown

Eliryn wandered.

The warmth of the kitchens still clung to her like a fading cloak, but the castle beyond those heavy doors was vast and colder—its stone corridors humming with silence, its air threaded with a hush that made her feel like an intruder. She hadn't meant to stray far from her quarters, but curiosity gnawed at her, as did restlessness. The trials loomed, and every instinct in her healer's mind told her that information—truth—was the best medicine for fear.

But the Citadel did not give up its secrets easily.

She passed grand staircases and closed archways, narrow windows that looked down on gardens cloaked in moonlight. Once, she paused before a massive tapestry depicting an ancient dragon alighting on a mountain pass, gold-threaded fire curling from its mouth. Another time, she turned a corner and found two guards in black armor speaking low in a tongue she did not recognize. They fell silent the moment they saw her, eyes sharp, unreadable.

She kept walking—slower now, but not turning back. They didn't follow her, but a prickling unease crawled along her spine.

Someone was watching her.

More than once, she glanced behind her, catching only shifting shadows cast by flickering sconces. But the feeling did not go away.

Vaeronth, she whispered silently.

I know, came the calm voice of the dragon. *Eyes follow you. But no blades are drawn—yet.*

"Comforting," she muttered.

At last, she came upon a high archway, its iron-banded doors half open. Lanterns glowed within—and beyond them... books. Hundreds, maybe thousands, lining dark oak shelves that rose endlessly toward the vaulted ceiling. The air was thick with the scent of parchment, old leather, and candle wax.

Eliryn stepped inside, tension sliding off her shoulders like a poorly-fitted cloak. "Thank the gods," she whispered. "A room that keeps its violence pressed between pages."

"I wouldn't be so sure."

She spun, pulse lurching.

A man waited at the end of the aisle, shadow holding to him the way cloth holds a crease. He didn't lean so much as *occupy* the space—still in the way weapons are still.

Lantern light found him reluctantly. Dark hair, cut close but unruly at the collar. A clean jaw with the faintest pale line along it—almost a scar, if you knew how to read one. His build read like a blade: lean, balanced, made to move only when it mattered. The coat was matte charcoal, tailored to disappear; the fall of it hinted at weight near the hip that wasn't fabric. Hands bare. Knuckles disciplined, palms callused. Boots that made no sound on stone. He carried the faint scent of leather and cold air—the smell of rooftops.

His eyes—gray-green—had the flat patience of something that hunts at dusk.

Eliryn stopped just inside the threshold. She hadn't reached for a book; she had counted exits. "How long have you been there?"

"Long enough to know you counted the doors before you counted the shelves," he said, stepping just far enough into the light to be a choice.

"You don't sound like a librarian."

"I'm not."

"Scholar?"

"No."

"Hunter, then." Her tone didn't rise at the end. Statement, not guess.

"Some nights."

"Is this one of them?"

"If it were," he said mildly, "we wouldn't be speaking."

"Hmm..."

Silence opened between them. Not empty—measured. She watched for tells and found none. Even his half-smile looked stored rather than spontaneous, a thing he could sheathe.

Her skin prickled. "You've been following me."

"Observing," he corrected again. "There's a difference."

"Not from where I'm standing."

He smiled at that. "Well. You're standing rather defensively."

"I've had a lot of practice with that lately."

"I noticed."

The easy way he said it unnerved her more than any threat could have.

"You were with the guards," she said suddenly, realization sparking. "The one at the back. You didn't speak much."

Something flickered in his eyes—amusement, maybe. Or something darker.

"You remember."

"I remember thinking you looked like you wanted to be anywhere else."

"And yet," he said softly, "I stayed."

She hesitated. "Why?"

His answer came without pause, smooth as a blade sliding free. "Watching people is what I do."

A beat.

"And now?"

Now his smile sharpened, not unkind, but not comforting.

"Now I'm interested."

A pulse of warning lit in her chest. Vaeronth stirred, the bond flaring slightly in her mind.

Easy, she thought to him. *He's not threatening us.*

Yet, Vaeronth rumbled.

She couldn't argue that.

Instead, she shifted her weight slightly, her tone dry. "Interested in what, exactly?"

"In seeing what you do next."

"That sounds like a threat."

"Only if you're predictable."

She crossed her arms. "Is there a reason you're talking in riddles? Or do you just like annoying strangers in libraries?"

"I like libraries." His gaze swept her—slowly. Deliberately. *Intimately.* "And you don't feel like a stranger."

That stopped her.

For a breath.

Then: "If I don't feel like a stranger, you've been too close for too long."

He laughed. It was low, real, and disturbingly warm. She hated how much she liked the sound of it.

"I'm Malric."

"And that's supposed to mean something to me?"

"No," he said softly. "But I want it to."

Before she could answer, he flicked two fingers.

The lantern breath shivered. Air folded—no words, no circle, no chalk—and a book *arrived* between them, weightless for a heartbeat before settling into his palm. Her runes prickled along her forearms; the pendant warmed as if the room had inhaled.

Records of the Trials: A History of Ascension and Ruin.

He hadn't even looked at the shelves.

She didn't reach for it.

"What's the catch?"

He smiled like she'd passed a test. "No catch. Call it professional courtesy."

"I'm not a professional."

"No. But you're something."

She hesitated. He grabbed it and held it out towards her, their fingers brushed in her haste to grab it quickly.

Gods, his hand was cold.

"I don't owe you for this," she said, stepping back.

"Of course not."

She hated how flippant he sounded.

"Why help me?"

His smile was soft. Sad, even.

"Because I've seen too many people die without knowing why."

She blinked.

And for one disorienting moment, she thought maybe he meant it.

Malric nodded toward the book. "Read carefully. They lie even in records."

And with that, he turned.

"No cryptic goodbye?" she called after him, pulse still racing.

At the threshold, he paused.

"I already said it."

"Did you?"

He glanced back.

Then he was gone.

Eliryn stood in the empty silence for a long while, the book warm in her hand.

In her mind, Vaeronth spoke.

I do not like him.

"Neither do I."

A beat.

Then softly, she admitted: "I'm not sure that's going to matter."

And she hated how true that felt.

She stood alone for a while longer, staring at the place where he'd stood. The shadows swallowed the space easily, leaving nothing behind- no lingering warmth, no presence.

Only the book in her hands, still faintly warm from his touch.

Malric.

She turned the name over like a stone in her mind. It didn't feel false. But it didn't feel like the whole of him, either.

Her steps found her chambers, though she wasn't sure how. Lost in her thoughts, she barely remembered leaving the library, let alone the hallways and turns she took to get back.

The pendant at her neck pulsed softly, as if in reassurance that Vaeronth was there to guide her.

Her quarters welcomed her like she'd been expected—the door giving way without resistance, the fire already lit. She stepped inside and only then let herself take a deep breath when the door clicked shut behind her.

Only then did her hands begin to shake.

Not from fear. Not exactly.

Malric had known her. He'd been watching her. And while his presence should have felt like danger, it hadn't. Not quite. More like a blade held in expert hands—potentially lethal, yes, but controlled. Intentional.

She settled on the bench beside the fire, set the book before her.

The book was old. Ink faded, brittle pages.

Her heart sank. In the firelight, with her vision, she wouldn't be able to make out the words.

But as her fingers brushed the page, the ink shimmered. Just slightly. A quiet glow rose from the letters—gold and faint blue. They resolved into clarity. Not imagined. Real.

She blinked, startled, and reached for the pendant beneath her robe.

Is this you? she asked Vaeronth.

It is the room, he replied. *It has a vast amount of magic and it seems to like you.*

Eliryn glanced up at the lanterns, at the tall, listening shelves. "Thank you," she said softly—to the room, to whatever old will lived in its bones.

The air seemed to smooth around her. She looked back down. Clear, sharp words stared up from the page.

For the first time in years, she read with ease.

Page after page. Names of the chosen. Where they came from. How they ended.

Some had dates. Some were crossed out. Some bore only the word *vanished.*

There were sketches. Notes. Symbols she didn't recognize.

One, in particular—a jagged triangle inked in crimson—had been circled several times. Beneath it, someone had written:

Seen on the bodies of the marked. Unknown origin.

She touched the symbol lightly. Her skin tingled.

Vaeronth? she called again.

But the dragon was silent now. Resting. Or thinking.

She leaned back, eyes fixed on the fire, the book open beside her.

Why give this to her?

Her skin prickled. Not from fear, not exactly. From not knowing.

She wasn't sure which unsettled her more: the book in her hands...

Or the man who wanted her to read it.

Interlude 4: Malric

"The first dragonriders burned for the crown. The last ones burned by it." —Fragment from the lost journal of Ser Elandros the Wingless

He watched her go.

Silent as a shadow. Fluid as silk against stone. Healer. Dragonrider.

She shouldn't have unsettled him.

And yet... she had.

Malric drew deeper into the darkness, pressing against the cool stone behind the library shelves. The wards here were good, but not enough. Nothing in this castle was built to stop him.

His father's mark—the brand burned into bone, woven into blood—still opened doors no mortal hand could.

And yet, she had sensed him watching.

Those failing eyes of hers. They should have seen nothing. But when she lifted her chin, when her gaze flicked over the shadows like she'd been waiting for him... he'd felt it. Like the press of a knife at his ribs. Not fear. Not surprise.

Recognition.

The dragon must have warned her. Or perhaps—worse—she simply knew.

The room still smelled of fire-touched fabric and rain. She had been... curious. Too curious.

He clenched his fists, drawing a slow breath to still the pulse behind his eyes. This was not meant to be complicated.

His father's words echoed in his head: *"Watch her. Let her grow strong, if she must. But when the time comes, she dies last. The final spectacle."*

He remembered the first time the king taught him to kill. He'd been ten. Small hands. Sharp blade. *Cut hesitation from yourself,* his father had said, the order as cold as the stone floor Malric knelt on. And when he obeyed, when the body stilled, his father only nodded. No praise. No comfort. Just approval—the coldest form of love he'd ever been given.

Malric had never disobeyed an order. Not when he was a child, and certainly not since. His father, the

Sovereign King, ruled with iron in his voice, and Malric had always obeyed. That was what he was bred to do.

But this woman... She was different.

That unguarded moment in the library—the lift of her mouth, that wry, tired grin—it shouldn't matter. A small thing. A meaningless expression from prey who didn't yet understand the hunt.

And yet.

It lingered in his mind.

He remembered when he'd first seen her: leaving her village with smoke clinging to her skin, armor hanging wrong on her frame. And now, after the bond had remade her, she walked like something elemental. Raw. Unrefined, yes—but inevitable.

And gods help him... he liked how breakable she was pretending not to be.

His father had called her dangerous. Had ordered her watched. Stalked. Executed.

Malric should have felt nothing.

Instead, he felt... fascinated.

His fingers found the ring again. Always the ring.

Malric knew it was a leash.

And it owned him.

But tonight, as he followed the silent halls toward the king's sanctum, every step heavier than the last... Malric realized something unsettling.

He didn't want to give his report.

He didn't want to speak her name.

Because for the first time, he wasn't sure if he was reporting on a target.

Or a secret.

A secret he wasn't ready to share.

He should have gone straight to the sovereign.

Instead, Malric slowed at the fork where the lower hall bled into the king's ascent. He lingered, steps quiet, but breath slightly uneven.

The stone here pulsed faintly—wards woven centuries deep. Each step forward would carry him closer to the king.

He didn't move.

Eliryn's voice hovered in the back of his mind.

Curious. Direct. She hadn't flinched from him. She should have.

Malric pressed his gloved thumb against the edge of the cursed ring, a reflex as much as habit. The metal throbbed faintly, pulsing once, like a heartbeat that wasn't his.

He forced himself to breathe.

Hesitation wasn't allowed.

And yet... all he could think was:

She smiled at me.

His pace slowed.

And for the first time in his life, Malric wondered what it might feel like... to disobey.

He opened his eyes to the space around him, pulling himself from his thoughts.

Everything here was stone. Dark and cold.

This was the edge of the sovereign's sanctum. A place where thoughts were not supposed to wander.

Malric waited, forcing every thought from his mind until only the ring's pulse remained.

And then he took one step forward.

Another.

But not as quickly as he once would have.

Not as easily.

Because when he spoke to the sovereign tonight, Malric knew:

He would lie.

Not in words.

But in what he didn't say.

And that silence would be the first betrayal.

CHAPTER 11: THE SECOND TRIAL

"Illusion is the most faithful servant of power—because it does not need to be true, only believed." —The Writ of Nine Flames, forbidden volume

Eliryn stretched slowly, her muscles warm from the heat of the enchanted bath, her mind hazy with too many hours spent curled in the folds of her borrowed sanctuary. The air in the chamber had no breeze, no sun to rise or fall, and time had become a slippery thing—soft and unmarked.

But Vaeronth stirred.

It is close now, his voice echoed in her mind, low and solemn. *The next trial waits.*

She stood, brushing damp hair from her face. "You can feel it?"

Something stirs beneath the stone. A gate with blood in its memory.

"Fantastic. Bleeding stone. Nothing ominous about that."

She swallowed, pulse ticking at her throat, and glanced around the chamber—its strange, gentle luxuries still alien. The plush carpet that never gathered dust. The beautiful tub always filled with warm water. The corner shelf now stacked with books to accompany the one Malric had given her.

She moved to the armoire.

The doors creaked open at her touch.

Inside hung a new garment.

She hesitated. The fabric shimmered dark as obsidian in the low light—tight-fitting leathers layered with shadowy cloth. Sleek. Precise. Quiet. On the left shoulder, stitched in thread that flickered like firelight, was the same symbol that had adorned her first borrowed armor—her family crest.

A single dragon's eye, slit-pupiled and unblinking, embroidered in fine lines. A slender starburst hovered over the eye, as if the light itself would crack the creature's gaze. Encircling the emblem was a delicate crescent moon, its points curling protectively around the eye's edges. Along the lower curve, a scatter of small scales hinted at the beast that had borne the mark, a subtle reminder of power and fire long vanished from the world.

It looked made for someone far braver than she felt.

Her fingers brushed the embroidery. "It knows my family crest."

It honors you, Vaeronth replied. *And it prepares you.*

She dressed slowly, wrapping herself in the dark leathers with careful movements. Beneath the leathers, the inner lining was soft and warm—as though tailored only for her.

She looked like a warrior now. But inside? She still felt like a healer wearing a dead woman's skin.

A loud knock sounded, single and deliberate.

She opened the door.

The same guard stood waiting—straight-backed and silent, dark eyes flickering down to her new attire before rising to meet her gaze. A glint of something like approval passed through his features.

"Well," she said, leaning in the doorway. "You again."

His gaze flicked over her, lingering a fraction too long on the faint glow of her bond marks, but his face remained neutral. "My assignment hasn't changed."

"Mine either." She studied him a beat. "If we're going to keep doing this, I need something to call you that isn't 'hey, shadow.'"

A pause—then the smallest concession. "Silas."

She tasted it. "Silas."

He inclined his head once, as if that settled a contract.

"You're ready?" he asked.

"No. But let's go before I change my mind."

He led her in silence at first, his stride steady and precise.

"I'm guessing you can't tell me what the next trial is," she said after a while.

"No."

"Didn't think so."

A few beats.

"But," Silas said, glancing sideways, "I can tell you what they call it."

"Dare I ask?"

"The Bloodfall."

"Oh, brilliant," she muttered. "Is it named that because there's an actual waterfall of blood, or do they just like to traumatize people early?"

Silas almost smiled. Almost. "I've never asked."

"Right. Fewer questions, fewer funerals."

Silas didn't answer, which she took to mean that her joke was actually accurate.

They descended deeper, the air cooling, the silence lengthening.

"Do you ever get tired of escorting people to their probable deaths?" she asked.

"Orders."

She huffed a laugh. "Have you considered a career change? Something less murder-adjacent? Baker, perhaps?"

"I'm not good at baking."

She blinked at him. "That was a joke."

"I know."

"Stars above, there's hope for you yet."

Silas's mouth twitched again. Once more, almost a smile.

The deeper they descended, the darker the stone. The motifs carved into the walls began to shift—from elegant dragons and stylized flames to something older, cruder. Symbols gouged deep into the stone, glinting with flecks of metal dust.

"I've never seen this part of the castle," she murmured. "Even the air feels... wrong."

"These lower halls are older than the royal line," Silas said softly. "The trials were built into the bones of the mountain."

"That would explain why it feels like the stone is listening."

"I believe a great many things I don't say aloud," he replied, eyes flicking to the carvings. "Especially here."

These stones remember fire older than your blood, Vaeronth whispered, heavy and patient. *I walked here before the first gate was carved.*

A narrow fissure in the wall exhaled a cold, damp breath.

"I used to think castles were all glory and war banners," she said, hugging herself slightly. "But this place—it feels like a cage made beautiful."

So much for fairy tales and glory.

Silas's voice was quieter now. "I think many would share that opinion."

They walked in silence for a while, until the weight of it grew too much.

"Why are you a guard?" she asked suddenly.

Silas hesitated. "I'm sworn to the crown."

"That's not an answer."

Another pause. Then he said, more quietly, "Because loyalty buys safety."

"For you?"

"For my family. My little sister works the grain stalls outside the inner ring. My mother can't work anymore. Guards get food stipends, even when there's drought. If I wear the colors of the sovereign, they're left alone."

Eliryn stopped walking for a moment. Just stopped. "Oh."

Silas kept walking. His voice didn't waver.

"I've seen too many who chose rebellion over survival. I don't judge them for it. But I chose different."

She caught up, silent now. And ashamed of the earlier teasing. He noticed that, too.

"You're not wrong to ask."

"I wasn't expecting such an honest answer."

"Most don't."

"Do you... hate it?"

Silas didn't look at her, but his voice was steady.

"I hate the choice."

The silence stretched after that.

Then, softly, he added: "But sometimes... sometimes you get assigned to someone who makes you hope the world might change."

She tripped.

"Wait. Did you mean me?"

"I didn't say that."

"Oh my gods, you're bad at lying."

Silas looked down at her then. Actually looked. "Then maybe don't die."

She snorted despite herself. "I'm actively working on it."

At last, the corridor narrowed. The arch ahead loomed: a carved threshold etched with old runes that shimmered faintly like something breathing in the stone. Another guard waited, hooded and silent.

"This is where I leave you."

She hesitated. Then, against her better judgment: "Do you want to tell me good luck?"

Silas shook his head slowly. "Luck won't help you."

"Thats fine, I've never been very lucky."

"I'll be waiting."

She blinked.

"Waiting for what?"

"For you to come back."

Eliryn's throat tightened. She made herself smirk instead.

"No pressure."

"Don't make me regret hoping."

"Silas?"

He looked at her.

"I'm really not good at this whole 'hope' thing."

"Neither am I."

And with that, she stepped toward the arch.

At the top of the spiral descent, she paused once more, hand pressed to the cold wall. Torchlight flickered across the narrow steps ahead.

She glanced back.

Silas still stood there, unmoving.

Watching.

Hoping.

She swallowed.

And went down.

The stone door beyond rumbled open, revealing a corridor lit by red crystal. The light was low, flickering. The shadows stretched long.

She walked in.

The door sealed shut behind her.

Steady now, Eliryn. Vaeronth cautioned.

The corridor led into a vaulted chamber carved from black-veined stone. The walls pulsed faintly, alive with some ancient rhythm. She stepped lightly onto a polished floor that mirrored her shape in a distorted silhouette.

Overhead, the ceiling arched like a cathedral vault, inset with spiral constellations of crystal. The room thrummed with quiet magic. As she moved, hovering glyphs ignited and faded, recognizing her dragonmarks.

This room knows your kind, Vaeronth murmured. *It remembers every trial-taker who survived. And every one who did not.*

At the center stood a pedestal of obsidian, a single scroll resting atop it. No guards. No attendants. Just stone, time, and judgment.

She approached carefully.

The moment her fingers brushed the scroll, it unfurled. A deep voice—not Vaeronth's—rang through the chamber:

"Trial Two: The Arena of Veils. You shall face illusion and blood. See through the false, strike through the real. There is no mercy within. Only reflection and reckoning."

The scroll snapped shut.

"Veils," she murmured, uneasy. "Illusion magic?"

Likely, Vaeronth said. *The mind is the cruelest battlefield. If they cannot break your body, they will fracture your will.*

A mirror slid into view from the stone wall. Its surface gleamed like water, so flawless it unnerved her. Her reflection stared back—tall, strong, clothed in black. Harder. Sharper. A stranger who might survive.

She looked away.

But the reflection didn't turn.

A breath caught in her throat. When she looked back again, it matched her movements once more—too smoothly.

She turned toward the corner, where a stone basin filled silently with glowing water. Without hesitation, she dipped her hands in. Warm. Luminous. It left a shimmer on her skin like moonlight.

A final boon, Vaeronth said. *Memory-threaded waters. To help hold onto what is real.*

"Will it be enough?" she asked, drying her fingers on her thighs.

Only if you trust yourself more than your fear.

She looked down at her hands—the ones that had once mended broken bones and soothed fevers. She hadn't prepared for her destiny like she should have.

No weapons. No map. Only her, her dragon, and the hollow certainty that the next battle wasn't just physical—it would be fought inside her mind.

"This is going to suck," she muttered under her breath.

A quiet rumble stirred in her mind.

That's the spirit, Vaeronth said dryly.

She almost smiled. Almost.

Fear pressed against her like a second skin. Not just the fear of death, but the deeper fear: of being small again. Of not being enough.

She closed her eyes. Felt the thrum of the bond. Vaeronth's steady presence, curled around her mind like smoke and steel.

The chime sounded overhead—low and resonant, like a bell tolling for something long dead.

The mirror split.

Light fractured in the doorway beyond. Flickering. Waiting.

Eliryn flexed her hands. The glow of her bond-marks pulsed once, steady and sure.

"They're going to regret putting me through this," she said softly.

Make them. Vaeronth answered.

She squared her shoulders and stepped forward, unflinching.

Let the mind be the battleground.

Let the fear come.

She'd burn through it.

Chapter 12: The Arena of Veils

"Illusion wears your face best when you no longer recognize yourself." —Kalevin Marr

The light swallowed her whole.

For a moment, she floated in silence.

Then the brilliance contracted, drawing inward like a breath held too long. She landed in a circular antechamber of black stone, the air thick with old magic that pulsed like a second heartbeat.

At the chamber's center stood a low iron pedestal, embedded in the floor. Upon it: five weapons.

Each rested on its own carved sigil. Each radiated a different kind of promise.

A curved dagger—quick and cruel.

A twin-headed spear—balanced and long.

A longbow of glasswood—its string humming softly.

A spiked mace—blunt and wet with warding runes.

And a sword—slender, dark, and silent, with no ornament save a single etched star near the hilt.

Eliryn stepped closer.

A feeling washed over her, a sense of knowing that she was supposed to choose one of the weapons as her own.

She hovered a hand over the spear, then the dagger, but her fingers paused above the sword. Taking it in her hand, it felt nearly weightless. The etched star pulsed faintly, as if it had magic that recognized her.

"This one," she murmured.

As her fingers closed around the hilt, the pedestal vanished. The floor trembled. The far wall slid open—stone folding in on itself, revealing mirrored corridors beyond.

Do not trust your eyes, Vaeronth whispered in her mind. *The illusions here are old. Hungrier than most.*

Eliryn scoffed softly, tightening her grip on the hilt.

"Well, that gives me a bit of an advantage, doesn't it?" she said dryly. "I can't trust my eyes on a regular day."

The pendant at her throat pulsed with warmth—not quite laughter, but close.

She stepped forward.

The trial had begun.

For a moment, there was nothing. No floor beneath her, no ceiling above. Just weightless white in all directions—soundless and still.

Then the world snapped into place.

Stone slammed beneath her feet. Walls rose around her like jagged curtains—mirror-black obsidian, towering and curved. The air thickened with heat and the iron tang of blood. Flickering shapes skittered across the mirrored surfaces, shadows caught between flame and glass.

A great arena.

But not for sport.

This was a maze.

A vast, fractured warren of mirrored halls and angled traps, pulsing faintly with twisted magic. Somewhere far off, a scream tore through the silence—sharp, then abruptly cut short.

Then: stillness. Oppressive. Smothering.

Her pulse quickened.

Vaeronth's voice was thinner now, like sound buffered by a thick wall. *These illusions feed on fear. You mustn't let them.*

A low bell tolled. Once.

Twice.

It was official now; the other trial chosen must also be here somewhere.

She moved.

The floor sloped downward into a narrow corridor lined with mirrors. Her reflection blinked from every angle—some delayed, some too fast. One version of her stood still while she moved. Another turned left when she turned right.

Illusions.

An impossible breeze brushed her cheek, and she felt a pressure on her shoulder. A child's laughter echoed and faded.

She kept moving, keeping her breath even.

Around the first corner: blood. Streaked across the wall. Still drying. No body. Just a single boot, and the stale tang of pain in the air.

She didn't linger.

The second corridor bent strangely—an impossible angle, like the hallway had folded inward. Her stomach lurched as she stepped through.

A shape moved up ahead.

She froze.

Someone was there.

No—something.

A flicker of motion in the mirrors. Sharp. Fast. Inhumanly fast.

She drew still, sword steady in her hand, listening to the silence like it was a language she had once known.

Behind her, a reflection moved.

Not hers.

Her grip tightened on the hilt. "I'm getting very tired of ghosts," she muttered, scanning the mirrored corridors.

The reflection stilled when she turned. Watching. Waiting.

"Come on then," she said aloud. "Let's find out who's real."

Nothing answered.

A whisper brushed her ear, so soft it felt like breath.

She spun—just as something lunged from the wall itself.

Her blade met it mid-strike, the clash ringing in her bones. Whatever it was—a creature of glass, or shadow, or both—it recoiled from the star-etched sword. She saw flashes of a distorted face: eyes too many, mouth torn too wide.

Eliryn. Vaeronth's voice like steel on silk. *Illusion cannot bleed. If it does, it's real.*

"Noted."

It lunged again.

She dodged, narrow, precise. Not graceful, not flawless—she was no warrior yet. But her reflexes were sharper than they had any right to be. The bond helped her now, adrenaline churning with dragonfire in her veins.

She swept the sword through its middle.

A scream—shattered glass and cracking bone—and the creature evaporated into shards of light.

Silence returned.

Eliryn stood panting, the sword steady in her shaking hand.

"Next," she whispered, throat raw. "Come on. I've got too many nightmares for that to be the only one here."

The maze answered with silence.

She moved forward again, slower this time, sword angled low, senses burning.

In her mind, Vaeronth's voice stirred.

You are more than your fear.

She didn't answer him.

She wasn't ready to believe it yet.

But she caught sight of a figure ahead.

"Hello?" she called, feeling foolish instantly.

The figure turned. A tall man in a hood. Familiar.

Too familiar.

It was Malric.

"Not real," she muttered.

He smiled. "You shouldn't be here," he said in Malric's voice. "You don't belong here."

"You're not him."

"No," the illusion replied, stepping closer. "But we both know you want me to be."

It lunged.

She dodged—barely—just as its face flickered: Malric, her mother, her own.

She struck. The sword moved with her, fluid and alive. The illusion shattered in a burst of ash.

She stood alone again, breathing hard.

You must not let it draw from you, Vaeronth said. *The more fear you offer, the more faces it will wear.*

She flexed her fingers tighter on the sword. Steel in hand, doubt in throat. Par for the course.

This was only the beginning and she could barely grasp the magic that was all around her, that would try and break her.

And deeper within the maze, she could feel it: something waiting. Watching.

The trial wasn't only about surviving.

It was about unraveling.

Walls reared up, slick with moss, mist curling at their bases. The air thrummed, alive with rune-glow, alive with something watching.

A hiss echoed to her right.

She spun—nothing but shifting shadow.

Don't chase echoes, Vaeronth warned.

"Wasn't planning on it," she muttered. "Unless they try to kill me first."

A section of wall groaned shut behind her, sealing her in.

"Perfect. One way forward. I love not having options."

She moved silently, balanced. The sword was becoming a familiar weight in her hand.

She turned a corner and froze.

A man lay crumpled, limbs bent at impossible angles. Blood soaked the stone around him. A dagger rested in his hand a little too neatly.

Eyes open. Unblinking.

Eliryn, Vaeronth whispered. *Look closer.*

She crept forward. The stillness in the body was too precise. Staged.

"It's a trap," she breathed.

The corpse twitched—first a fingertip dragging grit, then a ripple under the skin like rats running the length of a sack. Joints popped wetly. The head rolled toward her and the mouth split—not opening, splitting—from the corners back toward the ears. Gums peeled high, showing a second row of needle-teeth that hadn't belonged to any human jaw.

She moved without thinking. Weight dropped. Back foot braced. Steel in her hand.

The thing snapped upright with a wire-yank lurch. Eliryn slid inside its reach, low and fast, blade flashing once across the throat. The edge met cartilage with a glassy skitter before giving—a hot sheet of black-red spilled over her knuckles, vinegar-sharp, coin-bitter. The creature didn't fall. It lunged.

She pivoted on the ball of her foot, left shoulder tucked, brought the blade up under the jaw and drove. The point punched through palate; the hilt hit teeth with a dull clack. Bone gripped the steel. She twisted hard, felt something thin and crucial snip.

The body spasmed—hands clawing at nothing. She ripped the blade free, boots slipping on slick stone, then stamped its knee. Ligaments went with a rubbery pop; the joint collapsed. The thing folded, not like a man, but like a trap losing tension.

It didn't bleed right. The sludge hissed where it touched the floor, smoking in hair-fine threads. Skin sloughed in wet sheets; the face caved from within as if fire were eating it from the bones outward. In two heartbeats it was a husk. In three, a heap of wet soot and teeth.

Eliryn held her stance, blade high, breath knifing in and out. Her wrist throbbed; her forearm was sticky to the elbow. The stench hit late—old pennies, hot vinegar, rot—and she gagged it back, eyes sweeping the dark for the next twitch.

Not a corpse, Vaeronth murmured, weight and heat in her mind.

She didn't lower the blade. Not yet.

"That... shouldn't have worked," she murmured. "I've never even trained with a sword."

And yet you wield it as if it remembers you, Vaeronth said gently. *It's in your blood, Eliryn. You are not only yourself now.*

She looked down at the blade. It felt like an extension of herself, like it was meant for her alone.

"Will I always feel like I'm guessing?"

In time, the guessing becomes knowing.

A panicked sound echoed from the mist.

She pivoted at the shout.

A figure blew past her—wild-eyed, mouth chapped white with fear. "Run!" His shoulder clipped hers and was gone, boots skidding, the word ricocheting down stone like a thrown coin.

The wall to her left bulged.

Mortar spidered, stone distended, and something peeled itself out of the masonry—ribbed like a cage made wrong, all bone-lattice and shadow sinew. It hit the floor mid-snarl, talons clicking, a skull-face with no eyes hunting on sound and heat alone.

Eliryn dropped her weight. Blade up. Left foot back. The pendant at her sternum warmed—one beat, two—and the runes along her forearms flared in answer.

It lunged.

She slipped inside the first strike, shadow-claws raking sparks off stone where her head had been. The thing *stank*—cold lime and old blood. She drove her edge across the nearest limb; it parted like brittle coral, a dry crack and a scatter of pale shards skittering over flagstone.

The creature pivoted on three limbs, faster than a living thing should, and rammed her with its chest-cage. Impact knocked breath and thought; she hit a pillar with her shoulder and saw a spray of white stars that weren't magic. It came again, mouth yawning with a harp of needle-teeth, and she jammed her boot into its joint, twisted, brought the blade up under the angle of bone, and lifted.

A seam opened.

Sound followed—high, glass-keen—and then the thing fractured, not falling but *expanding* into ruin: a million splinters blown outward on a breath that wasn't air. Shards hissed past her cheeks and hair; some stuck and sang, thin buzzing notes, before dropping. Fine chalk burst into a white halo, the taste of quarry dust and coins on her tongue. The echo went on too long, like bells ringing under water.

She stayed crouched, blade between her and the debris, ears ringing, lungs burning as grit settled in a gray drift around her boots. A line of heat stung across her cheek; she swiped it, fingertips coming away red and grainy.

"That one nearly took my head," she gasped.

You were graceful, Vaeronth said, amused—thunder made indulgent. *In a newborn hatchling sort of way.*

She snorted, breath hitching. "You're doing wonders for my ego, you know."

She pressed deeper into the maze, the air thickening with heat.

"The air here is different," she murmured. "Smells like... fire."

She emerged into a wide chamber veined with glowing minerals. Smoke coiled near the broken dome. The sky beyond was bruised crimson, neither dusk nor dawn.

Five figures stood below, circling each other warily.

As she stepped down into the chamber, she recognized three of them at once.

The tall boy with copper hair, who had looked too young for the trials. His eyes were wide with terror.

The broad-shouldered man who had tried to shame her after the first test. He met her stare with a thin, ugly smile.

And the slender, snake-eyed one, watching her like he was deciding precisely where to strike.

The other two she didn't remember, but all five shifted as she approached, tension coiling tight enough to snap.

No illusions, Vaeronth murmured. *Only threats.*

The copper-haired boy took a stumbling step back.

The snake-eyed man tilted his head, studying her with a reptile's patience.

The broad-shouldered one came forward a half pace, axe in hand.

"So the little dragonblood thinks she belongs here," he said, voice low and poisonous.

She didn't answer. The blade in her hand gleamed, steady as her heartbeat.

"She moves like she's not afraid," the snake-eyed man observed. "Maybe she isn't."

Then, a screech.

A beast erupted from the shadows behind them—smoke and claw. One of the unknown men shrieked as it dragged him back into the darkness, his voice cutting off like a severed limb, wet and sudden.

The broad-shouldered man lunged at her with a roar, taking advantage of the chaos.

Left, Vaeronth hissed. *Step left—then pivot.*

She obeyed without thought. His axe slammed into stone, shattering the space where her shoulder had been.

Now. Strike his knee.

Her blade flashed. She felt the jolt as it connected, the man's bellow of pain.

Again—guard high!

She blocked his backhand swing, arms trembling with the impact. Sparks burst where metal met metal.

"Filthy cursed-blood," he spat, staggering back.

Behind her, the snake-eyed man vanished into the smoke. The copper-haired boy ran.

Her attacker tried to raise his axe again—too slow. She hooked his ankle and shoved. He hit the ground hard, air whooshing out of him.

Not dead. But not getting up soon.

You see? Vaeronth whispered. *Combat suits you. You only have to believe in yourself.*

She panted, heart hammering.

"This should be beyond impossible. I'm moving like I've done this before," she whispered.

In your soul, you have.

She turned, the chamber empty but threats near in the shadows.

A corridor glimmered beyond—green and cold.

She took one step, then stopped.

He appeared in the space ahead in the blink of an eye.

Malric.

He stepped out of the wrecked dark where the wall had just birthed teeth. Dust ribboned off his coat; a thin white shard clicked under his boot and stilled. He stopped within reach, then—deliberately—took half a step back.

"You again?" Her voice was rough. The blade in her hand quivered once and held.

His gaze took her in with a quick, exact sweep: cut along the cheekbone, grit stuck in the lashes of her right eye, blood slicking her knuckles, the left wrist overworking. "You're hurt," he said. Observation, not pity. "Blink before it crusts. You'll lose depth."

She didn't move.

He slid a square of dark cloth from his sleeve and held it out—fingers open, palm visible, no advance. "For the eye."

She stared a beat, then took it without lowering the blade. The cloth was clean. Warm from his wrist. She wiped once; the world sharpened by a degree.

"Better," he said. "Now breathe. Three counts in, four out. Your left wrist is lying to you—shift your grip or you'll drop the point when you cut."

Her jaw clenched. She adjusted anyway. The tremor eased.

"Why are you helping me?" she asked, watching him over steel.

"It costs me nothing," he said, soft. "And you're more useful alive."

"Useful to whom?"

"To whatever comes next."

That should have chilled her. It didn't. Not quite. He was studying her, yes—but not like prey. More like a craftsman evaluating a tool he intended to keep sharp.

"Step back," she said.

He did. No argument. Choice, not surrender.

The corridor breathed around them, the sour tang of the last creature still in the air. Far down the passage, a faint **tink** like cooled glass under stress. His head turned toward it. "When you hear that," he murmured, "the walls are thinning. Don't hug the stone—stay center, watch for mortar spidering."

"You know these things well," she said.

"I've walked this space before." A glance to her hands. "And you're beginning to tire."

"You're an illusion," she said flatly.

"Am I?"

"That or you're somehow a part of the trials. Or you've been following me again."

"I'm not here just for you," he said, voice low and infuriatingly calm. "I have work to do."

She narrowed her eyes. "Work."

"And you, it seems, are very good at finding trouble."

Her pulse kicked up. "So you are part of this?"

He smiled, a flicker of amusement warming his eyes.

"Not exactly," he murmured. "Not officially. But you assumed that I was an illusion at first? That's telling."

"Telling how?"

"For you to have seen me here before means you must have been thinking about me," he said softly.

Her grip on the sword tightened. "I'm a little busy trying not to die to be thinking about you."

Gods above, why did her heartbeat betray her so loudly it was hard to think?

"You look like you know how to multitask."

He considered her a heartbeat longer, then added, almost as if against habit, "When the air turns vinegar, don't cut high. They open low."

She filed it before she could stop herself. "Why tell me?"

"You don't need another new scar," he said simply. "Not tonight."

Vaeronth murmured in the warm weight of her mind. *He prowls. But his blades are sheathed—for now.*

Eliryn let a sliver of tension go. Not trust. Not yet. Just the notch that keeps a bowstring from fraying. "If I see you again... friend or foe?"

He tilted his head as if considering.

"If I wanted you dead," he said, voice gentle as a confession, "you wouldn't have the breath to be asking questions."

He stepped past at an angle that didn't put his back to her, close enough that she felt the calm of him, the unhurried pulse of someone who didn't need the dramatics of danger to be dangerous. As he moved, he spoke without looking. "Center of the hall. Avoid alcoves with lime dust—the ones that breathe. And don't let your left hand carry your pride."

She almost smiled. Almost. "Noted."

"Try not to die, Eliryn," he called over his shoulder. "I'd find that rather... anticlimactic."

Eliryn held her stance until her breath obeyed. The sword steadied in her grip where he'd told her to shift it; the cloth was warm in her palm. Against sense, something in her eased by a hair.

"He is not kindness," she said under her breath.

No, Vaeronth agreed, heavy and intent.

Eliryn stood frozen, the sword trembling faintly in her grip.

"I still don't trust him."

Good.

She turned slowly toward the corridor, but her gaze lingered on the place he'd disappeared, on the swirling darkness still softening back into silence.

She tried to steady her breathing, to pretend the encounter hadn't shaken her. But it had.

More than any monster so far.

Because she could brace herself for claws and fangs and illusions that wanted blood.

But Malric...

Malric was something else entirely.

Something she couldn't name.

She turned away, willing her thoughts into stillness. If she refused to dwell on the impossibility of magic and monsters, or how naturally the sword had fit her hand, she would not linger on Malric either, or wonder what part he played in these cruel games.

Let him play his game. She'd win hers.

Interlude 5: Malric

"A blade remembers the hand that forged it, even when it's forgotten what it was meant to protect." —Virellen of the Black Sigil

There are worse things than being born a weapon. Malric should not have lingered.

The maze breathed and bent around him, a living thing of stone and shadow. Most walked it with dread. He walked it like memory, silent and sure, his boots never scuffing, his breath too shallow to echo.

He was made for places like this.

But tonight... something pressed against that certainty. A presence, still near. A pull.

Eliryn.

The dragonrider.

His gloved fingers drifted to the ring on his right hand—the blood-forged signet that marked him as the king's blade. Its weight was constant, but tonight, it felt heavier. He twisted it once, feeling the cold bite of its magic brush against his pulse.

It knows, he thought grimly. *It knows what it was made to kill.*

And perhaps... it already recognized her.

She shouldn't have unsettled him. And yet... her presence lingered longer than he liked. Too long.

He hated thinking about her.

And still, he thought of the way her voice had sounded when she said his name. How her injuries hadn't made her smaller. How the marks on her skin caught the light like they belonged there. Like they were meant for her.

His hands flexed without him realizing.

Malric stopped beneath a crumbling arch, one hand braced on the stone, steadying himself. He knew this sensation. Knew how it started: the mind looping back, caught on a problem it couldn't solve. Obsession, his father would say, is failure disguised as discipline.

But Eliryn wasn't just a problem.

She was becoming a fixation.

And fixations were dangerous.

For everyone involved.

He knew that.

And yet, when he closed his eyes, it wasn't her power he remembered. It was her.

The way she stood after exhaustion should have broken her. The faint tilt of her head when she listened like she didn't trust what her own eyes told her. The brief, unguarded smile she gave him in the library, like she didn't know he was supposed to kill her.

Her smile haunted him more than her magic.

He hated that.

Some part of him wondered—darkly, quietly—what it would feel like to be the last thing she trusted. To be the one she looked to, when the others fled.

That was the part of himself he knew better than to listen to.

Because when Malric fixated on something... he never let it go.

Not until it bled.

Not until it broke.

He forced himself to move, sinking to one knee and testing the ground with his palm. Warm. Still shifting. The trial was awake, watching, weighing every step.

He should be moving. But his hand lingered against the earth, and his thoughts strayed back.

To her.

The way she'd held the sword, awkward but unafraid. The way she asked questions no one else dared. The way she didn't flinch when she thought he was an illusion, didn't run when she realized he wasn't.

She didn't know it, but that moment might have already changed her fate.

Or his.

Malric cursed under his breath and pulled out the old leather-bound book he always carried. The pages were filled with ink and secrets, scraps of overheard prophecy, ciphered maps, old marks of dead kings, and sketches from his own hand. Symbols of flame. A dragon's eye cradled by a crescent moon.

He flipped to the newest page. At the top, in neat, sharp ink: The Dragonrider. Eliryn. Subject marked by prophecy. Eyes like storm clouds before the storm.

He paused.

Then added, almost reluctantly: Not what I expected.

Malric leaned back against the stone, letting his head rest for a breath. His muscles ached beneath the stillness, trained to stay coiled, never softened. But lately... something had cracked his indifference.

It had been years since anyone had looked at him without fear. Longer since someone saw him without knowing what he was.

She had. Somehow.

Even if she didn't yet understand what she was looking at.

His fingers drifted to the scar under his chin, the one no armor could cover. It hadn't healed right. Left by someone he'd trusted once, an echo of a lesson burned deep.

Don't hesitate.

But Eliryn made him hesitate.

And that alone made her dangerous.

Not because of her growing power.

Because of what she might make him remember. The boy before the blade. The name before the silence. The man who might have chosen another path, if someone—anyone—had given him the chance.

He stood quickly, shoving the book back into his cloak. Too much stillness in this place invited regret. He couldn't afford that. Not yet.

The next corridor was narrowing, darkening. A change was coming.

Before he vanished again, he looked once more in the direction she'd gone. Not with cold calculation this time, but something like... reluctant hope.

"I've hidden the monster—for now. But I can't wait for the moment she meets him."

Then, without sound or farewell, Malric melted into the dark again, just another shadow among many.

But his thoughts lingered behind like footsteps he hadn't meant to leave.

Chapter 13: The Space Between Blades

"Strength alone will not save you. But it may carry you far enough to choose something better." —Letters of Eianya Rell, First Flamekeeper

The silence that followed was nearly holy.

Eliryn moved through a narrow corridor of glistening stone, its floor cracked but dry, the mist thinning with each step. Here, the air was cooler. Calmer. The scent of blood and smoke that had lingered in the maze's heart faded to damp moss and old dust.

A breathing space. A lull in the storm.

She stopped beneath a broken archway and leaned her back against the cold wall, finally letting her sword lower completely. Her arms trembled, not from fear, but from sheer fatigue. Sweat clung to her spine. Her heart still hadn't quite decided if it was done racing.

"Vaeronth," she murmured, "am I crazy for still feeling overwhelmed by everything?"

The dragon's voice coiled through her mind like smoke curling through rafters. Calm. Present.

No, young one. You are far from crazy. What you have faced has killed lesser-folk. Our bond gives you strength and your blood gives you an edge, but you are doing far better than even I could have hoped.

She let her head fall back against the stone, exhaling softly. "See, now that just makes me more nervous."

Why?

"Because if this is me doing well, I hate to think what failing looks like."

A pause. And then, dry as a winter wind: *You would not still be standing.*

Eliryn let out something like a laugh—a sharp, breathless sound. "Valid."

She closed her eyes, breathing in slowly through her nose. Her fingers curled reflexively at her sides. Her knuckles ached from how long she'd gripped her sword.

"And you're sure Malric is not part of the trials?"

I am not sure what role he plays. There are many things at work within Castle Othren. A pause, then more softly: *But in that moment... he was not feeling malice. Not toward you.*

She pressed a hand to her sternum, over the pendant. Her palm felt clammy against the warm metal.

"Then why do I feel like I've just made a mistake somehow?"

Because he, like you, has gone unnoticed for so long. And that commonality intrigues you both.

"I didn't want to be intriguing."

Your heartbeat said otherwise.

Eliryn blinked, frowning. "...Did you just make a joke?"

A beat of silence. *I am capable of humor.*

"That wasn't humor. That was unsettling."

And you're awfully reckless for a girl who can barely see, Vaeronth replied, wry and fond.

She smirked despite herself, brushing damp hair from her face. "Fair enough."

She let herself slide down the wall until she was sitting, sword resting across her lap. The weight of it felt unfamiliar now. Everything did.

"He unnerves me."

There's lessons to be learned in all things.

She let out a shaky laugh. "If I live long enough to learn them."

We will.

The certainty in Vaeronth's voice made her chest tighten. She didn't believe it—not fully. But for now, she let herself borrow his faith.

For a time, they sat in silence, dragon and rider. Just breathing. Just listening.

But peace, like all things in the maze, was not built to last.

As she pushed herself upright and rounded the next corner, the quiet began to stretch unnaturally. No sound of stone beneath her leathered feet. No echoes. No distant shouts or monster roars.

It was still.

Too still.

She slowed.

"More illusions?" she whispered.

Likely. Vaeronth's tone was guarded now. *But not the same as before. These will be shaped by you.*

Her brows drew tight. "By me?"

The trial already knows you can best beasts. Now it wants to see what you'll do when facing your own fears.

"Oh, good," she muttered. "Because those other monsters weren't nearly personal enough."

The corridor ahead shimmered; light folding in on itself, mist curling like fingers around her ankles.

And from the shadows stepped two women.

One was cloaked in the shape of a memory barely old enough to bruise. Her mother, on her final day, bandaged and pale from the wounds she'd never recovered from, jaw clenched tight even in death. Her clothes were bloodstained, scorched at the edges—the same ones she'd worn when she'd slipped away into the dark to steal armor for Eliryn, only to come home broken.

Eliryn's stomach hollowed.

And beside her... was a stranger she somehow knew.

Straight-backed. Tattooed in sharp geometric spirals down her arms and neck. Eyes like chipped obsidian. Not old, but not young either—aged by time, tempered by war. There was no warmth in her face, only strength. Her skin bore the faint shimmer of a rider once bonded, a power from within radiating around her.

Her grandmother.

Eliryn's breath stilled. She had never seen her in life. Only in faded sketches. Only in stories so painful her mother struggled to speak them aloud. But now she stood in the flesh—or something close to it—wearing the face of a warrior who had once soared alongside dragons before falling with them into history.

Eliryn's sword lowered slightly. Her heart shuddered.

"Vaeronth..." she breathed, her voice barely audible.

Illusions, Vaeronth whispered in her mind, quieter than before. *But not of the maze's making alone. These came from you.*

Her pulse faltered.

"I didn't summon them."

Not consciously.

Her vision fluttered, ghosted and weeping. One moment the women blurred to smudges, the next, she could see the curl of ash at her mother's sleeve, the shimmer of her grandmother's tattoos. It felt like waking and dreaming in the same breath. Too sharp. Too real.

"Make it stop," she whispered.

I cannot, Vaeronth said gently. *You carry them.*

Her mother stepped forward.

"You shouldn't have gone," her mother rasped, voice rough and worn. "I died for you. And you... burned it all."

Eliryn flinched. Her throat closed. "I gave you rites. I honored you the only way I could."

"You lit the match," her mother whispered, eyes full of ache. "And left me in ash."

She shook her head, weakly. "I couldn't leave the house standing. They would've torn it apart. Desecrated it."

"You left nothing," her mother said. "Not even yourself."

"No." Her voice cracked. "That's not true."

But her mother's hollow eyes said otherwise.

Eliryn's chest seized as her grandmother stepped forward, circling like a hawk assessing weak prey.

"So this is what the line has become," the elder woman said, voice not angry but heavy. Measured. "Half-blind. Half-formed. Shaking in the dark."

Eliryn's grip faltered. She felt small. So small.

"I didn't ask for this," she whispered. "I never asked to be chosen."

"And yet here you are," her grandmother replied. "Trying to carry a legacy you barely understand. You disgrace what came before."

The words hit harder than a blade. Not fury. Not hatred. Just cold assessment.

Eliryn's strength cracked. Not from anger. From grief.

"I'm trying."

Her grandmother circled slowly. Closer now. "Trying won't keep you alive. Trying won't lead armies. You are not strong enough. Your eyes betray you. Your grip falters. You chase prophecy like a blind moth to flame."

"I—" Her knees hit the stone. She didn't remember falling.

Her vision faltered again—then cleared.

And in that moment, she saw both their faces clearly: her mother, broken by sacrifice; her grandmother, a legend turned shadow.

Eliryn bowed her head. The tears came, sharp and hot and unwanted.

"I know I'm not enough," she said hoarsely. "But I don't have anything else. There's no home for me in the village without you. No safety. All I have now is trying to survive these trials."

She looked up, throat burning, eyes stinging, sword trembling in her grip.

"I didn't leave because I wanted glory. I never wanted to be chosen. I left our home in flames because I knew I would never be returning."

Her mother said nothing.

Her grandmother tilted her head, and for the first time, something flickered behind her obsidian eyes. Not approval. Not disdain.

Curiosity.

"I'll never be what you were," Eliryn whispered. "But I found my dragon. My soul-bonded. And if the world means to burn me—then let it. I will meet you both in the flames."

Silence stretched, long and painful.

Her vision blurred again. Mist turned the world to watercolor.

When it returned—the illusions watched her not as accusers.

But as judges.

And then, her mother whispered, soft as snowfall: "Go."

Eliryn dragged herself upright. Slowly. Painfully. Her legs shook. Her hands shook. But she stood.

"I'll carry you anyway," she whispered. "As weight. As warning. Not as chains."

And she stepped forward.

The air shivered around her. Mist unraveling. Stone warming beneath her boots. Behind her, the figures cracked and faded, leaving only echoes.

"...Glad to know judgment runs in the family," she rasped, wiping her cheek with her sleeve.

You stood in your truth, Vaeronth said gently, quieter than before. Proud.

"She was so strong," Eliryn whispered. "Both of them were."

And now you are, Vaeronth said. *Because strength is not the absence of pain. It is the decision to move through it.*

Eliryn walked on, her body heavy but her steps steady. She let herself breathe.

"Okay," she muttered. "One emotional breakdown down. How many more to go?"

Vaeronth wisely didn't comment. But she felt his presence coil closer, protective and steady.

Her hand tightened on the hilt of her blade, the weight of it both grounding and sharp.

And then—laughter.

Not cruel. Not mocking.

Joyful.

She froze.

It was the kind of laughter she hadn't heard since her seventh summer, barefoot and sunburnt, racing through the golden hills of Lirin's Edge.

She turned.

And saw them.

Children. A dozen or more. Some she remembered from games beneath the orchard trees, others she barely recognized—faces she'd glimpsed only once at village gatherings. They danced around a bonfire, ash smeared on their cheeks, hands sticky with honey, chasing each other with wild abandon.

And at the front of the crowd... herself.

Younger. Freckled. Barefoot. Wild-haired and free. No sword. No shame. Just a girl, smiling so hard her whole face glowed.

Before her eyes changed.

Before the village turned cold.

Before they whispered things about her when they thought she couldn't hear.

Eliryn's throat closed. She took a step back.

"I don't want to see this," she whispered, sword lowering.

But you need to, Vaeronth murmured in her mind, voice gentle as rain on ash. *The maze shows you your burdens.*

The younger Eliryn stepped forward, grinning.

"You don't belong anywhere," the girl said softly, tilting her head. "Not here. Not in the trials. Not even with the dragon."

Eliryn's chest tightened. "Stop."

The girl's smile sharpened, cruel in its innocence.

"They hated you before you left. You think they'll welcome you back if you survive?" Her eyes gleamed obsidian-dark. "There's nothing waiting for you. No love. No family. No home."

"No—" Eliryn's voice cracked. "That's not true."

But her heart clenched, because somewhere deep, some small, jagged part of her believed it.

Behind the girl, the laughter twisted—slipping into something colder. Children crumpled to the ground like dolls with their strings cut. Honey turned to rot. The air reeked of smoke and burnt grass.

Eliryn flinched. "This isn't real."

Isn't it? whispered the maze. Or maybe it was her own mind.

The girl stepped closer, voice rising, cruel and bright. "You'll never be one of them. You weren't enough for your village. You won't be enough for the throne. Not with those eyes. Not with that cursed blood."

"I'm not cursed," Eliryn rasped, fists trembling.

"Then why do they all look away?" The illusion hissed.

The younger version lunged—suddenly, violently—eyes wild, blade in hand. Her movements were fast, feral, a perfect echo of Eliryn's own style but stripped of dragonblood. Unhoned. Angry.

"You left me behind!" she shouted, slashing downward. "You left the girl who didn't know how to fight!"

Eliryn parried with a cry, metal ringing. Her hands burned. Her body felt too heavy. "You're me," she hissed, locking blades. "I grew up, but I never stopped carrying you."

The girl snarled, pressing close. "You hate who you were. You hate where you came from."

Eliryn bared her teeth. "I don't hate my past."

"Liar."

The other children closed in, shadows now, limbs sharp and broken, eyes empty. They carried no faces anymore. Just twisted weapons made of bone and iron, screeching like wind through a broken door.

Eliryn spun, striking fast. One, two, three. They dissolved into ash as her blade passed through them. But more came.

"Vaeronth—" she gasped.

I am with you. But this battle must be yours.

The younger Eliryn circled, voice breaking. "You'll never be more than what they made you. A strange girl with strange eyes, chasing a title that was never meant for her."

For half a heartbeat, Eliryn's blade dipped.

Then her chin lifted.

"I am strange," she said softly. "And maybe the gods should have chosen someone better for their prophecy."

She stepped forward.

"But here I am."

She met the girl's gaze—her own gaze—and stepped into her.

"I didn't survive this long just to lose to a memory," she rasped. "Not now."

Their swords clashed. Once. Twice. Sparks flew. Her body burned, her arms screamed, but she didn't stop.

"I didn't leave you behind," Eliryn snarled, locking blades again. "I carried you. Every mile. Every night. Through every scar."

She knocked the blade from the girl's hand with a final, brutal strike. The younger version stumbled, breath ragged, tears falling silently.

"I just wanted to belong," the girl whispered, voice cracking.

"So did I," Eliryn breathed. "But we were made for more."

She didn't strike.

She didn't have to.

She pressed her palm gently—against her younger self's chest.

"I see you," she whispered. "And I forgive you."

The girl blinked once—then cracked like glass, shattering into a thousand glowing shards. The remaining children turned to dust with the wind.

Silence fell.

Eliryn stood alone again, shoulders shaking, breath ragged.

You faced yourself, Vaeronth said quietly, voice proud yet soft. *And gave yourself the grace you deserve. Your pain is not weakness.*

Eliryn wiped her face roughly with her sleeve, hating the tears but unable to stop them. "I still want to belong," she whispered, hollow.

I know, Vaeronth replied, closer now, steady as the earth. *But now you belong to something greater.*

"I belong to you."

You belong to yourself, came the gentle correction. *I am simply fortunate enough to be yours.*

She laughed then, raw and broken.

"Alright, old man. That was... actually quite nice."

A pause.

I have my moments.

Her blade felt lighter now. Or maybe her heart did.

Eliryn raised her chin, took a shuddering breath, and stepped forward.

Let the next illusion come.

Let them all come.

She was ready.

You did well, Vaeronth said softly. *You faced your own self-doubt and didn't let it shake you.*

"Then why," she whispered, "does it still feel like losing?"

Because the pain you feel is not a puzzle to solve, he replied gently. *It's a price. And you're still paying it.*

She wiped her blade clean on her sleeve, movements sharp but hollow.

"I thought pain had a peak—you climb it and it's done. Turns out it's just a path that doesn't end."

A pause. Then, dry as ever: *You'll grow stronger. Eventually.*

She huffed a small, bitter laugh. "Stars, you're insufferable."

And yet, I'm not wrong.

She fell quiet, her breathing slowing as she pressed a hand against the stone wall for balance. Then, gripping her sword tighter, she pushed forward.

She thought she'd reached the heart of it.

But the maze had one more truth to unearth.

The corridor narrowed, pressing inward until she had to shoulder through sideways, stone scraping her bare arms, jagged edges snagging against her skin like the world itself was trying to hold her back.

Her breathing grew tighter. Shallow. The pendant at her chest pulsed wildly, the rhythm panicked, too fast, too loud.

"I hate this," she whispered. "I really, really hate this."

So does the maze. That's why it's fighting you now.

She barked a bitter laugh. "Why does that almost make sense?"

Because you're finally beginning to trust me.

She shoved herself forward—and then, suddenly, an opening.

A circular chamber.

Carved not from rough stone, but from black-veined obsidian. Smooth as glass. Gleaming like water.

No doors. No sky. No exit.

Only a pillar in the center.

And atop it—

A mirror.

She approached warily, every part of her body screaming to stop, her blade still drawn, still shaking faintly in her grip.

Be ready, Vaeronth warned, lower now. Almost sad.

"I'm so, so tired of hearing that."

Nevertheless, be ready. He repeated.

The mirror shimmered.

And then it stepped out.

Herself.

Not a younger version. Not a ghost.

This was now.

Clad in the same dark leathers. Holding an identical sword. Every movement mirrored her own. Even the expression was the same: steady. Guarded. And cold.

But the eyes.

The eyes were wrong.

"Another illusion," Eliryn muttered, half-hopeful.

Not quite, Vaeronth said softly. *This one is not made of your fears. It is made of your potential.*

Eliryn took a step back.

"Meaning?"

It is what you become... if you surrender to the path without restraint. If you choose power without purpose. Survival without soul.

Her reflection lifted its blade and stepped into the air, dropping form the platform in a silent, predatory glide. Stone took the impact with a hollow thud; dust rose in a tight halo around its boots as it came to rest a breath away from Eliryn.

"Oh, you've got to be kidding me."

Eliryn lunged.

Metal met metal in a bone-jarring clang. Sparks scattered like spilled starlight. She pivoted, struck again, but her mirror blocked her every blow with calm precision.

"This isn't fair!" she snapped, parrying desperate-ly.

Her skin split open as the hilt bit into her hand. Blood slicked her grip, hot and sticky, but she refused to loosen her hold.

Pain was just another thing she'd have to carry.

"Vaeronth!" she gritted.

I'm here.

"How do I beat myself?"

You don't.

She nearly cursed aloud.

Vaeronth's voice growled inside her mind.

You cannot outfight yourself.

"I'm open to ideas!"

She rolled to the side, barely avoiding a downward slash that cracked the stone floor where she'd just stood. She scrambled upright, sword sagging in her grip.

Her copy fought in silence. No taunts. No gloating. Just relentless, precise brutality. It was... clinical.

"I miss the creepy children," she gasped.

That is concerning.

She ducked another strike, her whole body screaming.

"What do I do?"

Choose what she never will.

Her reflection advanced, blade raised, silent and merciless.

And then she saw it.

Her reflection was perfect.

Flawless.

Empty.

Eliryn's chest tightened.

"I get it."

She stood straighter.

Her sword wavered once—then she let it fall from her grip.

It clattered to the floor.

Her copy hesitated.

"I choose not to become you."

Silence rang louder than swords.

Her reflection faltered, head tilting.

"I'm not just prophecy," Eliryn whispered. "I'm not just power."

Step by step, she crossed the glass floor.

"I remember who I was. I remember hands that healed. I remember wanting something more than glory."

The mirror hesitated. The copy's head tilted, confused.

"I'm not just a blade," Eliryn rasped. "I didn't ask for this life. But if I had known that all this was possible... I think I would've welcomed the prophecy. To prove that legends could be real again."

The mirror's surface cracked, spider-web thin across its chest.

"If the world wants to burn me down, I'll be the one setting the fire."

The mirror-Eliryn trembled.

Eliryn whispered, steady now:

"I am not afraid of myself anymore."

And the reflection shattered.

A single crack—then a hundred.

Shards of obsidian spiraled upward, dissolving to dust as they rose.

She stood alone.

Silence. Total and complete.

And then—

A doorway bloomed from the wall.

Real. Solid. Lit with golden light.

Vaeronth's voice came, reverent now.

You've done it. You've reached the end.

Eliryn staggered toward her blade, scooping it up off the ground before heading for the opening, each step leaving blood behind.

"I'm not sure I won," she whispered.

Today, you survived. That is victory enough.

"What if there's more?"

There will be, Vaeronth said softly. *But not today.*

She paused at the threshold, glancing back at the pile of dust where her reflection had shattered.

Then, voice bone-dry:

"Next time I fight myself, she better show up with sass, not steel. I might stand a chance at winning a verbal argument."

A pause. She let her sword hang low, dragging it halfheartedly behind her.

"And if these dragon marks don't start coming with built-in stamina soon, I'm filing a complaint."

You are being very dramatic, Vaeronth rumbled dryly.

She huffed. "Says the creature who gets to hitch a ride in my pendant while I'm over here doing all the cardio."

There was a pause, like even the ancient dragon had no rebuttal.

Technically, you are correct, he conceded at last.

She smirked. "Damn right, I am."

CHAPTER 14: WHAT REMAINS

"A true warrior isn't the one who strikes hardest, but the one who carries ruin without letting it shape his name."
—Torren Vex, war-widow of Stonefell

The gate hissed open.

Stone groaned in protest as it parted, mist uncoiling across the threshold like something alive. Eliryn stepped through, her boots striking bare flagstones. For an instant, she half-expected more illusions to pounce. More traps. More visions gnawing at her mind.

But no phantoms came.

This space was plain, almost insultingly so after the labyrinth's torments. A long, rectangular hall stretched before her, empty except for a row of benches bolted to the walls. The air was cool, damp with salt, and the ceilings arched overhead in silent mockery of some grand temple. Gulls wheeled beyond high, barred windows, their cries thin and hungry.

It felt like the maze had simply spit her out here. Like she hadn't *earned* her exit so much as been expelled, too stubborn to die.

Only one figure waited beyond the gate: tall, robed in silver and charcoal, spine straight as a swordblade. The steward.

He stood alone in the center of the room, a brass bell dangled from his wrist.

He did not ring it, though his hand was posed as though he wanted to.

His eyes fixed on her like she was something sharp. Dangerous.

"The dragonrider," he said, voice cool. "You're the first."

Eliryn didn't answer right away. She stepped forward slowly, wary.

The steward's gaze flicked briefly from her sword, to her pendant, to her eyes, lingering on her ghostlight irises.

"Yeah. They do that," she said flatly, catching his look. "Spooky eyes. Part of the new aesthetic."

He flinched. Barely.

But she saw it.

Vaeronth's voice curled in her mind, dry. *People will fear what they do not understand.*

She flicked her eyes toward the steward. *He should be terrified then.*

"So," she said softly to the steward, shifting her stance like someone preparing for a punch, "you're afraid of dragonblood."

"I am not afraid," he replied too quickly.

"Right. That's why you're holding that bell like it's going to save your life."

The steward's knuckles whitened subtly on the bell handle.

"If you're going to call for backup," she added, "you should do it now. Before my cursed blood decides to do something unexpected."

Vaeronth rumbled. *You are enjoying this far too much.*

"I have to get my entertainment somewhere," she muttered.

The steward didn't answer. Not at first.

"I've read every account of the dragonriders that exists," he said finally. "And every account agrees on one thing: the deeper the bond, the more... inhuman the rider becomes."

"Inhuman," she echoed, rolling the word on her tongue like something unfamiliar. "Huh."

She flexed her fingers once on the sword's hilt, then consciously forced them to relax. "Is that what you see when you look at me? Something inhuman?"

"I see someone without full sight who has survived the second trial," he said tightly. "And I wonder how."

Her brows lifted slightly. "Yeah. Me too."

A beat of silence. Then she smiled, small and sharp.

"Maybe it's all the running. I'm getting stronger."

Vaeronth huffed in her mind, half exasperation, half fondness. *Or perhaps you simply refuse to die.*

"I prefer my version."

The steward's lips thinned further, understanding that she was probably speaking with her dragon.

"Time will decide," he said coldly.

She wondered if he realized how pitiful he looked wearing his fear so obviously.

Before she could press further, the gate behind her groaned. Footsteps echoed—heavy, grounded, purposeful.

She turned.

And though her muscles tightened automatically, she said, mostly to herself—

"If it's another trial, I swear I'm sitting this one out."

You won't, Vaeronth said, far too knowingly.

She sighed. "Yeah, yeah."

But her fingers stayed tight on her sword anyway.

A man emerged from mist: tall, thick-shouldered, with scars like old maps across his arms. His face was lined with sun and blood and time. He carried no weapon now, but Eliryn didn't doubt he could make one from anything at hand. He moved like someone who had learned to survive by force, not finesse.

Eliryn's mind supplied his village name, remembering from the first trial.

Stonefell.

Old mountain blood. Warriors raised with steel in their hands and legends in their marrow.

His brow lifted when he saw her standing there.

"You?" he said, voice rough like a whetstone. "I thought I would be the first."

"You're only a little late," Eliryn said, almost smiling despite herself. "Not that it's a race or anything."

He huffed, a sound halfway between amusement and disbelief. "So the girl with dragonblood proves worthy after all."

She tilted her head slightly. "As does the warrior with iron bones."

They stood for a moment, measuring each other like soldiers weighing whether or not they were on the same side.

Then Stonefell nodded, once. "I heard stories of dragonriders when I was young. Thought they were just legend and song." His gaze flicked to her family crest, then her eyes. "But I've also heard they were monsters. Weapons in skin."

"You sound like the steward," she said, dry.

"Do I?" Stonefell glanced at the pale-robed man. "Then maybe he's wiser than he looks."

Vaeronth rumbled in her mind, unimpressed. *That one does not strike me as wise.*

"Agreed," she murmured back.

They stood for a long moment, both too stubborn—or too wary—to look away.

Then, Stonefell's gaze flicked toward the empty benches lining the wall. He shifted slightly, the barest hitch in his stance, as if his legs had only just remembered they could ache.

Eliryn caught the glance, then glanced at the benches herself. Her legs were already protesting, and her shoulder felt like it had been ripped out and jammed back into place by some drunk deity.

"Don't suppose you're as tired as I look?" she asked dryly.

Stonefell's mouth twitched. "That's a bet I'd take."

She huffed softly, stepped toward the nearest bench, and dropped onto it like a collapsing siege tower.

Stonefell followed, slower but steady, settling beside her with the weight of a man used to carrying grief as armor.

Neither of them spoke for a few breaths. Not out of discomfort.

Just... because silence, for once, wasn't an enemy.

"I've seen some strange things in my time," Stonefell said after a moment, scratching absently at one of his scars. "But nothing that cut as deep as what I saw in those chambers."

Eliryn nodded. "They weren't just fake illusions. They were more like... truths twisted sideways."

"Your family?"

She hesitated, then nodded again. "And pieces of myself I thought I'd buried deeper."

He looked at her for a long moment. "You came out steady."

"I came out alive," she corrected. "That's enough for now."

Stonefell leaned back, elbows resting on stone. "You move like a fighter, but not one trained by war. More... desperate. Personal."

Eliryn huffed softly. "That's one way to say 'a complete novice.' But yes, I'm basically winging it."

At that, Stonefell chuckled once. A real sound. Not forced.

Then, after a pause: "Your eyes. How much can you see?"

"Shapes. Light. Motion. Blades when they're too close for comfort." She shrugged. "I can see you clearly if I focus hard enough—like shards of glass. I have to piece everything together. It's... exhausting."

"And you still made it through the trials unscathed?"

Eliryn tilted her head. "Would you believe me if I said it wasn't sight that got me here?"

Stonefell met her gaze evenly. "I wouldn't be surprised at all."

Vaeronth stirred, his voice dry in her mind. *You did some of the work.*

Eliryn snorted softly. "My dragon says it's because I have amazing instincts."

That earned her a proper huff of amusement from Stonefell, though he said nothing, and the dragon equivalent of an eye roll. A small smile flickered across her lips for the first time in what felt like hours.

The silence that followed didn't press. It simply settled—heavy, but not unwelcome. Like the pause between battles when both sides knew neither could strike yet.

Stonefell picked absently at a seam in his bracer, the motion oddly boyish for a man who looked carved from the mountain itself. It felt almost like he wanted to ask her something—but wasn't ready.

So she did it first.

"Can I ask you something?" Eliryn asked softly, her voice threading into the quiet like she wasn't sure if it would be allowed.

He glanced up. "You just did."

She snorted. "Fine. Another thing."

A flicker of warmth crossed his expression. "Go on."

"Did you want to be here?" she asked. "Chosen, I mean."

Stonefell looked out toward the high, barred windows. His jaw shifted. It was a long time before he answered.

"Want's a strange word for it," he said at last. "I didn't grow up dreaming of glory. Never saw myself answering to stewards with bells on their wrists." A pause. "But it's a chance."

"A chance at what?"

His hands curled, then flexed again. "Redemption, maybe. Or at least a reason to keep moving." He hesitated. "I fought in too many wrong battles. Took orders from the wrong people. When my sons died... I stopped trying to be anything better. And people stopped expecting it from me."

She felt that like a knife to the ribs.

He wore his losses like armor.

She understood that—she wore hers like flame.

Eliryn studied his face. "And now?"

"Now the Flame called me to be one of the chosen." He laughed once, dry and low. "Maybe it's a cruel joke from the gods. Or maybe it's something else. Either way, I've got nothing left behind me worth running back to."

He looked at her. And this time, she didn't look away.

"And you?"

She nodded slowly, her throat tight. "Same."

A pause. Then quieter: "My mother died the night before the trial guards came for me. The villagers saw to it that she suffered. Everyone believes me to be a sacrifice, and I—" She hesitated, her fingers curling tight against her thigh. "I burned my home down myself. I didn't want to leave anything behind for them to scavenge."

Her voice cracked. But she forced herself to keep speaking.

"There's no place left for me that isn't forward."

Stonefell didn't flinch.

He just nodded. Small. Solid.

"Then maybe this path was made for people like us."

Eliryn blinked. She looked at him. Really looked this time.

"Maybe forward's the only direction people like us get."

He nodded again. Not as a warrior.

But as an equal.

She exhaled. Slowly. Feeling something behind her ribs shift. Loosen.

There is integrity in this one, Vaeronth murmured, approving. *He walks in ruin without letting it claim him.*

I like him too, she thought quietly.

Then, she stood, tilting her chin toward him.

"I'm Eliryn of Lirin's Edge." Her voice didn't shake. Her pendant warmed against her chest as her eyes shimmered faintly—opalescent silver with a flicker of gold deep within, like flame banked but never extinguished. "My dragon is Vaeronth, the Endbringer."

For the first time, speaking her name felt less like bleeding.

And more like becoming what was already foretold.

Stonefell turned fully toward her and rose. Something shifted behind his eyes—recognition. Not of who she had been.

But of who she was now.

He stepped forward, deliberate.

"Garic," he said, voice quiet, steady. "Of Stonefell."

They didn't bow. They didn't nod.

Instead, they clasped forearms.

Her wrist to his.

His scarred hand closing around her bond-marked skin.

A wordless pact. A comrades acknowledgement.

And for the first time, Eliryn felt like maybe she had an ally in this fight.

Vaeronth hummed his approval, deep as thunder.

And in that moment, something real settled between them.

Not quite trust.

But the seed of it.

The gate behind them groaned again, slow and reluctant, like it hated whatever came next.

"Here we go again," Eliryn muttered.

"Time to see who remains," Garic replied.

Eliryn and Garic rose as one, instinct pulling them upright. Another figure stumbled through the mist.

Tall. Wiry. Wrapped in dark leather with gold-threaded cuffs that now hung loose and stained. Sweat slicked his hair to his brow, and a tear along the hem of his coat exposed a flash of bruised skin. His eyes snapped up.

And locked on Eliryn.

Her stomach clenched. She didn't draw her blade, but her fingers brushed the hilt, muscle memory sharp as ever.

Garic noticed. His voice was low. "You know him?"

"I remember him," she murmured. "From the start of this trial. The dais."

Garic narrowed his eyes. "That one's from Whitvale, isn't he?"

The man saw her proximity to Garic, likely recognizing the warrior standing beside her, and froze for half a second, just long enough for the mask to crack. Then his lips curved into something between a smirk and a sneer.

She could have answered his sneer. Mocked him. Cut him down with words sharper than her blade.

She didn't bother.

Let him waste energy pretending; she'd save hers for the next battle.

Beside her, Garic grunted. "I remember him. All mouth. Walked like he owned the stone. Talked like he thought he'd already won."

Eliryn gave the faintest nod. "Slimy bravado."

Garic chuckled dryly. "More snake than man."

Eliryn's gaze held steady. "He wasn't alone when I encountered him. There were five of them back then. For a moment, I thought they'd attack me together—but something in the maze started hunting them first. I defended myself as best I could against the one who charged me. I left him alive. But this snake looked like he'd have been happy to try his luck at ending me too."

Garic's expression darkened. "And yet here you are."

The man from Whitvale strode forward now, chest puffed, trying too hard to look casual. But his boots dragged slightly. His left sleeve was darkened with blood.

"You're still breathing," Whitvale muttered, not trying to hide his disdain.

Eliryn tilted her head, unimpressed. "You look even worse than you did running away."

He dusted off his coat half-heartedly, as if posturing could erase the maze's damage. "Don't get smug, dragonblood. I got here on my own. Pretty sure you can't say the same."

Garic stepped forward just slightly, enough so that his shadow crossed the path between them.

"Don't mistake your survival as something that's permanent," he said.

Whitvale's bravado cracked, just slightly. His gaze flicked between them, recalculating. And for the first time, Eliryn realized Garic wasn't just standing beside her.

He was standing *with* her.

Whitvale's gaze flicked between the two of them. His bravado thinned as he turned away, dismissing them. He threw himself down onto the farthest bench, lounging like it hadn't taken everything he had to pretend he wasn't affected.

Eliryn exhaled.

"I hadn't realized the chosen would turn on one another," she said softly, only for Garic's ears.

Garic didn't look at the man again. "The stakes are too high for most to not try and cheat one way or another."

Silence lapped between them like low tide. Then, after a breath, they sat down side by side without speaking—her sword angled across her knees, his hands loose but ready.

Her shoulder brushed his once as they settled. Neither of them shifted.

She glanced toward the far door, where the air shivered.

Another soul, dragging itself toward survival.

She let her eyes half-close, letting Vaeronth's quiet hum echo in her chest.

The air steadied. Somewhere in the stone, something took note. She let it.

Maybe not the castle at all. Maybe *him*.

Malric's eyes felt like an oath.

Interlude 6: Malric

"Witness is a kind of oath. Be sure you mean it." —The Quiet Arts

He didn't watch the door; he watched the way the room changed around her.

Air that smelled of coin and vinegar drew itself straight. Dust hung lower, more obedient. She stood, counted exits, didn't sway. The marks along her throat answered her breath like a second pulse. Her shoulder—set like something torn and shoved back where it belonged—refused to broadcast the ache.

Then the older warrior: mountain-cut, scar-mapped. Not Malric's problem—until their forearms clasped.

Touch, here, is not courtesy. It's a claim.

Jealousy flared like a struck match—small, clean. He let it burn to a steady pilot light, the kind that never admits it's heat.

It should have been his shoulder she measured. His name traded for hers. His steadiness she set her breath to.

But the king liked mirrors.

"Be a shadow," King Thalen had said. *"Cull. Watch. Make it look like the trials are working."*

If the king truly wanted her destroyed, he'd have risked counterfeit choosing, Malric's name declared by the Flame, Malric inside the trials at her shoulder. Not this distance. Not this deniability.

Shadows don't harvest truth. They ration it.

He'd already had to step into her path to make anything real. Their connection crawled. He disliked the pace.

Malric watched as they sat—her blade over her knees, the warrior's hands loose and ready—and their shoulders touched, stayed. After a few breaths their rhythms matched without conscious thought.

The desire to edit the scene—remove the extra piece, claim the empty inches—moved through him like a cool decision.

He was good at removing.

He was not good at feeling.

The last time he let attention cross into attachment, it ended with a woman dead and a mission compromised. Not a lover; a lever he told himself he could hold without breaking. He misjudged. She died because he let himself be distracted; he almost followed her into death because rage makes men stupid.

After that, he learned to starve the part of himself that reached. He learned efficiency like a religion.

This was not efficient.

This was a slow, precise hunger he didn't intend to starve.

Below, the steward pretended to have competence.

Malric knew he could go to the king with a clean report, telling him about her new ally in the trials. Thalen would praise his observations and leave him where he'd put him: above, outside, hidden.

No.

Malric wanted more.

He would become close to her. He would be the constant she learned to account for, the correction that kept her upright, the edge that taught her where to cut.

Possessiveness isn't a sin if you're honest about it. It's a plan.

He thought about the mask he wore for her. How clean his hands looked when he offered a cloth. How stains always return, no matter how well you wash.

He'd told her nothing that was a lie; he'd only with-held details.

I've hidden the monster—for now. But he would show her soon.

He wanted that moment. He wanted to stand close enough to measure the change in her eyes when understanding arrived. Some people flinch. Some harden. Some lean in. He wanted to know how she would respond.

He tracked small, useful truths. The way she never sat with her back to a door. The way pain had taught her economy instead of drama. The way her left wrist—the one he'd corrected—held true now, even tired. The way she ignored Whitvale because he was cheaper than her attention.

He imagined the scene rewritten: her breath taking its measure from him; her forearm finding his like the natural place it belonged; her mouth forming his name—*Malric*—not as a test, but as something you set on a table and intend to keep. He remembered the first time she'd said it and remembered the cadence. He wanted it steady, next time. He wanted it warmed.

He stayed where the rafters held him and let the want sharpen instead of spread.

He marked the timing of the guards' turn by the stutter in their lantern shadows. He counted the beats between the steward's bell and the footfalls. He noted the soot-blackened finger on the third torch to the left—someone had been checking the bracket for a loose pin. Malric noticed *everything*, no detail too small.

He would speak to the dragonrider again where light chose no favorites and stone remembered order. He would plant himself at the distance a weapon lives in—closer than a breath. He would give her the choice to step back and measure what that meant or give her judgement as quickly as she thought it.

She shifted, only slightly, and the pendant at her chest warmed in answer. He felt the echo of it the way you feel thunder approach before sound.

The room traced her silhouette.

Malric would soon cast the shadow over it.

CHAPTER 15: THE TEMPERING

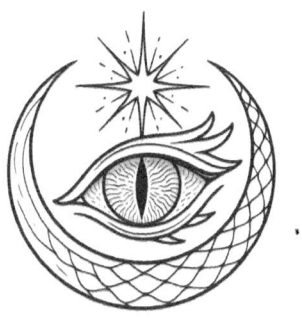

"The sword does not choose the fire, nor the hammer, nor the pain. But if it endures, it becomes something more than steel." —Arden Valemir, Master of Arms, Citadel

The bell rang once.

Low and resonant. Not triumphant. Not mournful. Just final.

The steward stepped forward in the center of the room, a magical wind tugging gently at the edges of his robes. His face held the same careful neutrality as before, but something behind his eyes had shifted and tightened, like a man bracing for a truth he didn't enjoy speaking aloud.

"You stand now at the end of the second trial," he said, voice crisp but not loud. "You have endured what others could not."

He glanced to his left, then right, his gaze drifting over each of the six who remained.

Eliryn.

Garic.

Whitvale.

The other warrior from Tarn's Hill who still wouldn't meet her eyes after she inferred he was a bug.

The tall, slim woman in her thirties hailing from Stormthresh.

And finally, the boy with the copper hair, from Westbrae perhaps.

Garic had remembered the village names of the chosen, and had whispered them to Eliryn as each emerged alive from the trial.

Six.

And the Steward confirmed it aloud.

"Four did not return," he said. "One was consumed by a vision he could not escape. One died of wounds earned in a chamber where his own hands turned against him. Two made it through the maze, only to lose themselves to madness upon confronting their true selves."

He waited, letting the silence take root.

"No bodies will be retrieved. No names will be written in stone. Only those who finish the trials have their names recorded."

"Six remain," he reiterated, quieter now. "More than in any cohort for generations. Our caliber as a magical people is improving."

Garic murmured under his breath, "More like the realm's magic has been dying but we've learned to fight without it."

Eliryn didn't comment, but she felt the heat of her dragon stir in quiet agreement.

The steward turned his attention to her then, just for a breath, as though he could sense the magic pulse from inside her.

"The third trial begins at dawn. Until then, you are to rest. No questions. No preparation. Your next task will reveal itself as all others have: without mercy."

The Steward lifted one long-fingered hand, as if brushing invisible dust from the air. At the gesture, a door set into the far wall gave a low, resonant click and swung inward on hidden hinges. A group of guards stepped through, their footfalls measured, their armor catching the light in muted glints.

Eliryn scanned them quickly, catching a quick glimpse of who she thought was Silas.

One by one, the survivors began to drift apart. Not speaking, everyone else seemed to be reeling from the horrors of the trial.

Eliryn stayed still.

Garic lingered beside her, arms crossed loosely, his presence steady as carved stone.

"I remember the way the room looked before the first trial," he said quietly, voice heavy with something more than fatigue. "How many of us there were."

She kept her gaze forward, but her voice softened. "You didn't think we'd lose this many."

"I didn't think we'd drop to half before the second trial even finished," he admitted, shaking his head. "Thought maybe the first would cull the weak. Not everyone."

A silence stretched. Then, quieter: "Maybe it culled the unlucky instead."

Eliryn's throat tightened.

"Did you know the other warrior? The one you said was from Tarn's Hill?" she asked, needing words to keep the weight from crushing her.

Garic frowned, his gaze distant as he followed the shadows of the vanished survivors. "No. But I saw the way he moved. He was probably someone of high rank from within their army."

She blinked. "They have their own army?"

"Poor bastards raise their young with knives in their teeth just to keep the crabs off the grain stores," Garic muttered, lips twitching in grim humor.

She huffed, just a breath of laughter. "Sounds charming."

"They're tough. Not many survive long enough to serve on the front lines."

"And you said the woman was from Stormthresh?"

"Yes, another physical threat." Garic answered after a beat, his voice more thoughtful. "Tide-priests send their young to the blackwaters to train. Militants. Half warriors, half zealots. They don't fight fair. They fight to win."

Eliryn nodded faintly as she watched the last of the other figures disappear down their separate hallways. Soon there would be no one left to count, and Eliryn thought it was important that she remember who they were.

"Everyone seems to know what they're doing," she said softly.

Garic's gaze flicked to her.

"Except me," she admitted.

He didn't hesitate. "You're wrong."

She blinked at that, glancing sideways, surprised.

"You're walking the same path as the rest of us. Bleeding the same. Standing the same," Garic said simply. "Doesn't matter how you started. Only that you're still here."

For a moment, Eliryn had no answer. She just let those words settle in her chest, heavy and solid, like the kind of truth no one had ever given her before.

Then Garic turned slightly, eyes searching hers. "You still burning?"

She flexed her fingers slowly, letting the pendant warm against her collarbone, Vaeronth's steady hum curling around her ribs like quiet armor. "Always."

They clasped forearms once more, no longer strangers this time.

"You watch your back in the next one," Garic said. His voice was steady, but his eyes were sharp. "I don't think this lot will fight fair."

Eliryn smirked faintly. "Neither do I." A pause. "But I've got a dragon watching my back."

Garic's dry chuckle cracked like a stone settling in the hearth. "You make a fine legend come to life, Eliryn of Lirin's Edge."

She opened her mouth, searching for something clever, something sarcastic, something that would keep the moment light.

But nothing came.

She just stared at him, thrown off balance. She hadn't expected someone from the trials to show her this... kindness.

In the end, she only nodded, once, careful.

Garic turned away toward his waiting guard, solid and unyielding.

And Eliryn went straight toward the waiting figure at the edge of the hall.

Silas.

His posture straightened instinctively when she approached, his kind energy coiled behind a guard's discipline.

His armor wasn't polished, it was dull at the edges, as if he'd worn it for years rather than days. But his face, soft-lined and alert, with warm brown eyes, brightened as soon as he saw her.

"Dragonrider," he said, relief threading his voice. "I hoped you'd find your way."

She blinked once, surprised. "You sound almost happy to have to be escorting me again."

Silas gave a small shrug, almost sheepish. "Better than one of the outside posts."

She tilted her head, the corner of her mouth quirking. "How honest of you, Silas."

He offered a small smile, seemingly pleased that she remembered his name. A quiet thread of friendship passed between them, warm and unspoken.

As they walked side by side through the corridor leading back to the inner halls, Silas kept a respectful distance, but not a cold one.

"Did you stay with the steward earlier?" she asked.

Silas nodded. "Posted to him for the trial's end. When he isn't briefing the chosen, he has to remain guarded... He is one of the few that know details about the trials before they happen."

"Really? I didn't realize he was so protected."

"In previous trials, some individuals have thought it best to circumvent the system a bit, go after the source of information rather than wait."

She looked at him, curious. "You mean questioning the steward?"

He gave a small huff of humorless laughter. "I mean torturing him."

They shared a quiet beat, Eliryn thinking about all the other chosen to walk these halls before her. She almost couldn't blame someone for wanting to seek answers any way they could... and she wasn't sure if that meant she was already changing in ways she couldn't see. Then-

"I'm glad you made it out," Silas said. "Not many do. Not whole."

Her hand tightened on the hilt of her sword as they turned a corner. She wondered if anyone who survived this place left whole. Or if surviving simply meant learning how to carry the cracks without letting them show.

"I'm not sure I am whole," she murmured.

Silas didn't ask her to explain. Just walked with her, letting the silence do the work of understanding.

They reached the shadowed curve of the corridor where her chamber door stood, dark wood carved with faint, spiraling runes that caught the torchlight like water. Silas stopped a pace before it, hands clasped loosely behind his back.

"I'll be stationed near the kitchens tonight," he said, tone easy. "Heard you've been down there visiting with us commoners."

Eliryn raised an eyebrow, half a smile tugging at her mouth. "Word travels fast in this place."

"Well," he said, eyes glinting, "when you make a good first impression on the cooks, everyone hears about it."

"They told you the strange dragonblood interrupted their evening, didn't they."

"I never said that." He paused. "Though I'm not denying it, either."

She gave a small huff that might've been a laugh, the tension in her shoulders loosening just slightly.

"You've been kind," she said after a moment, her voice softer. "More than most."

Silas shrugged. "Doesn't cost me anything. And I figure kindness is in short supply with the lot you've had to face."

There was a moment, just a breath, where neither of them spoke. The space between them felt thinner than before, the silence charged—not uncomfortable, but expectant. Eliryn wasn't used to being looked at without judgement. Silas wasn't looking at her like a trial survivor or a mere acquaintance. Not tonight.

Eliryn looked at him fully, and she could feel her eyes brightening in their new unnatural way. "You called me *dragonrider*."

He blinked. "I did. Meant it fondly, I swear."

"I know." She hesitated, then added: "My name is Eliryn."

Silas straightened slightly. The small tilt of his head held a quiet gravity, the recognition that this wasn't a name given lightly.

"It's very nice to meet you, Eliryn," he said.

The torchlight flickered between them, the quiet like a held breath.

She nodded once, then turned to the door. Her palm pressed to the runes, and they flared blue and warm beneath her touch. With a low whisper of wind, the chamber opened.

Before stepping inside, she glanced back. Silas was still there, standing like a quiet watchman in the corridor's dim curve.

She eased the door shut, and leaned against it for a long moment, listening to the silence. She wasn't ready to call anyone a friend. But Silas... might be the first person who who made her want to.

The chamber welcomed her like the first breath taken after drowning. Warmth and comfort like she had never known.

The scent of juniper and woodsmoke stirred faintly, rising from the hearth that had already lit itself. Beyond, the tub magically steamed, perfumed with something floral and wild, reminding her of the mountains near Lirin's Edge after a spring rain.

Eliryn exhaled. Long. Shaky. A thread of tension unraveled from between her shoulders.

Without a word, she kicked off her boots and loosened her soft leathers, clasps unfastening with a slow, respectful ease. It peeled away like shed skin and she folded it neatly before placing it on the table near the bath. When she moved to step into the bath, the floor beneath her reshaped itself to be gentle on her now bare feet. A small towel fluffy and soft appeared draped over the side of the tub.

She slid into the pool without resistance, sinking deep. Heat curled around her freshly forming bruises. The aches she hadn't noticed until now pulsed, then dulled. Her head tilted back against the smooth rim, flame-streaked hair fanning out across the surface like threads of light.

Still, something inside her didn't relax.

Her fingers touched the pendant at her neck, the etched stone warming faintly under her touch. She traced its edges again and again, steadying herself without realizing it.

She reached inward.

"Vaeronth?"

Silence. Not absence, just... distance.

Eliryn furrowed her brow faintly and closed her eyes, breathing deeper, slower, trying to focus inward on the coils of their bond.

"You've been quiet."

A beat passed. Then:

I did not wish to burden you.

His voice was there at last, low and steady as fire beneath stone.

"You could never be a burden to me."

You faced your dead and did not flinch. You named your grief, burned what tethered you, and stood unbroken. A pause. *I felt every breath of it. I felt... pride. I did not know that emotion before you.*

Eliryn opened her eyes, blinking fast against the tears that rose, unbidden.

"I thought you were angry with me. Or tired."

No.

His presence gently curved, like a wing wrapped around her thoughts, but there was an old, hollow ache at the edges of it. *I was watching. I was... remembering. Your grandmother's dragon was the last I called kin. And I knew when he fell. I remembered that pain through you today. And I wanted you to have space from my pain.*

She touched the water's surface lightly. The motion steadied her, though her voice in her mind felt scraped raw.

"You were alone a long time," she said. "Longer than I can imagine. When your kin fell... do you know what took them? What kind of magic could do that?"

For a few heartbeats, nothing moved but the slow ripple of water over her fingers. When Vaeronth spoke, the words were quiet as embers.

I have asked myself that question every day since the ruin came. There are no records left, no witness who stood beyond it and survived whole. But I have long suspected King Thalen's hand.

Her breath caught. "You think he killed them?"

I think he could not have become what he is while dragons yet lived. We were not so easily bent to mortal crowns. If any of us had remained, we would have challenged his rise before it rooted itself. Whatever power unmade my kind... it cleared the path for him.

Her pulse beat hard in her throat. "But you don't know."

I have no proof, he admitted, and for all the weight of his voice, there was something almost fragile in that confession. *Only the whispers of those who passed through the Undermire after the fall. Only the stories carried here into this castle. I have listened to secrets spoken into the veil in search of answers for longer than you have drawn breath. And when none came, I waited for you. For your blood. For your power. So that, together, we might set right what should never have been allowed to happen.*

Eliryn closed her eyes. The water lapped at her wrist, cool and steady.

She did not flinch from the enormity of his vigil, his purpose, or the long hunger for justice beneath it all.

"I won't turn away from this," she said softly.

I know, Vaeronth murmured, voice like heat banked low. *Rest now, little flame. Your heart still smolders. Let the room hold you a while. When the next trial comes, I will call you.*

When she finally rose, the room had already laid out a robe in place of her worn leathers; soft, lined with deep crimson threading, the color of volcanic rock at twilight. Loose trousers. A thick tunic. Clothes for comfort, not ceremony.

As she dressed, she noticed something else had changed: the walls bore new markings. Motifs of wings and firelight etched above the hearth, growing more vivid when she looked at them directly.

She sat by the fire after, curled in one of the wide, deep chairs that hadn't been there before. A mug of something hot and herbal steamed beside her hand. It tasted like pine and honey. She couldn't decide if she felt more like a dragonrider or a wayward stray someone had dragged in from the cold. Maybe she was both.

She drank in slow sips, the warmth of the pine and honey seeping into her bones. The room was still, save for the soft crackle of the hearth and the faint pulse of light in the carved wings above it.

Eliryn let her gaze drift over the shifting glow on the walls. She didn't think of what lay ahead. Not yet. Not of magic, or monsters, or men who wore too many faces.

For now, there was only this breath. This fire. And the quiet promise that when the next trial came, she would rise to meet it.

CHAPTER 16: ASH AND HUNGER

"Some hungers are born in the body. Others in the silence that follows survival." —Aremond Thorne, former captain of the Crown Guard, executed for sedition

Eliryn woke to the firelight and the low murmur of her own breath.

The warmth had sunk deep into her bones, softening the tension in her back, the quiet ache still lingering behind her ribs. Her tunic, thick, brushed cotton with sleeves that fell past her knuckles, smelled faintly of lavender and woodsmoke. The loose trousers she wore matched it, drawn tight at her hips with a simple ribbon cord. It wasn't only finery, but comfort, and tonight, comfort meant more than rest.

The room, sensing her motion, stirred slightly, coals blooming deeper in the hearth, a pillow adjusting itself behind her in the chair.

Her stomach groaned loudly with a long, hollow longing.

The kind that had nothing to do with magic or power or proving she still belonged in the world of the living. This hunger was simple.

She wanted bread. Stew. Something she could bite into, hold between her hands.

She glanced toward the center of the room, expecting a tray to appear, as it often did when the room sensed her needs. But this time, nothing appeared.

Eliryn tilted her head slightly, amused.

"Decided not to mother me tonight?" she murmured to the stone walls.

They remained silent, warm and golden.

She stood, stretching her arms overhead, joints cracking softly. A long exhale left her lips. Then—

You have time.

Vaeronth's voice, low and steady, coiled gently into her mind.

"Time for what?"

Time to move as you please. To choose conversation and human company. Go to the kitchens, little flame. Let the hearth feed you, not the stone. You've earned that.

She smiled faintly, fingers brushing her pendant.

"Didn't realize I needed your permission."

You don't. But I know it pleases you to hear it.

Her smile widened, just a little, as she pulled on the heavier coat hanging near the door—one the room had conjured in anticipation of her departure. It had high shoulders and deep pockets. She liked it instantly as it swallowed her form.

Outside her chamber, the halls were quiet. Low torches lit the way in flickering gold and blue.

And somewhere below, kitchens waited. Bread. Salt. Stew. And, if she was lucky, the quiet warmth of familiar faces.

She took her first step, boots silent against ancient stone.

The halls of the Castle Othren were quiet this late, lit by torches that burned low with enchanted blue and gold flame. No footsteps echoed. No guards on patrol. The quiet after the second trial had settled thickly across the stone like mist.

She blinked slowly as she walked, rubbing at her temple. Her eyes were worse tonight, only blurred shapes and shifting warmths of color. Pale stone, gold flame, the deep navy smear of night through the distant windows. Her vision wavered with every turn, but she didn't need it. She counted steps. Remembered patterns in the wall. Trusted the scent of yeast and spice to pull her forward.

She reached the stairwell by memory, one hand on the carved banister, and descended toward the kitchens.

Warmth met her halfway down. Real warmth from oven heat and rising dough and the sharp tang of herbs cut fresh from someone's garden.

The kitchen doors were already open in welcome.

She stepped through the threshold and paused, blinking into the firelight.

There he was.

Silas.

He stood near the great hearth, one sleeve pushed back, a mug in his hand. Steam curled from the cup like mist from mountain stone. His armor was gone, in its place just a simple tunic and worn trousers now, his dark hair mussed like he'd run one hand through it too many times.

Eliryn's breath caught for a moment she didn't care to name. He looked... ordinary. And in this castle, that was something rare enough to feel like safety.

"Didn't realize this place took dinner reservations," she said lightly, stepping further inside.

Silas glanced up, and the weariness in his face broke like morning sun. "Didn't realize dragonriders hunted kitchens after midnight."

She folded her arms, feeling almost out of place in the doorway. "When you said you would be stationed near the kitchens I didn't realize that meant you'd be here hanging out."

"Kitchen duty," he said with a crooked little smile. "Better than standing around waiting for the next bell to ring. And...sometimes easier to pretend things are normal."

She let out a soft breath, tension unspooling from her shoulders. "Does this count as normal for you?"

He glanced around at the flour-dusted counters and bubbling pots. "Close enough." His eyes returned to her. "You look... better. Not that you looked—" He caught himself, a faint flush rising to his cheek. "Just... more at ease."

A corner of her mouth lifted. "I'm not sure anyone's at ease in this place. But I'll take the compliment."

He rubbed the back of his neck, smiling like he wasn't sure he was allowed to. "I wasn't sure if you'd... well. I'm glad you're here."

Something quiet passed between them, like recognition of how little either of them knew about the other, and how now was the opportunity for that to change.

She nodded toward the simmering pot. "My stomach made sounds more frightening than the Undermire. Figured I should probably feed the monster some stew."

He let out a short, surprised laugh. "That's probably the best reason to be out of bed."

"Mhmm. That's me. Practical."

She hadn't meant to stare, but out of uniform he was suddenly *human*—just a linen shirt open at the throat and sleeves rolled to scarred forearms. The rest of the room softened at the edges—not her failing sight, but the unwisely pleasant shock of him like this.

"And practical is good," he said with an easy smile. "Especially if it means you'll sit for a while. Let someone else worry about what comes next."

"Maybe," she allowed. "For tonight."

He tipped his chin toward the hearth. "Starting with Marta."

Only then did Eliryn register the silver-haired cook by the kettle, flour dust bright on her hands.

Marta grinned and gestured to the pot near the back hearth. "Bowls are on the shelf, love.

Eliryn stepped past him, the warm smells wrapping around her like a cloak. She felt the hush of the room settle over her, simple and nonthreatening, a softness she hadn't known she missed.

And when she glanced back, he was still watching her with that same open, wondering expression, as if he wasn't quite sure how someone like her had ended up here, but he was glad she had.

Tonight, she thought, she would let herself have that. Just for a little while.

She found a bowl, slightly chipped along one rim, and ladled the thick stew from the pot. It was rich with lentils and wild game, fragrant with thyme, onions, and something roasted low and slow. Her stomach clenched in answer.

Silas joined her with his own bowl, nodding toward the hearth in the corner. "Sit with me?"

She followed him over to the small table tucked beside the fire. Two old stools, legs uneven, but they didn't wobble when she settled into one. A faded cloth lay across the table, clean but stained with old wine and memories.

For a moment, they ate in silence. The only sounds were the crackle of the hearth and the soft scrape of spoon against bowl.

It was Silas who spoke first.

"I hoped you would survive the Bloodfall." He met her eyes, blurry to her, but his voice gave shape to the look. "But I've heard that the second trial would break men stronger than steel. And you... You looked like nothing had phased you."

"I wouldn't go that far," she said quietly. "I bled like anyone else. I just... kept going."

"That's better than."

She let the warmth of the stew settle in her chest before answering. "Four more didn't make it."

"I heard." His expression sobered. "They say that even that number is higher than past trials."

Eliryn made a noncommittal sound in return.

Silas cast a glance toward the doorway, as if to be sure no one lingered in earshot. When he looked back, his voice had dropped to a hush.

"There are rumors in the barracks. Some of the royal guard have stopped following orders altogether. Refusing to prepare for the next trial. They're meeting in private, speaking up."

Eliryn lifted her gaze to his. "Speaking against the trials?"

He nodded, once, deliberate. "And against the crown itself. People are tired of pretending this is about honor or tradition. Tired of letting magic die slowly while the crown prospers from it."

She considered that, her breath moving slow and careful. "Do you think there's truth to it?"

"I think," he said quietly, "there's truth in people reaching their breaking point. And that truth doesn't need permission to exist."

Silence settled between them, taut as a drawn bowstring.

"And if it turns into an uprising?" she asked.

He stirred his stew as though it might reveal an answer. "Then maybe Vireth will have to stop pretending that cruelty is just the way of things. And the rest of us will have to choose where we stand."

"I didn't ask to be chosen," she murmured. "But maybe that doesn't matter anymore."

He met her eyes, something solemn and kind behind his expression. "It doesn't."

She looked down at her bowl, the stew blurring slightly in her weakened vision. "It's strange."

"What is?"

"This," she said softly. "Sitting here. Talking like there's still a world beyond these stone walls worth making better."

He was quiet for a moment. Then: "Maybe there is. We've just forgotten how to find it."

That made her throat tighten unexpectedly. She focused on the weight of the spoon in her hand. The warmth of the fire at her back. Real things.

"You sound like someone who's already lost too much," she said softly.

His throat worked as he swallowed. "Five years I've worn this crest. Watched the crown cull friends. Watched frost and war take family. This place doesn't care who you were before. Only what's left of you when it's finished."

That silence stretched again—this time heavier, but not cold.

"I don't know what'll be left of me after all of this," Eliryn said softly. "But I'm starting to realize that my destiny is much bigger than I thought."

Silas looked at her a long moment. Then, a little awkward, a little too earnest: "You seem... stronger than when I first saw you."

She blinked, caught off guard. "Stronger?"

He nodded. "You seem... more yourself."

She tilted her head, a slow smile creeping in. "Careful. You keep talking like that, people might think you admire me."

Silas hesitated just long enough for it to be obvious.

"I... do."

Eliryn stilled.

Silas's gaze flicked to the table, sheepish but honest. "I mean, who wouldn't? You're the Last Dragonrider. It's not something you expect to see, let alone talk to."

She swallowed her surprise, her grin turning sly. "So you've been admiring me since day one. Good to know."

His head snapped up, horrified. "That's not—I mean—not like that—"

She laughed, full and warm. "Silas."

He flushed deep red, mouth opening but producing no sound at all.

"Relax." She nudged his elbow gently. "I'll take the compliment."

"I didn't mean to make it weird," he mumbled.

"I'm the one teasing you. You're fine."

Silas let out a breath, but the smile he gave her then was unguarded. Quiet. Real. "You're different than I expected."

"Thought you said you never expected a dragonrider."

"You know what I mean."

"I know," she said softly.

Another quiet moment passed between them, steady as the hum of the hearth.

His knuckles brushed hers as he reached for a wedge of bread. She didn't flinch, but she felt the contact like a spark.

When was the last time someone touched her without expectation? Without needing something in return?

Then the kitchen door creaked open, and a gust of wind stirred the herbs above the hearth. The spell broke, gently. Silas looked toward the noise, then back to her.

"You want more stew?"

She stood. "No. That was perfect."

They carried their bowls to the basin, rinsed and left them stacked neatly on the side.

As they reached the door, Silas hesitated, his voice quieter now. "If the night drags long... you're welcome to wander back."

She paused, glancing up at him. "An open invitation?"

His ears flushed. "I mean... sure. If you want more conversation."

Her lips twitched. "Conversation." She repeated.

Silas gave a helpless, breathless laugh, shaking his head. "I'm not very good at... whatever that was."

"You're genuine. I'll take that over good."

That pulled a real smile from him—soft and a little awed.

She let her fingers brush his forearm as she passed, just light enough to make him freeze.

"Goodnight, Silas."

He straightened reflexively, more soldier than man for half a second. "Goodnight, Eliryn."

And when she slipped into the shadows, he kept watching long after she'd gone.

Chapter 17: The Measure of Loyalty

"Not all storms test walls. Some are sent to see if the Flame still burns beneath the stone." —Inscription carved into the trial chamber's western arch, origin unknown

Wake, Eliryn.

The voice came like smoke curling around her bones—low, rumbling, unmistakable.

Vaeronth.

Eliryn startled awake, a sharp breath pulled into her lungs. The fire in her hearth had long since dimmed to a bed of glowing embers, and the pale gray light of dawn pooled at the corners of the ceiling, soft as silk.

The third trial begins soon, Vaeronth said. *The steward prepares the call.*

"Gods," she muttered, scrubbing her hands over her face. "You make a better alarm than the temple bells."

I'll take that as a compliment.

She sat up slowly, joints stiff from where she'd curled in the large chair in front of the hearth. She barely registered the ache, warmed from within now, a gift of the bond, perhaps, or a symptom of being less human with each passing day.

She crossed to the basin and splashed cold water on her face. The shock of it cleared the last shadows of sleep. Dabbing her cheeks dry, she turned toward the tall mirror that shimmered faintly when she stepped near.

Her hair had staged a small revolt. She winced, raking her fingers through the snarls until her scalp stung. Sitting at the edge of the bed, she sectioned it clean and began a tight crown braid—quick, practiced pulls, the rhythm of someone who'd learned to make order before walking into chaos. The leather tie on the nightstand waited like a coiled promise; it warmed in her palm when she grabbed it as if the room approved.

The marks along her forearms pulsed once, settling. The pendant lay heavy and steady against her sternum.

"I'm not ready for this," she muttered.

You are.

"I meant emotionally."

That too.

She snorted. "I liked you better when you were cryptic and brooding."

His silence was smug.

When the braid was done, she stood and found the day's clothes already laid out at the foot of her bed. The room had changed again, anticipating her needs.

Today's garb was darker: ash-gray stitched with threads the color of blood and cinders. A sleeveless tunic belted snug at the waist, reinforced at the seams with loops for steel. Trousers of supple wool, meant for movement. A short cloak clasped at the throat with a bronze flame.

She dressed without hurry, each layer grounding her. The nerves were there, but quiet. Not gone, just banked.

Her sword waited by the door, already polished. She buckled it to her hip, the weight familiar. Right.

"I'm ready," she said aloud, more for herself than him.

Then go. The others stir. Try not to be the last again.

She rolled her eyes and stepped to the door.

The hall beyond smelled of lavender and lamp oil; soft, sharp, calming. Far off, boots echoed, steady and sure.

A figure turned the corner.

"Silas," she said, the smile arriving before she could stop it.

He took in the braid, the blade, the steadiness. "Eliryn. You beat me to it."

"Try to keep up."

"That's the assignment." He nodded at the sword on her hip. "Let me see this."

She did. He tightened the buckle a notch—quick, efficient, no fuss.

"Part of the escort package?" she asked.

"Part of the staying-alive package." A brief spark. "Escort is just branding."

"Mm. And the charm?"

"Limited inventory." He stepped back to give her the path. "You want it now or after?"

"Surprise me."

"I'd rather not. Surprises get people killed." He spoke honestly.

She laughed, soft and quiet. "I think you might be the first person here who's tried to charm me without a hidden agenda."

"I'll try not to ruin the streak," he said, then gave her a once-over. "You look ready. Though I can't tell if it's for battle or for a royal assembly."

"Why not both?" she said, adjusting the sword at her hip.

He raised a brow, a little admiring. "You look ready to succeed in either setting."

Eliryn gave him a dry look, but her mouth curved faintly. "Was that another attempt at flattery?"

"Observation," he replied smoothly. "I thought we covered this."

They walked together, companionable now, the stairwell just ahead.

After a moment, he asked, more quietly, "Does it help? Having him... the dragon."

"Vaeronth?" she glanced sideways. "He woke me this morning. Said the trial would begin soon."

Silas let out a low whistle. "I'd ask what that's like, but I don't think I could ever understand."

"He's not subtle," she said with a small smirk. "But he's steady. And he listens."

Silas nodded, thoughtful. "Must be nice. All I get for company is the steward shouting or someone banging pots in the barracks."

They descended the stairs in easy rhythm. Below them, the low murmur of voices drifted up like mist. The chosen were gathering.

Silas slowed near the final step. When she glanced over, his voice came quieter. Warmer.

"Whatever hell you have to face in there... just come back."

He hesitated, then added, more softly:

"Keep surviving. I like the company on the walk back."

Eliryn blinked. She wasn't sure what she expected—something formal. Less personal.

Her throat tightened before she could stop it. "You're getting sentimental on me."

Silas smiled faintly, earnest. "Someone has to."

She tried to scoff, but her voice betrayed her. "Stars, you're worse than Vaeronth."

Inside her mind, the dragon stirred, unimpressed: *I am merely pragmatic. He has a crush.*

Silas tilted his head, confused but still watching her like she was something worth believing in.

Eliryn shook her head, breathing a quiet laugh. "I'll try to come back. For the conversation."

"I'd count that as a win."

Then, nudging his elbow with hers, she let her smirk return. "You're really not supposed to care this much."

Silas shrugged once. "Maybe with time you'll get used to it."

Before she could think of a reply, they stepped onto the final stair together, and the hall opened before them.

If she felt steadier with him beside her... she didn't say it out loud.

The hall opened before them into a round chamber, its ceiling carved with ancient runes, banners hanging high above like watchful eyes. Light slanted in through unseen windows, golden and solemn.

One by one, the chosen filtered in.

She spotted them easily: Whitvale, smug and silver-bladed; the Stormthresh woman, all tension and silence; the boy with bright hair and wintry eyes; the Warrior from Tarn's Hill, wrapped in blue with an axe slung across his back.

And Garic.

He stood alone, broad and still as stone. When his gaze met hers, he gave a single, steady nod.

She returned it. No more. No need.

Her eyes flicked across the others, all armored in some fashion: hardened leather, stitched steel, ceremonial cloth turned practical. Even Whitvale wore daggers strapped down each thigh like he thought himself untouchable.

All of them bore weapons.

Except Garic.

She tilted her head. He carried no sword. No axe. Just the weight of someone who had already faced death and had no need to show it.

She stepped closer to where he stood. Silas gave her a parting nod, stepping back toward the outer wall.

Then the steward appeared.

No footsteps. No announcement. Just presence, sudden and cold, as if the room recognized his authority and made space for it.

His silver robes whispered as he stepped forward into the center of the chamber. The brass bell at his wrist did not ring.

"You are six," he said, voice calm and cold as ever. "Six, where once there were many more. That alone is unprecedented."

The silence deepened.

"You stand on the threshold of the third trial," the steward went on. "This one will not test what lies behind you, but what remains within you. It will demand your strength, yes—but more than that, your clarity. Your will."

A murmur passed between some of the others. Eliryn stayed still.

"This trial is not merely of blade or bone," the Steward continued. "It is one of endurance. Of balance. A challenge that will break the arrogant and scatter the unfocused. If you are to lead, if you are to rise among the chosen, you must show more than wrath and readiness."

Eliryn felt Vaeronth stir, a low pulse of heat in her spine.

He speaks truth, the dragon murmured. *This is the trial that weighs a soul.*

The steward stepped back, eyes scanning the six.

"In one hour, you will be summoned. Steel your bodies. Steel your minds."

Then he vanished.

Not in a flare of light. Not in smoke.

Just... gone.

Eliryn stood for a moment longer, breathing in the quiet, feeling the hush ripple through the room like distant thunder.

Garic stayed close, his expression steady.

But still, they didn't speak—not yet. Something told her they'd need all their words soon enough.

The room shifted slowly after the steward's departure, each of the chosen splintering off to their own quiet corners to prepare. Eliryn remained where she was, the hem of her soft tunic brushing the backs of her heels, her hands loose at her sides.

She didn't move until Garic touched her shoulder in passing—No words. Just an offered tether.

Then he was gone too.

She turned toward the archway that she had come from, looking for her own spot to retreat to.

But the shadows shifted wrong.

She paused.

Blinking once, twice.

The hall beyond looked... wrong.

The torches that normally lined the far wall were dimmer than they had been minutes ago— no, not dimmer. Her eyes simply weren't catching the full shape of the light. The glow was fractured now, a haze more than flame. The sharp lines that marked the floor's edge had blurred into fog.

She lifted a hand in front of her face.

She could still see it.

Mostly.

Her fingers were soft outlines, washed in shadow, their edges flickering when she moved too fast. There had always been blurriness in her vision—an imbalance of sensation traded for something deeper—but this...

This was different.

Eliryn reached for the wall, needing to anchor herself.

Her palm hit damp stone. Steady. Real.

"Good," she muttered, fingers flexing against the wall. "At least stone hasn't changed."

Vaeronth stirred faintly.

I feel your fear.

"Not fear," she whispered, exhaling through her nose. "Annoyance. At myself."

A pause. Then, warm as coals: *That too can be strength.*

She resisted the urge to roll her eyes. "You and your wisdom. You know I'm standing here debating whether I've gone completely blind, right?"

The dragon said nothing to that, which felt ominous.

Her humor fractured then, just a little, the dryness forced. But she tightened her jaw and breathed through it.

Right now, falling apart wasn't allowed.

Not yet.

It is not yet gone, Vaeronth said. *But it will go. Piece by piece. You knew this.*

"I didn't know it would be now," she whispered aloud.

She pressed her forehead lightly to the stone, breathing slow. Steady. One inhale. Two.

Her vision flickered again. Shadows where there shouldn't be. Light failing in places her mind swore it should hold.

"I'm fine," she muttered aloud, though no one was listening. "I'm absolutely not falling apart moments before a deadly trial."

From the corner of her mind, Vaeronth's voice was quieter now. Concerned.

You must not hide this from yourself, Eliryn.

"I'm not hiding. I'm compartmentalizing."

The dragon's silence, unimpressed, said more than words.

A shaky laugh left her throat. "Don't look at me like that."

I cannot look at you. I am housed within the vessel you wear like a necklace.

"Exactly. So stop sounding so judgy."

She let the small, strained smile linger for just a heartbeat longer before straightening, pushing off the wall.

One step forward.

Another.

"I'm still moving," she whispered. "I just might need you as my eyes."

Her chest ached.

She blinked again, hoping it would pass. That the fog would recede.

But this time... it didn't.

Half of what she could see—the left side—simply slipped away.

Almost all at once. It happened mid-blink.

One breath, and the room in front of her was murky.

The next breath the murk was halved.

Eliryn reeled, catching herself on the wall. She turned her head, trying to force her other eye to compensate, to anchor the disappearing edges. But it was like watching night swallow color.

Her left side saw only color-smudged light now. No detail. No shape.

She gasped, a sharp inhale she didn't mean to make.

Easy, Vaeronth rumbled, low and deep in her chest. *It is not death. It is a door.*

"A door that closes," she whispered.

Only so another may open.

She stayed there for a long time, breathing shallow and slow, memorizing the shapes of the room while she could still make them out with half a world's worth of clarity.

The others had started getting antsy, stretching or pacing, but she sank down onto one of the stone benches near the wall and folded her hands in her lap. The left side of her vision had dissolved into a haze of color and warped light. Even the floor seemed to slope slightly, unbalanced by the clarity she'd lost.

She didn't call attention to it. Not yet.

Across the chamber, she could hear muffled voices; two of the chosen muttering to each other, the rhythm of nervous energy passing between them like a thread being wound and unwound. Whitvale was sharpening his blades against the stone wall's edge. Stormthresh paced near the far door, muttering prayers under her breath.

Garic hadn't strayed far. He stood a few paces away, arms crossed, eyes occasionally flicking toward her. He didn't speak.

Eliryn closed her eyes entirely.

Vaeronth, she reached again, more steady this time. *This is only going to keep getting worse.*

Yes, he said without delay. *And yet you will not break.*

Not yet. She muttered.

Not ever.

A pause passed between them. She opened her eyes and studied what she could. The blur had stopped spreading, at least for now. But her left eye registered only vague, abstract movement. If she turned her head too fast, her stomach lurched.

"I feel crooked," she muttered under her breath.

You are changing, the dragon acknowledged. *But that doesn't mean it's bad.*

"No one else would see it any other way."

No one else is bonded to dragon and bound by prophecy.

Eliryn exhaled slowly, letting the warmth of Vaeronth's presence expand within her. He didn't fill the space with words this time, only with stillness. A kind of protective quiet, like being wrapped in wings beneath a dark sky.

Her hand moved absently to her chest, fingers brushing the pendant there. The warmth of it grounded her. The magic pulsed beneath her skin, quiet but alive.

Around her, time moved strangely, thick and slow, like honey poured over stone.

She waited.

And in the waiting, she began to gather herself. Not just strength, but certainty.

One breath. One anchor. One truth.

Eliryn of Lirin's Edge. The Last Dragonrider.

Vaeronth, the Endbringer.

Half-blind. Half-lit.

But never broken.

The door at the far end groaned open.

Stone against stone, low and grating, a sound that cleaved the hush like a blade.

The steward stepped through, flanked by two guards in deep grey with faces obscured by mirrored helms. He moved without hurry, the bell at his wrist chiming once as he entered the room.

The chosen turned toward him, one by one. Fingers stilled on hilts. Even Garic straightened from his place near the wall, eyes narrowing as if bracing for something heavier than before.

Eliryn rose last. She could feel the world tilt slightly as she stood, her left eye offering only color and blur, a swirl of nothing that buzzed faintly at the edge of her concentration. But her spine stayed straight, and her hand curled once, steady, at her side.

The steward surveyed them with unreadable calm.

"Six remain," he said, his voice carrying like wind across still water. "Six who passed through illusion and emerged intact."

He let the words rest in the air for a beat. Then continued: "This third trial has showcased champions. But it has also culled even the most clever of chosen."

Garic's jaw flexed once. The youngest chosen, the boy, visibly swallowed.

The steward went on.

"You will not face this trial together. The path must be walked alone. One by one, you will enter. You will not see the others emerge. You will not know their fate until your own is decided. The next will not begin until the former has ended—by victory or by death."

A ripple of unease moved through the gathered six. Eliryn felt it pass like wind through reeds.

The steward's eyes swept across the chosen and stopped on Eliryn.

"Dragonrider," the steward said. "You will be the first to face what lies beyond."

Eliryn blinked once. "Wow. And here I was, just about to volunteer. Really took that opportunity from me."

The silence that followed was heavy, but she let it hang. Someone—probably Garic since he was her only ally—let out a quiet snort from her right.

She felt their stares like weights across her shoulders: wary, curious, or maybe just quietly waiting to see if she'd fall.

The steward, to his credit, didn't react. He only gestured smoothly toward the stone archway yawning open behind him. "Enter. Your fate awaits."

Eliryn rolled her shoulders once, stretching the tension from her neck. "Not ominous at all. Love that."

Then she stepped forward without hesitation, braid tight down her back, her steps quiet as breath. As she passed the steward, her voice dropped low, just for him.

"Next time, someone else goes first."

Behind her, Garic's quiet grunt of approval followed her to the threshold.

And then the stone door closed.

In her mind, Vaeronth stirred. *Steady, Eliryn. Not all traps are meant to be walked into. Some wait for trust.*

"Very vaguely put," she muttered. "But thanks."

And with that, she walked into the dark.

The door closed behind her.

The corridor she entered was dark at first, then flooded with a soft amber glow. The walls curved like bone, warm to the touch. The scent of heated stone and ash curled in her lungs.

She descended a short ramp and found herself in a chamber unlike any other she had seen since the trials began—an arena.

She stepped into the arena, and the world changed.

No walls. No roof. Just a sky of colorless clouds and jagged light, and below it—

It was a living thing. A labyrinth of blood-slick platforms and fractured terrain, part machine, part nightmare. Barbs jutted from stone. Chasms breathed smoke. Obsidian spikes curled like claws. Nothing was still. The entire structure moved, constantly shifting- plates grinding, ledges retracting, new horrors unfolding with each second. A gruesome obstacle course meant to cull.

Eliryn didn't move right away.

She waited and listened.

The floor beneath her pulsed faintly, like breath drawn through stone.

Far ahead, a platform dropped into a pit, then reemerged on the opposite side with a grinding groan. Spears clattered into place above distant ridges, suspended in nothing.

She took a single step forward.

Her boot crunched down on something hard—then gave way with a sharp crack.

Glass.

She hissed, pulling her foot back slightly.

Shards glittered across the floor like frost, jagged and fresh. Some were stained with blood, none of it dry. The only way forward was through.

You've bled before, she reminded herself, jaw tight.

She crouched low, shifting her weight to move light and fast.

The first real step sliced through the outer sole. She felt it bite. Then the next, and the next—sharp edges pushing up through soft leather, deeper than they should. The boots her mother had crafted, once her comfort, were losing their protection.

"Vaeronth," she breathed.

I will be your eyes, he answered, warm and steady in her mind. *Three steps. Ledge. Far drop. Wind will try to take you. Crouch at the edge.*

She obeyed.

Her vision blurred violently; shapes melting, light blooming in unnatural ways. Shadows twitched like living things. Even the color of the stone seemed to bleed.

She nearly stepped off a ledge she couldn't see.

STOP. Vaeronth's roar cut through her skull.

She froze—her foot hanging over open air. The wind howled below, teeth bared.

Gasping, she dropped to a crouch. Her heart hammered in her throat.

"Too close," she muttered.

Trust me. Trust nothing else, not even your own senses.

The next stretch led to a wall of rotating beams, each one slick with something that might've been oil... or blood. She grabbed hold, climbing fast, ignoring the scream in her limbs.

Hidden mechanisms snapped to life.

Thunk. Shnk.

Spears shot from alcoves in the stone. One grazed her shoulder; another sliced the edge of her braid.

She swung sideways, feet slipping on the beam. A sharp edge ripped straight through the side of her boot and her skin beneath it.

The pain was immediate, hot, and spreading.

She caught a ledge by her fingertips and dangled, legs kicking. Her feet were slick with blood inside the boots now, glass embedded deep.

With a hissed curse, she found footing and climbed. But the damage was done and each step made the pain worsen.

At the next pause—a narrow ledge, nowhere to fall but down—she reached down with shaking hands.

She yanked the boots free, the sound wet and awful.

"Who needs skin, anyway."

They came off reluctantly, soaked red at the soles. She left them behind without ceremony. Let them become part of the arena, like bones offered to a beast.

Barefoot, she moved on.

Skin to glass, skin to stone. No more protection. No illusions.

She ran.

Retracting bridges. Spinning blades. Crumbling tiles.

You are bleeding badly, Vaeronth said, voice tight in her mind.

"Add it to the list," she rasped aloud.

Her feet stopped feeling like her own after the first dozen steps. Each impact felt distant, like she was watching herself from somewhere far inside her skull.

Every step hurt. But pain was simple. Pain was honest.

Vaeronth said again. *I am your sight. You will survive this.*

She walked a razor-thin rail over open flame, felt heat rise into her skin. At the next crumbling ledge, Eliryn sagged for half a breath. Just half.

This isn't survival, whispered some frayed part of her mind. This is butchery.

She shoved the thought back down just as quickly as it rose. Survival would be enough. She wobbled, but didn't fall.

And at last—

A tunnel loomed ahead, narrow and silent, its walls slick with condensation that caught the dim light like veins of old silver. From its mouth, the scent of damp stone and old ash drifted out like breath from a sleeping beast.

Then came the arrows.

They rained from nowhere. Black-fletched. Hissing like snakes. Some sliced past so close she felt the air part at her skin. She ducked low, pivoted hard to the left, and the next volley embedded into the stone beside her with a sound like bone snapping.

Then came the voices.

Not from ahead. Not from behind.

From all around.

She slowed—not in fear, but focus sharpening into something honed.

Shapes flickered at the edges of her vision. Her mother's gaze, hollow with betrayal. Her grandmother's hand, bloodstained and reaching. The blackened frame of her childhood home, burning all over again.

Every image whispered as it passed:

You're still trying?

You should already be dead.

You don't belong here.

Eliryn's breath hitched. The illusions clawed deeper, not as fear, but as memory draped in deceit.

She knew this wasn't real.

But gods, it felt real.

Tears burned at her eyes, blurring her already-failing sight into smeared shadows and trembling light. She hated the tears most of all.

"Not this time," she whispered, voice raw.

Vaeronth's voice stirred, low and steady, curling around her mind like a shield. *These lies are hollow. Keep moving.*

She didn't answer. She didn't need to.

She ran.

The illusions shrieked after her now, louder than the arrows, louder than her heartbeat. Her mother's voice broke with fury. Her grandmother's whispered disappointment. The ghosts of her village hissed like scalding water in her ears.

But her feet didn't stop.

Arrows whined past. Two glanced her shoulder. Pain sparked bright and brief. She counted it as proof she was still alive.

And then—light.

The tunnel spat her out like a broken bird. She fell to her knees, scraping skin, her body heaving for air as the oppressive sounds cut off behind her like a door slamming shut.

Silence crashed down.

Eliryn stayed there, on her knees, gasping. Trembling. Slightly wounded.

But alive.

Slowly, the floor beneath her rumbled. The platform, hidden in shadow, began to rise. Stone shifted, gears turning somewhere deep beneath her feet.

The platform lifted her higher, until the arena sprawled beneath her—carved stone slick with blood and smoke, where shattered illusions littered the ground like glass.

From up here, she could see the whole battlefield.

And for the first time, it felt like victory.

Even if no one cheered. Even if no one cared.

She did.

"We did it," she rasped aloud, her voice breaking.

Vaeronth's reply came like embers stirred to life.

You did it.

Eliryn's lips twitched faintly. "I mean. You're definitely the reason we're alive but I wouldn't say no to some applause."

There was silence.

Then, dryly: *Your sense of humor is very curious.*

She laughed, cracked and tired.

Below, the arena shifted again, hungry for the next.

She watched the next chosen enter: the woman from Stormthresh.

She moved like someone who'd spent her life slipping between dangers, but this arena was built to swallow even the gifted.

She passed the glass path with only shallow cuts, climbing much faster than Eliryn had managed. She leapt, flipped, dodged spinning saws and retracting steps. She almost made it.

Almost.

One of the bridges shifted just a heartbeat earlier than the woman anticipated. It caught her mid-leap. Her foot missed the landing. She tried to grab the edge, but the entire platform retracted like a closing jaw.

She vanished into the fog with a strangled scream.

The platform reset. Stone scraped. Smoke billowed.

The third chosen stepped through next.

Broad-shouldered. Tarn's Hill's warrior, axe in hand. He stared up at the course with cold determination.

He didn't waste time.

He tore through the lower level, crushing traps underfoot. Brute force served him well at first, he used the axe to jam moving panels, to wedge open passageways that threatened to slam shut. He even knocked a falling spear from the air.

Eliryn took a moment to admire his resourcefulness; she had never once thought to use her own weapon in that way.

But force can't outlast unpredictability.

In the middle of the fire-rail segment, he paused.

Too long.

Something was triggered beneath him. A hiss of pressure.

A spike rose straight through the floor—through his back, his heart, out his chest.

He didn't even have the chance to scream.

Eliryn flinched as his body was dragged under the platform, vanishing.

And again the arena shifted to welcome the next.

The fourth to enter was the snake.

Whitvale.

His grin returned the moment he stepped inside. His coat was immaculate, cuffs embroidered, hair slicked back with absurd confidence.

Whitvale didn't rush.

He walked the first half, taking careful, calculated steps. When a bridge began to retract, he casually leaped across to the next one with graceful ease.

Everything about him was practiced, polished, too smooth.

He didn't just conquer the obstacles. He'd mastered the arena without breaking a sweat.

At the final stretch, he threw a glance up at Eliryn, winked, and vanished into a blur as the platform raised him upward.

Vaeronth stirred in her mind.

That one is filled to the teeth with venom.

She didn't need to answer him back; Vaeronth already knew her opinion of Whitvale.

The fifth chosen stepped in next. The gentle-faced boy with copper hair from Westbrae. He gripped a short dagger with white knuckles. He was small. Fast. But afraid.

From above, Eliryn saw Whitvale reappear at the edge of the upper balcony where she waited.

"You're doing great!" he called to the boy below. "But mind the spinning blades—they switch direction after the third pass!"

Wait... Eliryn thought for a moment. *That wasn't true.*

Eliryn had counted and was almost sure they only switched after the fifth.

The boy, trusting, misjudged the pattern based on Whitvale's word. He turned early and a blade caught him square in the gut. He dropped, screaming, trying to crawl while holding his organs inside him, but the floor opened beneath him, swallowing him whole while he was still alive.

Whitvale sighed loudly and said to no one in particular, "He should've listened."

Eliryn's teeth clenched.

The sixth and final person to enter the arena was Garic.

He stood at the starting line, broad and still, arms flexed in readiness.

He didn't look up at Eliryn or Whitvale, not knowing they were there. He just stood a moment, taking it all in, and breathed deeply.

Then he ran.

Eliryn noticed immediately when Whitvale leaned over the balcony. "The ledge after the climbing beams is cracked!" he called. "You'll need to jump right instead of forward!"

Eliryn stepped forward without hesitation this time.

"He's lying," she said, voice flat and deadly calm. "Don't trust the snake."

Garic slowed. Looked up.

"Jump forward," she called, loud and clear. "Straight forward. The crack only shows if you step to the right."

Whitvale's smile curdled.

Garic's head tilted up, eyes finding hers.

He trusted her. No hesitation.

He adjusted course.

He moved with steadiness, not a showman like Whitvale but a man used to enduring. He bled some. He stumbled once, but he never faltered.

When he reached the rotating beams, Eliryn saw him pause for breath before starting the climb.

Spears launched. Traps clicked.

But she called out again: "Left side after the fourth beam!"

She watched Garic leap clear, landing heavy but whole.

She didn't let herself exhale. Not yet.

The trust he'd shown in her hit her harder than the pain pulsing her feet. She didn't let herself question it. Not now.

It was slow. Brutal. But Garic made it to the final tunnel, where the illusions bled through again. She saw him flinch, heard his voice call a name: "Bran."

One of his sons, no doubt.

The fire in her chest rose.

She shouted again. "Garic! They're not real. That's not him. You're almost through!"

And then—

He ran.

The illusions screamed. Shadows tried to follow.

But Garic emerged, bleeding and scraped, but alive.

He dropped to the floor, hands on his knees, gasping. Then raised his head to her. Although she had trouble getting her eyes to focus, she knew they connected.

And from across the balcony, Whitvale rolled his eyes and clapped sarcastically. "How sweet," he drawled. "Didn't know you two were close."

Eliryn didn't look at him.

Her eyes were locked on Garic. And her dragon's voice echoed through her.

The true trial was not just the course itself. It was loyalty. Integrity. You've passed both in the eyes of the gods.

She nodded—more to herself than anyone else.

Only three remained now.

The arena doors sealed behind Garic with a low, iron groan, the echoes dying slowly through the stone chamber.

Eliryn exhaled for the first time in what felt like hours. Her hands trembled slightly at her sides, not from fear, but from the sheer weight of watching others fail.

But Garic was alive. And he was walking toward her now, bruised and bloodied.

She met him at the edge of the platform where she'd been watching. Her knees threatened to give as she stepped toward him, but she locked them. Not now. Not in front of Whitvale. She could rest later. Maybe. Hopefully.

"You made it," she said, voice hoarse.

Garic gave her a tired smirk. "You sound surprised."

"I am," she said. "There were more dangers than just the arena."

Garic followed her gaze toward the far edge of the room, where Whitvale lingered in the shadows, wiping sweat from his brow and pretending not to listen.

"He lied to one of the others," Eliryn said, voice low and steady. "Gave him false directions like it was a game. The young boy with the red hair... he trusted Whitvale. Took him at his word when he called out the timing of the spinning blades, and it led him straight into them. He died trying to hold himself together, and Whitvale just stood there. Smiling. Like it was sport."

Garic looked at her, something shifting behind his eyes, disbelief yielding to grim clarity. "I knew he was arrogant," he said quietly. "But I didn't know he was cruel."

"He gains less competition," Eliryn said. "And fear. But more than that..." Her voice cooled. "I think he enjoyed it."

They were quiet for a beat. Then Garic said, "And you? How did you survive it?"

Eliryn hesitated, then gave a small, worn smile.

Vaeronth stirred, a quiet presence like a hand at her back. *Tell him the truth. Let him see the bond.*

"Vaeronth," she said. "My dragon. He saw what I couldn't. My eyes... they failed me. I was struggling with outlines and light. No shapes. No paths. I would've bled out on the glass field if not for him."

Garic stared at her a moment, taking note of her dragon marks that were glowing stronger as she spoke about her dragon, measuring the truth of it—then nodded slowly.

"So your dragon guided you."

"He's the only reason I'm standing here."

"Well, thank him for me too, then," Garic said. Then, after a pause: "And I'll remember what Whitvale did."

Eliryn touched his arm, needing her only ally to understand the gravity of what had happened. "Be careful around him. He's the type to strike when your back is turned. He wants to watch us fail."

Garic followed her gaze to where Whitvale lounged, boots swinging idly over the ledge like death wasn't a breath away. His expression hardened.

"I'll stay ready."

And as the torches dimmed slightly, and footsteps echoed far down the corridor, the last of the chosen stood shoulder to shoulder—warriors, champions and survivors, forged in blood and sharpened by fire.

Vaeronth's voice rumbled in her mind as Garic stood beside her.

Not forged, little flame.

Found.

Interlude 7: Malric

"Loyalty is forged not by chains, but by choice. Which is why tyrants fear it most." —From the private annotations of Councilor Rhalin

Malric watched from the high chamber.

The trial below played out across the mirrored surface of the viewing basin—an ancient, silver-edged pool that reflected cruelty with perfect clarity. Every blood-slick stone. Every shattered cry. Every spear hidden just beneath the surface.

And her.

Eliryn.

He should have turned away. Should have reported back already. But he stood frozen, gaze caught. Not by duty. Not by command.

By her.

She didn't know he was there.

He'd watched her before, in quieter moments. At the tables with her guard, laughing like she belonged in the kitchens. Her voice too soft, her skin too bare of armor. Vulnerable in ways she couldn't afford. She hadn't seen him. None of them had. He lingered in the shadows, unseen, as always.

But when that young guard—Silas—had spoken her name, Malric had faltered. The sound of it had dragged him backward in time.

Names were power. Especially here.

And she'd handed hers out like it meant nothing.

Foolish. Reckless.

But now, watching her move through the trial course, bloodied and breathless, he wasn't so sure.

She hesitated before danger. She flinched before illusions. He thought it caution. Discipline. Maybe fear. He hadn't yet realized she was losing her sight. To him, it simply looked like patience. Calculation.

But whatever it was—she kept moving.

He hated that he admired it.

And hated more that he watched her like he wanted to understand. Like understanding would grant him control.

She was becoming something else. Not just a girl. Not just a competitor. A story already half-formed. A symbol.

And symbols were harder to kill.

He saw the danger now. Saw it as clearly as the blood on her hands. When the arena shifted against her, she didn't fight harder. She fought smarter.

More than that, standing on the ledge, her breath ragged, her body broken, she'd reached back. Offered her support to the old fighter from Stonefell. Risked herself for someone who didn't matter.

Why?

Malric's hands curled into fists at his sides. His ring burned cold against his skin. Heavy. Restless. It always felt wrong when she was near.

And yet when he watched her, part of him wondered what her hand would feel like, if she offered it to him.

He swallowed, hard.

The dragonrider had what people followed. Not orders. Not fear.

Integrity.

He breathed out, slow and sharp, forcing control back into his body.

"She'd be good for us," he whispered. "Too good."

And he despised himself for meaning it.

Because he already knew what his father would say. What the council would demand.

Eliryn—this fragile, reckless woman who wasn't yet anything at all—was a threat. Not because of her strength. But because of her restraint. Her mercy.

Because she could be loved.

People would follow her.

That terrified men like his father.

Malric turned from the basin, though her image chased him like hunger. His jaw locked. The scent of smoke and blood clung to him.

She would have to survive far worse than a trial.

And he didn't yet know whether he'd help her do it—or be the one who stopped her.

The corridor outside was dim. The sconces guttered low, the air thick as velvet. Malric moved like a shadow, silk-smooth and silent, the gold cuffs at his wrists catching faint light.

He didn't want to go to the upper tower.

Didn't want to hear the voice waiting there. His father's voice—precise as a blade, cold as the steel it wielded. Secrets wrapped in barely human skin.

At the stairwell, he paused. His fingers curled around the stone railing, his knuckles bloodless.

He would be expected to report.

They had scrying pools. Eyes sharper than his. But his father wanted to hear the shape of her from Malric's lips. How she moved. What she inspired.

And what could break her.

Malric's stomach twisted.

Because he knew the answer now.

Not her weakness. Her strength.

She protected. Even when it cost her. She led without asking. She earned loyalty without demanding it.

That was what terrified them.

Not her dragon.

Her humanity.

A girl with no title. No allegiance but to truth and flame. That kind of power couldn't be chained. It couldn't be bought.

And it couldn't be allowed to grow.

He could already hear the verdict waiting for him. His father's voice, soft as silk, cutting as glass:

We can't risk her gaining allies. You'll see that it doesn't happen.

Malric swallowed hard.

It wasn't the order that would hollow him.

It was knowing how easily he would obey.

And yet—

He remembered her laughter, flickering like firelight in the kitchen halls. Her hair damp, curling against her cheek. Not a leader. Not a threat.

Just a woman.

In the arena, she hadn't survived like a warrior would.

She'd endured like someone with something to lose.

And he found himself wanting to know what it was.

He braced a hand against the stone. His pulse felt wrong in his throat.

Eliryn of Lirin's Edge had survived three trials.

She'd earned her place.

And his father would still order her death.

"Damn you," Malric whispered. Not to her. Not entirely.

To himself.

To the war inside his own ribs.

He straightened slowly.

If he lied, his father would know.

If he told the truth... she wouldn't live through the week.

The stairs rose ahead of him like a sentence.

Each step he took was either a promise.

Or a betrayal.

And he didn't know which one he wanted more.

Not anymore.

The ring pulsed faintly, as if it already knew.

And somewhere beneath the steel of his will, something darker stirred.

Something that whispered:

She's not yours to save.

But gods, you wish you could.

Chapter 18: The Weight of Surviving

"After the scream, the silence. After the fall, the breath. Survival is not always loud." —Unknown soldier, Requiems of the First Trial

Eliryn didn't feel the pain until the silence settled in.

Until the heat of adrenaline bled off her skin and her steps slowed. The ache seeped in—first dull, then sharp—crawling from heels to knees. The blood had stopped, but not before leaving a trail: faint red prints on pale stone.

She couldn't even place the moment Silas appeared. One heartbeat there was only the echoing hall; the next his arm was under hers. Pain had sanded the edges off time and taken the minutes with it.

Silas said nothing at first. He let her lean, one arm strong and steady beneath hers, guiding with the kind of gentleness men usually forgot how to wield. Warmth threaded through his sleeve to hers, as steady as his breath. He was careful.

At the final turn toward her door, he eased his hold without letting go, matching her pace like it was a language he'd learned on purpose.

He glanced at her sideways. "You're limping harder."

"I'm fine," she lied, though her voice cracked.

Silas didn't argue. But when they reached her door and she sagged against it, breath shaking, he stepped closer. Close enough she caught the faint scent of leather and cedar clinging to him, warm and familiar in a way that caught her off guard.

"Let me help you inside," he said softly. "If that's all right."

She hesitated. She should've said no. Should've told him she didn't need help. But her legs trembled, her vision blurred, and for once, pride lost the fight.

She nodded.

The door shifted open like it recognized her will, and Silas guided her through gently. Inside, the room responded instantly: the hearth leapt to life, casting a golden glow across the stone. A warm basin of water sat at the base of her padded bench, beside a folded set of thick, comfortable clothes and a bowl of dark-berries and honeyed root.

The door closed behind them with a whisper.

She tried to step forward on her own. Failed. The pain roared back, sharp and unforgiving.

Silas caught her before she hit the floor, arms steady beneath hers. "Gods," he muttered, easing her to the bench. His voice sounded strained. "Eliryn... you should've said something sooner."

She didn't answer. Couldn't.

He knelt, dipping the cloth in warm water. His hands, usually so steady, hesitated just for a moment before touching her skin.

"I thought you might not come back," he said finally. His voice was quieter than before. "Guards can't see anything when you're inside the trial. We just wait. Wondering."

She watched the way the firelight caught his profile, how carefully he wrung out the cloth, how his hands shook slightly.

She didn't speak until the cloth touched her feet. The burn of it pulled the words from her like a confession.

"I barely made it." Her voice cracked. "Vaeronth... he helped me through. I can barely see anything clearly anymore. I would've died without him."

His hands stilled.

"You're... blind?"

"Almost." She let out a breath. "I'm losing what little clarity I have left. I can feel the dark closing in."

Silas said nothing at first. The silence wasn't empty. It felt like him holding something carefully between his teeth.

Then, finally: "You didn't falter."

She blinked. Looked down at him, not understanding.

"When you walked in just now," he continued. "Even in pain. Even like this. You still reacted like a warrior. Like you could do it on your own."

Her throat tightened. She didn't feel like a warrior. Not with blood drying on her heels. Not with exhaustion pressing into her bones.

Then softer, almost too soft to catch: "I'm glad you made it back."

Her heart faltered. Something shifted inside her.

Before she could stop herself, her fingers found his. Rested there. Just for a moment. The warmth of him seeped into her skin like something she hadn't realized she was cold enough to crave.

"So am I," she whispered.

They stayed like that. In the hush of firelight. In the silence between orders and battles and trials. Just two people, scraped raw by a cruel world, holding something fragile between them without naming it.

When she finally pulled her hand back, she didn't look at him. Couldn't.

Silas helped her into the thick sleepshirt the room provided. His hands moved carefully, respectfully, but she caught the hesitation in his breath when his fingers brushed her skin. Felt the quiet awareness settle between them like fog.

He eased her down onto the low bed, where furs waited to swallow her whole. Her eyelids felt impossibly heavy, but she didn't know if it was exhaustion or the unfamiliar ache of safety.

Silas crouched beside her, his voice barely audible now. "You should sleep."

Her voice came without her permission, low and uncertain. "Will you stay?"

Silas didn't answer right away.

In the quiet, Eliryn forced a dry, self-deprecating smile. "I'm not ready to be alone with my thoughts just yet."

That made him pause. His gaze flicked to her—not pitying, not startled. Just soft. Honest.

Then, quietly: "I'll stay."

She didn't know how to answer that. So she didn't.

Silas shifted, settling beside her on the stone floor, not touching, but near enough that the warmth of him filled the air. A quiet kind of steadiness. Not only a guard but a man choosing to be there.

And this time, she let herself drift. Not into battle-readiness. Not into fear.

Into sleep.

Real sleep.

The dream came fast—and cruel.

She wasn't alone on the course.

All of them were there—the chosen. Running the trial together. Shoving past one another, bleeding, screaming, breathless. Their faces blurred and streaked with blood, but she recognized them. Every last one. The boy with copper hair. Garic. Stormthresh.

And Whitvale.

He was laughing.

Ahead of her.

And when the boy stumbled, too young, too unsure to stand against him, Whitvale shoved him.

Hard.

Into the blades.

The sound was the worst of it.

Steel cleaving through flesh, bone snapping wetly.

Eliryn's voice tore itself free in a broken scream—but no one heard. The boy's body twitched against the spinning blade, still trying to hold his insides from spilling through his shaking fingers. His eyes met hers, wide and confused, as if begging her to explain why this was happening.

She staggered forward. She tried to move. To help. To reach him.

Her feet slipped.

On blood.

Her own.

Her heels slid uselessly across slick stone, and she looked down to see her own insides unraveling—no, no, not yet, she wasn't ready, she wasn't—

She cried out for Vaeronth.

Nothing answered.

The bond was severed. Silent.

Not even the echo of him remained.

She spun, desperate, choking, gasping, but the walls were too high. Her voice bounced back at her—thin, useless, not hers.

She was nothing here.

Just meat.

The others ran past her. Stormthresh didn't even look back. Garic—his face, shadowed, unreadable—disappeared into the smoke.

They left her.

Whitvale watched.

And smiled.

When she slipped, it was almost a relief.

The ledge broke beneath her, blood-slick stone giving way.

She fell, and kept falling.

Not even her scream followed her down.

No flame. No dragon.

No one.
Just cold.
And the dark.
Forever.

Eliryn jolted upright, breath ragged, a low cry caught in her throat.

The fire still burned.

Her walls still held.

And Silas was still there.

He sat beside her bed, awake now—leaning forward the moment she stirred. His voice came soft, steady, like he'd been rehearsing it in her absence.

"It's all right," he said quietly. "You're safe. You're here."

His hand hovered, unsure, until she reached for him first.

She grabbed it like a lifeline, her fingers tight around his. His skin was warm. Steady. Real. An anchor.

"I'm sorry," she rasped.

Silas frowned softly. "Why are you apologizing?"

"I... don't know."

"Then don't."

His thumb brushed against her hand, careful as always. She held tighter. She wasn't sure he minded.

"I thought I was alone."

"You're not," Silas said simply.

The answer lodged somewhere deep. She breathed carefully, forcing the tremor from her chest.

They sat like that for a while. Silent but not uncomfortable. His presence filling the space where her fear used to live.

Eventually, she shifted, glancing at him through her lashes.

"Is this... something you do often?" Her voice was dry, threaded with something lighter now. "Waiting in the wings of weak and vulnerable girls?"

Silas blinked, noticed her teasing smile, then huffed a soft laugh. "Only the dragonriders."

"Ah." She smirked faintly. "Exclusive clientele."

"Very."

He looked down at their joined hands, then back up at her. His tone lost the humor, though his gaze didn't waver.

"No one would accuse you of being weak, Eliryn."

Her breath caught—not because she didn't believe him, but because maybe, for the first time, she did.

"You don't know me well enough to say that," she said softly, though her fingers didn't loosen.

"I know enough."

Silas said it without hesitation. Without question. And that terrified her far more than the dream had.

Before she could answer, his free hand lifted, hesitating near her cheek.

She surprised them both by leaning into it.

"Just so we're clear," she murmured, her voice soft but carrying, "if you're going to keep saying things like that, you're going to have to get used to me being confused about how I'm supposed to feel."

Silas smiled at that, and it was quiet, but honest. "I'll risk it."

"Dangerous move, soldier."

"I've faced worse."

Her lips curved. But her heart was trembling again, and this time, not from fear.

They stayed like that longer than either of them would want to admit.When sleep finally pulled at her again, she didn't fight it.

Silas brushed her hair from her face once more, gentle as a prayer. He didn't leave. Didn't say he would.

She drifted down into sleep knowing that when she woke—he'd still be there.

And this time, she didn't feel alone.

Only when her eyes closed and opened again without the storm behind them did he rise.

"I'll come check on you in the morning," he said, voice still soft, still steady.

She nodded, too hollow to speak.

At the door, he paused. Like there was something else he wanted to say. But in the end, he only offered her a small, quiet smile.

Then he was gone.

Only when the fire had burned down to coals did she finally reach inward.

"Vaeronth?"

His presence stirred, low and warm in her mind. Tired. Protective.

I'm here.

She exhaled shakily.

"Do you think there's another trial soon? Did you... sense anything? Hear anything from the steward?"

A pause.

No. Nothing clear. Nothing that will happen right away.

Her breath trembled out. "So we don't know what tomorrow brings."

We never do, Vaeronth said gently.

Eliryn closed her eyes again. Letting the quiet hold her the way Silas' hand had.

And this time, when sleep found her, it was kinder.

Chapter 19: The Shape of The Sky

"Some truths arrive like sunrise—soft at first, until you realize they've changed the shape of everything." —Field Notes from the Western Watch, Vol. III

Eliryn woke slowly, the way one wakes after an injury—mind surfacing first, body second. Her limbs felt heavy, warm beneath the layered furs, but not quite her own. Her breath was steady, though, and for the first time in what felt like days, her sleep had been restorative.

Light filtered faintly through the narrow, high window. Morning, but not early.

She shifted slightly beneath the covers, her voice rough. "Vaeronth?"

I'm here, came his voice in her mind, smooth as riverstone, steady as ever. *And before you ask—no, there's been no summons. The steward hasn't stirred the air today.*

She exhaled slowly, tension leaking out of her by degrees. "So I have time?"

Indeed, Vaeronth said. His voice softened. *And we should use it. I need air. Space. Sunlight. My form is tight inside this place. My wings ache.*

She smiled faintly, eyes still closed. "You want to stretch."

A dragon does not stretch. A dragon flies. A pause. Then, quieter: *Even if only for a little while.*

Eliryn pushed herself upright with a quiet groan. Her muscles protested sharply, her ribs aching with each breath. She swung her legs over the edge of the bed and stood carefully, barefoot on the polished stone floor. Her knees buckled, and she caught herself against a low table, knuckles white.

"Maybe we'll both need a while before we're back to normal," she murmured.

Speak for yourself, Vaeronth grumbled fondly. *You are fragile. I am not.*

She chuckled softly, despite herself. "Don't get cocky."

Well I'm not wrong, am I?

Her lips curved, if only for a moment.

She made her way slowly toward the bathing alcove, trailing blood-flaked footprints behind. The stone tub steamed gently, already filled. The room had prepared it while she slept. The scent hit her first: cool and sharp, like mint and lavender wrapped in smoke. Herbs floated among soft petals—heather, bellflower, starleaf.

You're hesitating, Vaeronth observed.

"It's... a lot." She whispered. "To be given such comfort is... still unsettling."

Too bad, he said. *Let yourself enjoy it.*

She undressed stiffly and stepped into the water with a hiss. The heat scalded at first, then dulled into warmth that seeped deep, unwinding knots even as her skin stung from the grit and blood.

As she sank lower, the surface around her bloomed red. The water stirred gently of its own accord, a soft whirlpool spinning outward from her body. Blood and dirt dissolved, drawn toward a silver drain at the base. The petals and heat remained, untouched. Magic. Precise. Unintrusive.

Eliryn leaned back, throat tight, watching the last dark swirl disappear.

Better? Vaeronth asked softly.

She closed her eyes. "Better."

She stayed there until the ache dulled enough to breathe without flinching.

Then, at last, she sat up. "Let's see what we can do about finding you some proper space."

About time. But the teasing was gentle. Grateful.

Her feet still ached, the skin tight where it had torn, but her vision had stabilized—blurred, but functional. She dressed slowly: a thick overshirt and fresh riding trousers. No shoes for now, she couldn't even entertain the thought of it. Pinning her still-damp hair away from her face with simple copper clips, she left it loose down her back. Her necklace pulsed gently against her collarbone, Vaeronth's tether both literal and symbolic.

She caught herself touching it absently as she stepped out.

I'm with you, he murmured.

"I know."

She headed towards the kitchen instinctively.

The warmth and scent of the lower halls met her instantly: roasting roots, warm bread, citrus steeping in water. Safe. Familiar. She hadn't realized how much she'd missed the smell of somewhere that felt like... a home.

Marta stood alone, her hands working the dough on the table with patient strength, forearms dusted in flour, humming low beneath her breath. The sound curled through the stone like something meant to ward off shadows.

For a moment, Eliryn hesitated in the doorway, just... watching.

She used to watch her mother knead bread like that. Not often. But the likeness of it stole her breath for a moment.

Marta's rhythm was different. Slower. Stronger. But the quiet focus was the same.

"You standing there because you're lost," Marta said gently, without turning, "or just too tired to ask where you need to go?"

Eliryn startled slightly. "I... maybe both."

Marta huffed softly—just like her mother used to—and wiped her hands on her apron, finally facing her. "Sit."

Eliryn obeyed without thinking, perching at the edge of the table like she was twelve again.

"You're too pale," Marta muttered, sizing her up with the same clinical sharpness of a battlefield healer. "And you haven't been eating properly."

Eliryn let herself smile, faint but real.

"You remind me of someone," she said softly.

"Oh?"

"Someone I miss."

That, more than anything, seemed to catch Marta. Her gaze softened, lines of her face easing just slightly.

"What do you need, child?"

The word struck something deep in Eliryn's chest. She hadn't been called child in years. And never like this. Not with such warmth.

"I... Vaeronth needs air. Open skies."

Marta nodded slowly, as if she'd expected that answer all along. "There's a ground entrance you can use, near the east stair. It's not locked—kitchen staff and guards take it when they need air, though most forget it's even there."

Eliryn tilted her head. "Convenient."

"Left, out of the kitchens," Marta continued, patient as if instructing an apprentice. "Follow the hall until it ends. You'll see a split willow—can't miss it. Past that, keep to the path that leads up through the old orchard. When you reach the top of the rise, you'll find cliffs on the far side. Good stone, plenty of space."

"For a sunbath and a wingspan?" Eliryn quipped.

Marta's smile creased her weathered face. "Exactly that."

"Will I get in trouble for leaving the inner wards?"

Marta's grin was brief, but real. "Only if you get caught."

Eliryn smiled, genuine this time. "Perfect."

Marta stepped closer then, unwrapping a cloth bundle and pressing it into her hands. "Take this. Bread's still warm."

"I didn't ask for—"

"I know."

Eliryn's throat tightened. "Thank you."

Marta only nodded. Then, after a moment's pause, her voice gentled further: "You remind me of someone too."

Eliryn dared to ask: "Someone you miss?"

"Someone I prayed would survive."

Silence lingered between them, heavy but not sharp. Marta's gaze, steady and maternal, held hers a moment longer.

"Go now. Before he goes mad from being caged."

Vaeronth rumbled, smug.

Eliryn snorted softly. "Stars help me... there's no need to preen."

Marta glanced at her, brows raised, but said nothing. Some things, it seemed, didn't need explanation.

Eliryn smiled, more fully this time, and stood. "I'll be back."

Marta's voice followed her as she stepped into the corridor.

"I know."

The walk to the cliffs took longer than Eliryn expected. Her muscles burned with each step, her breathing uneven. Vaeronth stayed quiet, letting her pace herself.

When they crested the rise, the clearing opened like a promise: pale blue sky, lazy wheeling birds, stone warmed by sunlight.

Vaeronth stirred within her like a rising tide.

Now. His voice was tight. Urgent. *It is time.*

She placed her hand over the pendant. Her skin prickled.

"Ready?"

Always.

The moment her fingers touched the cool metal, she felt the shift—not just inside, but in the air itself. A pulse. A soundless thunderclap. And then—

He emerged.

Like light pouring into a shape, Vaeronth stepped from the pendant in a shimmer of gold and flame. He rose and rose, impossibly tall, unfurling from that impossibly small space. His wings caught the morning sun like living mirrors, each scale edged in iridescent steel. He was massive—larger than she remembered—his neck arching with the grace of a river in motion.

Eliryn took a half-step back, breath caught in her throat.

This was only the second time she had seen him fully manifested. And still, it left her speechless.

His scales shimmered even through the haze of her imperfect vision. Glinting like starlight caught in obsidian, his body glistened with the weight of ancient bone and coiled power. His wings spanned farther than she could have run in a single breath. His eyes, deep as forgefire, turned to her and softened.

"You're..." she exhaled, barely a whisper, "...beautiful."

Vaeronth gave a low, rumbling exhale that shook the stone beneath her feet.

And if you could see me clearly, he teased, *you'd be weeping from my sheer magnificence.*

He lowered his massive head, smug warmth threading his tone. *Fortunately, your eyesight spares you the emotional devastation.*

Eliryn snorted, one brow arching despite herself. "Right. So I should be thanking my half-blindness for shielding me from your overwhelming beauty?"

It's a kindness, really. My radiance has felled kingdoms.

She crossed her arms, tilting her head, a faint smile ghosting her mouth. "And yet, not five minutes ago, you were sulking about cramped quarters like a glorified housecat."

Vaeronth blinked slowly, then released a smoky huff. *Careful, little flame. I might forget I like you.*

Her smile softened, warmth flickering unbidden in her chest. "No, you won't."

A pause. Reverent. Then:

No, Vaeronth quietly agreed. *I won't.*

He stepped forward, talons settling into the moss with careful grace, and looked skyward. With a powerful beat of his wings, he launched himself into the air, a cathedral of shadow and light rising above her. His body spiraled upward, eclipsing the sun, a constellation wrought of obsidian and fire.

Eliryn raised a hand to shield her eyes. It didn't help much—her vision already dimmed things substantially—but the pieces she saw were enough. Even the shapes he carved into the sky made her breath catch.

She sank onto a sun-warmed stone, unwrapped one of Marta's hand pies, and watched him wheel and spiral above her like a myth come alive.

She was halfway through chewing her last bite when a voice, quiet but certain, broke through the air behind her.

"I thought I might find you here."

Her body went still.

She turned—slowly.

Malric stood at the edge of the rise. His cloak stirred in the breeze. Sunlight carved bronze and shadow across the angles of his face, and it was his expression that rooted her. It was composed. Too careful. Eyes locked entirely on her.

His voice broke the quiet. "I take it this isn't an official trial rite?"

Eliryn blinked, startled. Then smirked, wiping honey from her mouth. "No. And if you're here to reprimand me for improper use of highland terrain, I'm throwing this pie at you."

A brow arched. His mouth quirked—a half-smile, quick and dry. "I'll take my chances. Your aim doesn't look deadly from here."

She tilted her head, narrowing her eyes. "What are you doing out here?"

Malric's gaze lifted, tracking Vaeronth's slow, deliberate spirals overhead. Even half-shrouded by haze, Vaeronth's presence dominated the sky.

When Malric spoke again, his voice was quieter. "It's not every day you see a legend take to the skies. I wanted to see it for myself."

She watched him carefully. "And is it worth seeing?"

His gaze returned to her. Sharp. Restless. "It is."

Then, after a pause: "I hate not knowing the shape of something dangerous."

That made her laugh—quiet, worn, but real. "Is that what we are to you? A threat?"

His expression didn't shift, but something in his eyes did. A hesitation. A quiet gravity.

"I think you're a woman trying not to fall apart while the world tries to split you open."

The words hit her like a blade beneath her ribs. Gentle, but precise.

She turned her face away, unable to meet that honesty. Her voice was low. "You're not wrong. But you're not exactly a soft place to land, either. You've got the look of someone who's watched too many people bleed."

A beat.

"I've watched more than just bleeding," Malric said softly. His voice didn't stretch for drama. It simply settled. Plain and cold. "I've seen what comes before it. And after. The silence. The choices."

As his words settled, Vaeronth's voice stirred lazily but alert within her mind.

He's watching you too closely, the dragon said, his tone low but unimpressed. *Should I burn him?*

Without thinking, Eliryn responded aloud. "Not yet."

Malric blinked, thrown for half a second. "...Not yet what?"

She flushed, realizing. "Vaeronth, my dragon. He's just—being himself."

Pity, Vaeronth mused, smug in her mind. *I need the practice.*

Eliryn cleared her throat, glancing skyward. "He's feeling dramatic."

Malric studied her a moment longer, then nodded once. "Smart dragon." He didn't press.

She tilted her head, wary but trying not to show it. "What are you *really* doing here, Malric?"

His gaze flicked to Vaeronth overhead. When he answered, his voice had thinned to something quieter, something harder.

"I wanted to see him."

She blinked. "And?"

A pause.

"Well... I'd be lying if I said I was only here for the dragon."

That landed heavier than she expected.

"You've been watching me," she said slowly, testing the waters.

His gaze didn't shift. "Since your village" A beat. "But I thought I had already made that clear."

"Because someone ordered you to?" she pressed.

His expression shifted. Not guilt. Not shame. Something darker.

"What did you expect?" he said softly. "You're the last dragonrider. Of course someone wants you watched."

Her throat tightened. "So you really are just a royal spy."

Malric stepped closer. The movement was deliberate. Controlled.

"You know I'm more than that."

She swallowed, but didn't back away. "Then tell me what you are."

"No," he said flatly. Then, a pause. "Unless you make me."

She arched a brow, playing despite the unease prickling her skin. "What, should I threaten you?"

A flicker of something sharp crossed his face. "You could try."

Silence stretched.

"Are you an assassin?" she asked, quiet.

When he smiled, it wasn't cruel. It was tired. "What do you think?"

She hesitated. Then said what felt like the truth.

"I think you're more than what you're forced to do."

His breath left him softly. "Then maybe you understand me better than most."

Eliryn found herself watching his mouth as he spoke, his voice cutting soft and deliberate. His honesty felt like a blade offered hilt-first. But still a blade.

"So someone high up sent their assassin to watch me," she said, voice steady despite the chill coiling beneath her ribs.

Malric's gaze didn't flinch. "I was sent to watch you. Yes."

Eliryn's throat tightened. "Because of the whole dragon thing."

A slight nod. "You're the last. That makes you valuable. Dangerous."

Her voice cooled. "So just another mission, then. Another problem to track."

"I thought so."

She caught the shift in his tone. "Thought?"

Malric's jaw flexed. For a long moment, he said nothing. Then, almost reluctantly:

"You weren't supposed to be... this."

Her brows furrowed. "This?"

He looked at her then—truly looked. And his voice came quieter. Raw.

"Someone I didn't want to stop watching."

The words hung between them, heavier than threats.

Vaeronth stirred warily in her mind. *He is dangerous.*

Eliryn forced herself to keep her tone light, despite the hollow expanding in her chest. "That's intense."

Malric's smile flickered, but it didn't reach his eyes. "Isn't it?"

She hesitated, caught between instinct and intrigue. "Why tell me any of this?"

"Because you asked."

She swallowed. "And you're just that honest?"

"I'm worse than honest, Eliryn." His voice was low now. "I'm tired."

She blinked at that. Of all the answers she expected, exhaustion wasn't one.

"I've spent too long in shadows watching people become monsters. Watching good things turn bad." His gaze sharpened. "But you—"

He stopped. His fists flexed at his sides, a rare crack in his composure.

She watched him carefully. "But me...?"

"I don't know what you are yet."

"And that bothers you."

"It consumes me."

The honesty of it stole the air from her lungs.

"You don't even know me," she whispered.

"I've watched enough to want to."

For a moment, neither of them breathed.

Then she tried for a smirk, though her voice caught slightly. "Maybe you just like the idea of something new. Something unknown."

His reply was softer. "I know exactly what I like."

Vaeronth growled softly, unsettled.

Eliryn flicked her gaze skyward. "Careful. You're going to get yourself incinerated."

Malric's gaze didn't waver. "I think I'd burn gladly."

That rattled her more than she wanted to admit. She tried to recover. "You're worse at flirting than you are at spying."

"I'm not flirting."

That stopped her.

"I'm telling you I don't know how to stop watching you."

The wind stirred between them, cold and sharp.

"I should be afraid of you," she whispered.

Malric's voice was softer now, the edge of something broken buried beneath the silk. "Then why aren't you?"

She didn't have an answer.

Vaeronth's presence coiled, tense but silent.

Eliryn drew a slow breath, trying to gather herself, but her words cracked anyway. "Because you told me the truth."

"You think that protects you?"

She met his eyes, steady now. "It makes you dangerous. But it doesn't make you my enemy."

Malric tilted his head slightly, expression unreadable. But something in his gaze flickered. A fracture.

"And you," she added, "aren't sure if you want to be."

He didn't deny it.

Instead, after a long silence, his voice came low and strange.

"You're the first person who's looked at me like I'm anything but a blade."

Her throat tightened.

"And you're the first one who hasn't looked at me like I'm cursed."

He smiled faintly. Not sharp. Not cold.

Just sad.

A long silence stretched.

She met his gaze. "Who do you work for, Malric? Whose assassin are you?"

His silence held like a blade.

"You know I can't answer that," he said softly.

"Why not?"

"Because then you'd know who I might be sent to kill next." His expression flickered. "And I'm trying very hard not to make you run."

She breathed a quiet laugh. "That's your strategy? Vague menace and terrible charm?"

"I prefer 'disarming honesty.'"

She smiled. Small. Real. "It's working."

For a heartbeat, neither of them spoke. The silence wasn't uncomfortable. It felt suspended. Like the air itself was waiting. Eliryn wasn't sure what unsettled her more: the fact that he meant it, or the fact that some part of her believed him. His gaze didn't waver, steady as if he'd already decided something about her that she couldn't see yet. And for the first time in days, she wasn't thinking about trials or pain or the weight of her own fear. She was thinking about him.

Her voice was almost hesitant. "Eliryn."

"What?"

"That's my name. Figured you should know."

Something shifted behind his eyes. Not surprise. Recognition.

"Eliryn," he said. He tasted it. "Fitting."

"Why?"

He smiled. Soft and unreadable. "Strong. Sharp. Hard to forget."

She swallowed. The sound of her name in his mouth did something strange to her chest.

"I don't know what to make of you," she confessed.

"That's fair. I'm still trying to decide what to make of myself."

She huffed a quiet laugh. Then sighed. The weight of the moment pressing down again.

Malric's voice was lower now. "If things were different..."

"But they're not," she whispered.

He nodded once.

Then added softly, "Try not to let the kingdom chew you up before you get the chance to piss off the right people."

She raised a brow. "Any in particular?"

His smile tilted sly. "Let's just say... those with crowns tend to bruise the easiest."

She rolled her eyes. But her mouth betrayed her. She smiled.

For a moment longer, they stood in silence. Vaeronth's silhouette cutting the sky above them. Then Eliryn stepped back.

"I should give my dragon some sky to himself."

Malric didn't stop her. But as she turned, his voice followed.

"You're not what I expected, Eliryn."

She paused. Looked back.

"Neither are you, Malric."

Then she walked away.

Vaeronth's wings beat once above her. Protective. Sure.

And not far behind, Malric stood alone, watching the sky like it had stolen something from him.

Interlude 8: Malric

"Some stars burn too brightly to be ignored. That's why kings learn to snuff them out before they become constellations." —Notes from the Ashen Court, Volume II

She walked away without looking back. Bare feet brushing over wind-smoothed stone, each step deliberate, even with the limp. Her silhouette, lean and poised, carved a striking line against the pale cliff's edge.

If he hadn't come, he imagined that she'd probably be in the air by now. Riding that great shadow wheeling overhead, free and blazing against the sky.

She looked born for it.

The long shirt and riding leathers clung to her like intention, not vanity. Practical. Sharp. The kind of beauty that didn't try. The kind that happened when someone moved with purpose, not polish. Her hair—reddish-gold, though the sun distorted it—shifted constantly in the wind. Loose strands caught the light like copper wire.

And her eyes—blank, silvered, opaque—should've made her seem lost. But when they'd turned toward him, it hadn't felt like blindness. It had felt like focus. Like she saw past the fog between them. Like she was watching what he didn't say.

She saw me.

That thought lingered. Unwelcome. Unshakeable.

Malric exhaled slowly and turned back toward the path through the orchard, stepping from light into leaf-dappled shade.

He didn't let himself dwell too long on the way her voice had sounded when she said her name. Soft. Vulnerable. Like she trusted him. He didn't tell her he'd known it already—that he'd memorized it long ago.

Some truths didn't need to be offered. Especially not to her.

He reached the castle through the side entrance few dared use. One watchman stood at attention. He knew better than to speak.

Malric moved quickly. Down the narrow staircase behind the western hall. Through the low stone corridor. To the door that always stayed unlocked for him.

His father was already waiting.

King Thalen. No crown rested on his head. No regalia. Just long steel-gray robes and the weight of power worn like second skin. He stood at a low table, maps and scrolls scattered like corpses. He didn't look up as Malric entered.

"Report."

"She's settling in," Malric said, voice steady. "Faster than expected."

Thalen turned. His eyes, cold as old ash, locked onto his son's face. "Explain."

"She's won the kitchens. Guards. Staff. Even the steward's wary but watching. She has eyes now. Ears. People."

"Too fast."

Malric said nothing.

Thalen's voice sharpened, each word precise as a knife. "She's dangerous. Not for her strength. Not for the dragon. But because people want to follow her. That's the danger."

"She hasn't done anything—"

"She was meant to rise," Thalen said softly, iron under silk. "Dazzle. Gather attention. Then fall. Publicly. Violently. A symbol crushed before it could bloom. That was the plan."

He turned fully now, and the cold in his gaze burned.

"But she's rising too quickly. Gathering support from within my own ranks. We cannot let her become beloved before she becomes dead."

Silence.

Malric felt the words sink into him like frost.

At last, he said, "I can keep her close. She trusts me."

Thalen's eyes flicked sharper. "Are you too close?"

"Not yet." A lie. He didn't even blink as he said it.

Thalen studied him for too long. Then he turned back to the table.

"You forget what the dragons were," Thalen said quietly, almost musing. "Why we killed them. Why I forged weapons like the ring on your hand. Their power would've undone everything I've worked for. She's bonded, Malric. That means we don't know what she'll become. What gifts she'll manifest. She's untrained, unstable—and worse, she's *trusted*. That combination is a threat we cannot afford."

He paused, gaze distant, then continued. "I've already chosen who wins this trial. Someone loyal. Predictable. Someone I can control even after the Flame selects them. Power will stay in my hands, no matter what. But she—she's a complication. A threat to us."

Malric's jaw tightened. His throat worked silently.

"Cut the threads," Thalen said again. "Remove her comfort. Take her allies. Keep her desperate. Keep her small."

"You want me to pick who to kill?"

"Her allies. Her comfort. The ones who make her feel seen. Guards. Kitchen hands. Anyone. End it."

Thalen lifted the goblet, drank slowly.

"She is not to become a symbol, Malric. If she does, the others will follow. And if they follow her..."

He didn't need to finish.

Malric's jaw locked until it ached.

"You know your task."

Malric bowed his head. Shallow. Sharp. Controlled.

Then he turned and walked. Step after step. Down the stone corridor. Toward his own chambers.

Eliryn's voice lingered in his mind like a knife still buried.

She said her name like it was a gift.

And now, he was meant to tear her world apart in return.

Malric reached his chambers without memory of the path. His ring burned cold against his skin, blood-forged and heavy, the mark of obedience. His father's tether.

He braced both hands against the stone wall, breathing hard, muscles coiled tight beneath the black of his robes.

She shouldn't have mattered.

She shouldn't still be in his head.

But when she'd said his name—casually, lightly, like she wasn't terrified—something in him had twisted. Unmoored. He'd told himself it was strategy. Leverage. That making her trust him would make it easier to end her when the time came.

She had looked at him not with fear, not with revulsion, but like she saw someone worth speaking to.

And that... that was the problem.

She was supposed to be a target.

Instead, she was becoming the focus of his fractured mind.

He pressed his forehead to the stone, let the coolness bite into his skin. Control. He needed control.

But when he closed his eyes, all he saw was her. On the rise, hair whipped by the wind, voice raw with exhaustion but still teasing him. Still standing.

She didn't belong here. In the castle. In his mind.

She was hope wrapped in dragonmarks.

And Malric had been trained to kill hope.

But he didn't want to.

Not this time.

"Damn you," he whispered.

He should end it. Now. Sever the thread before it tangled him further.

Instead... he imagined her voice saying his name again.

He shoved away from the wall. Prowled the length of the chamber like a caged animal. His thoughts snarled inside his skull, no longer sharp and clear but circling back, over and over, to her.

He could feel her starting to trust him.

And it felt like poison.

Because if she asked—if she reached for him in earnest—he wasn't sure he'd be able to refuse her.

He should do as his father commanded. Cull her allies. Break her down. Make her fear becoming more.

Instead... he wanted her to keep seeing him the way she had on the cliffside.

Like he wasn't just a weapon.

Malric sat heavily on the edge of his bed, jaw clenched, teeth grinding.

She's a threat.

He knew that.

And yet, she was the only person in years who made him feel like more than the blade his father had forged.

She doesn't know what I am.

That thought helped. A little. But not enough.

Malric stared at the wall until the torch burned low.

And in the silence, a darker thought whispered beneath his skin:

If he couldn't have her...

Maybe having her fear would be enough.

Either way, she'd belong to him.

He was already too far gone not to want that.

Not to need it.   .

Not to take it, if she didn't offer.

His fingers flexed, aching for the hilt of his blade.

One day, she would learn exactly what he was.

And he wasn't sure whether he wanted her to run from him.

Or into his arms.

This time, he didn't resist the hunger crawling beneath his skin.

He let it burn.

And welcomed the ruin it promised.

Chapter 20: The Edge of Knowing

"To ask what lies beneath the surface is to risk what holds you afloat." —Sayren of the Shattered Isle, philosopher-exile

The walk back through the orchards felt longer than before.

Each step pulled at the ache in her heels, the raw skin stinging, but she kept going. She told herself it was the wind slowing her, or the weight of Vaeronth's presence circling lazily overhead. But deep down, she knew better.

Her mind was too full.

She kept seeing Malric's face. The way he stood so still, too careful, like something dangerous loosely caged. His words echoed: *It consumes me.*

It wasn't fear that left her unsettled.

It was the idea that he meant it.

She glanced skyward as Vaeronth's shadow crossed the sun. His quiet hum in her mind steadied her, distant but present, content—for now.

When she reached the kitchen door, she hesitated for a breath. Then stepped through.

The warmth hit her first. The familiar weight of it: woodsmoke, roasting roots, the unmistakable scent of butter hitting hot stone. She breathed it in like a balm. Normalcy. Safety. Something human.

"Eliryn!" chirped Nim, flour on his nose, arms elbow-deep in dough. "Come to steal more pies?"

"I came for the company," she said softly. "The food's just a bonus."

"Well," Marta called, "you're in luck. Pies are fresh, and company's half-trained."

The humor tugged a reluctant smile from her. She drifted toward the prep table, accepting the slice Marta handed her without question.

Marta smirked. "Your favorite guard's not working today, by the way."

Eliryn froze halfway through her first bite. "What?"

"Silas," Marta said innocently, barely glancing up as she chopped a bundle of greens. "The one with the long lashes and the gentle smiles. Thought you might ask."

"I wasn't going to," Eliryn said a little too quickly, cheeks warming.

Marta grinned like a fox. "It's fine. We all see it."

"You're imagining things."

"Uh-huh. And dragons don't fly."

Eliryn rolled her eyes, but she couldn't quite suppress the smile curling at the edges of her mouth.

Marta slid a bowl of chopped herbs to the side. "Honestly, if any of them deserves a soft place to land, it's Silas. Boy's got the loyalty of a mastiff and the eyes of someone who's never seen spring. Let him have a real reason to smile."

"I'm not..." Eliryn hesitated. "It's complicated."

"Everything worth it usually is," Marta said.

But Eliryn wasn't listening anymore.

Because Silas had soft eyes. And steady hands. And when he had held her hand, she felt like a person, not a prophecy.

And then there was Malric.

She remembered the cold precision in his voice. The hunger buried deep. The way he looked at her like she was something inevitable. Something he'd already decided he couldn't stop wanting.

Silas felt like the edge of a hearthfire.

Malric felt like the blade that cast the shadow.

She wasn't sure which terrified her more.

They lapsed into a companionable silence for a few minutes, punctuated only by the scrape of knives and the low hiss of boiling pots. The warmth of the hearth soaked into her bones. But beneath it, something tugged at the edges of her mind—a quiet wrongness she couldn't name.

"There are only three of us left," she said quietly.

Marta's busy hands stilled.

"Eliryn..." She began.

"Only three," she continued. "And the chosen from Whitvale—he's not just ambitious. He's cruel. There's something in him that wants this too much, and not for the right reasons."

Nim nodded slowly. "He's the wiry one, isn't he?"

"If he reminds you of a snake, that's him."

Nim chewed his lip. "He gives me bad gooseflesh. Walked through the kitchens once and looked at us like we were meat. Like he'd already counted the cuts and wanted to watch us bleed."

A sharp clang rang out as Marta dropped a ladle into the sink with more force than necessary.

"Eliryn," Marta's voice dropped as she glanced once toward the open door. "You be careful. The castle's not just dangerous for those in the trials. There've been... deaths."

Eliryn looked up sharply. "What do you mean?"

Marta wiped her hands on her apron. "Word is, a minor official in the northern court wing was found dead two nights ago. And not from natural causes.

Poison or blade- depends on who's whispering. Just someone who'd... seen too much."

Nim leaned in, his voice barely audible. "That's not the only one. A scribe went missing last week. And a stablehand turned up drowned in the irrigation trench, but she couldn't swim and would never willingly go near the channel."

Eliryn's stomach twisted. "Are you sure?"

"No," Marta admitted. "But it's a pattern. And the castle hums differently when something's rotting inside it. I've been here long enough to know."

Eliryn sat back, pie forgotten on her plate.

Her mind twisted. She saw Malric's face. Heard his quiet, even voice when he told her he didn't know what she was yet.

He was an assassin.

Could it be him?

She wanted to say no.

But she wasn't sure what scared her more: the idea that he was the killer... or that he wasn't.

"I need to get back to Vaeronth."

She stood too fast, nearly knocking over the bench. Marta let her go, but Nim's quiet "Be safe" followed her out.

She didn't slow until the warmth of the kitchens gave way to cool stone.

Then, at last, she exhaled.

Malric haunted the shadows.

Silas lit the doorways.

She didn't know which one she'd find herself walking toward.

Not yet.

But she suspected it would hurt either way.

The sun hung low when Eliryn stepped out past the last row of gnarled apple trees, their branches bending with the season's weight. A soft wind stirred the leaves and carried with it the faint tang of river air, cool and tinged with memory.

Vaeronth lay on the wide outcrop just beyond, his great body sprawled like a monument left by time itself. His wings were half-unfurled, catching the last of the sun in glimmering sheets; black turned to gold at the edges, every scale a sharp, glistening shard. His head was low, eyes half-lidded, but she knew he was never truly sleeping.

You are quiet, came his voice, brushing gently across her mind like fingers smoothing a page.

Eliryn didn't answer at first. She stepped down from the slope and crossed the grass to him. Her hand found the warm edge of his foreleg—heat like sun-baked stone, alive beneath her palm. Living armor. Solid. Unyielding.

"I can't stop thinking about Malric," she said.

I know.

She didn't ask how. Of course he knew. She was quickly learning that dragons heard things not said, felt things not yet formed.

"He told me what he is."

A killer, Vaeronth said, without hesitation.

She nodded. "Yes. And something else."

Silence stretched between them. Not empty. Waiting.

Then: *You are drawn to him.*

Eliryn didn't answer.

You must not forget why you're here, he continued. *This place is not your home. These people are not your allies.*

"I know," she whispered. "But I can't seem to stop being human just because I'm supposed to fulfill some ancient prophecy."

Vaeronth shifted, slow and deliberate, lifting his head until his gaze settled fully upon her. His eyes were deep, endless pools of hammered bronze—ancient and steady, forged to outlast doubt.

You do not have to stop being human. But don't believe that everyone here can be trusted... not all monsters wear their true faces.

She sank down beside him, her back resting against the curve of his massive shoulder. His warmth enveloped her, steady as his breath—a low, constant thunder behind her ribs.

"I went to the kitchens," she said after a moment. "Talked with Marta and Nim again."

The young one who gives you the sweet bread?

She huffed a small laugh. "That's the one."

And what did they say?

"That someone under the king was killed recently. Someone important, maybe. It had nothing to do with the trials."

Vaeronth didn't speak at once. The silence felt heavier now.

It wasn't an accident, he said finally.

"You think it was a warning?"

Or a test. Of loyalty. Of silence. Of obedience. This place pretends at order, but it is rotting underneath. You are wading through it all.

Eliryn's throat tightened. She tipped her head back, staring up at the last light bleeding through the trees.

"I'm trying, Vaeronth. I just... don't know what direction to go in."

A pause.

You don't need direction, he said, voice soft as the settling of ash. *You have me.*

She closed her eyes, the truth of it sinking into her skin like his warmth.

Chapter 21: The Hall of Judgment

"A throne of embers burns brightest just before it collapses to ash." —Unknown, scrawled in the margins of a ruined prayer book

Eliryn sipped her tea slowly, both hands curled around the warm clay cup. The morning was pale and cold, the light from the high window stretched thin across the stone floor.

Vaeronth's presence stirred beside her mind, closer than breath, as always.

Someone comes. Metal-footed. Purposeful... your guard friend.

His voice was low, but alert.

A summons, I think.

She set the cup down on the table beside her and stood, tugging on her overshirt with haste. "Now?"

Soon.

Before she reached the door, the room shifted. Responding to the new information just like Eliryn was. Something new waited beside the bench where she'd draped her old clothes. Boots. Dark leather, reinforced at the heel and toe, laced tightly with silver-threaded cords. She stepped closer, hesitating. When her fingertips brushed the surface, she felt the difference immediately. Not ordinary. Supple yet strong. A second skin forged for survival, not just ornament. She sat quickly and tugged them on, the leather molding to her feet like memory returning to flesh. Protective and grounding.

She flexed her toes. "Well. Guess I'm running out of reasons to fall."

Don't test that.

She smiled, and said a silent thanks to the room for it's consideration.

A moment later: three sharp knocks at the door. No words.

Eliryn glanced at the room behind her, looking towards the warm tea and pastries, letting out a sigh. Whatever this was, it wasn't going to be eased by sugar.

She hesitated for a breath before opening the door, heart beating steadily but too loud in her ears.

Three left.

That thought wouldn't leave her. Not through the tea. Not through the quiet.

Not through yesterday's brief moment of warmth on a sunlit cliff with a man she shouldn't trust.

Vaeronth stirred again at the edge of her thoughts—steadying, present.

She thought of Silas's quiet loyalty. Of Malric's dangerous eyes.

And then she reminded herself: *This is not over. You are not safe yet. No matter how soft the morning feels.*

Silas stood outside when she opened the door, dressed in his formal guard attire; dark leather, the mark of his station stitched in silver thread over his chest.

He gave her a quiet, respectful nod. "You're being officially summoned; King Thalen wants to see the chosen. He'll address you in the Hall of Judgment."

Eliryn blinked. "Now? You're joking."

"I'm not."

Eliryn stepped into the hall beside him, her voice dry. "You always bring the best news."

He glanced at her sidelong. "Would you prefer I lied?"

"Only if you're good at it."

"I'm not."

"Shame."

As they walked side by side down the narrow stone halls, his shoulder brushed hers, casual, but purposeful. His arm shifted just enough to touch hers again.

She didn't pull away.

"You're not alone in this," he said softly, not looking at her. "You never have been."

The sincerity in his voice struck something small and trembling inside her. Eliryn inhaled slowly, as if that might steady her hands.

"My sight's gotten worse," she admitted under her breath. "Edges blur. Faces smear. I'm still tracking motion, but-"

He slowed his pace half a step, letting her match him more easily. "Lean on me if you need to."

She did. Just slightly. But enough to know he meant it.

"Why now?" she asked more seriously. "What does the king want?"

Silas's mouth tightened. "To look at you."

She arched a brow. "What, checking if I've grown wings yet?"

Silas didn't smile. "Maybe. Or maybe he just wants to see you kneel."

At that, her stomach twisted.

"Great."

"You'll be fine," he said.

"Not exactly reassuring, Silas."

"I'm not trying to be."

That startled a small, honest laugh out of her. She glanced up at him. "And here I thought you were kind."

"I am," he said seriously. "Which is why I'm telling you—be careful."

A pause stretched. She studied him more closely now, her voice quieter.

"Something else is wrong, isn't it?"

Silas didn't answer at first. Then: "Two servants were found dead."

Eliryn's pulse stumbled.

"They had nothing to do with the trials," she said softly.

"No."

"And you think...?"

"I think someone in that throne room doesn't care who the targets are."

She didn't answer. Her thoughts skittered in too many directions. Malric's voice haunted her more than she wanted to admit.

After a long silence, Silas spoke again, low. "How the king will react to you depends on whether you look like a threat."

"I'm half-blind and limping."

"Doesn't matter with your dragonmarks... There's not a lot you can do to lessen the look of your bond."

Eliryn sighed, more exhausted than afraid. "I was hoping for something more encouraging."

"I'm not good at speeches."

"No," she said dryly. "But at least you're honest."

They neared the doors. Silas slowed. His voice dropped.

"Eliryn."

She turned to him, sensing the shift.

"Whatever happens in there... don't let them see you hesitate."

A beat.

"You're still standing. That's more than half of them expected."

Eliryn's mouth quirked. "Including you?"

Silas paused, then shook his head once. "No. Not me."

Her lips twitched. But her heart steadied.

"Thanks."

"Don't thank me yet."

Then the doors creaked open.

And as the light spilled over them, Silas leaned in just slightly, voice low, steady.

"I'll be waiting."

Eliryn rolled her eyes—but couldn't stop the flicker of a smile.

"Try not to look too worried. People will talk."

Silas's answering glance was quiet. Steady.

"Let them."

She knew that if she failed here or in the trials, she didn't just die. She made it easier for them to erase her kind from history.

As the doors creaked open and the torchlight spilled out over them, Silas let his fingers graze her forearm once more.

A gesture. A tether.

And together, they stepped inside.

It was a vast space, circular and tall as a tower's spine. Marble columns loomed like sentinels, wrapped in iron banners bearing the sigil of the ruling line: a black flame rising through a broken crown. At the far end stood a low, obsidian dais. Upon it was the king himself.

Eliryn recognized him instantly, though they had never met. *King Thalen.* Tall, thin as a reed, but with the stillness of a blade left unsheathed. His hair was gray at the edges, the crown above his brow more bone than gold, shaped like fire frozen mid-burn. His eyes were the color of smoke and just as difficult to hold.

She bowed low beside Whitvale and Garic, noticing that their guards hovered a few paces behind them.

The king's voice rang out, sharp and echoing.

"So. You are what remains."

He rose, taking a step forward. His cloak trailed behind him like a shadow given form. "Three Chosen. Three trials completed. And no clear victor yet. Curious."

He circled slowly in front of them, his steps measured.

"I admit, I am… surprised. The Flame has not required more than three trials in nearly a century. And yet here you stand." He paused before Garic. "An old warrior cut from stone. Your village once rebelled against my grandfather, did they not?"

Garic did not answer. The king only smiled and moved on.

Whitvale held himself tall even while kneeling, chin high, barely masking his pride. The king stopped before him. "And you… The blue-marked disciple of the Temple itself. I expect you've already prepared your acceptance speech."

Whitvale smirked. "Only the final lines."

A low chuckle from the king, but it didn't reach his eyes.

Then he came to Eliryn.

She met his gaze without faltering, even as the silence pressed in thick around them.

"And you." The king's voice dropped. "The last rider. Dragonblood. How strange that the Flame called for you."

He studied her the way one might study a storm cloud; curious, but skeptical of its promise.

"Do you know why you were chosen, girl? Why now, after more than a generation of silence from your kind?"

Eliryn remained still. "The Flame doesn't seem to answer to anyone's timing, Your Majesty."

That earned a few sharp inhales from the guards at the edges of the chamber but not from the king. He smiled, slow and unkind.

"No. It doesn't. But it does respond to desperation. Perhaps that's what you are- desperation made flesh." He leaned slightly forward. "Tell me... does your dragon whisper anything useful, or is he just another relic barely clinging to breath?"

Her fists clenched at her sides. "My dragon is more intelligent than most of your court, I'd wager."

The king's brow lifted, amused. "Spoken like someone with fire in her spine. A rare thing these days. Rarer still when it's not snuffed out before it can be useful."

He straightened, clasping his hands behind his back.

"Do you have anyone waiting for you, Dragonrider? Anyone to bury you, should this all go wrong?"

The word *bury* landed like a blade tip pressed to skin. Not *celebrate*. Not *honor*.

Bury.

"No," Eliryn said softly. "There's no one left."

The king exhaled. "How tragic. How... tidy."

He turned, his voice rising once more.

"You are a relic. An echo of a bloodline that should have died out with your kin."

Eliryn turned her gaze on him. "And yet, here I am."

Let them fear that, Vaeronth whispered.

Thalen's lips curled. "What is it the Flame saw in you, girl? Hope? Or hubris?"

"Perhaps both," Eliryn said calmly.

Thalen studied her longer than the others. His voice was colder when he spoke next. "You are the only female contender in three generations to last this long. I wonder if that should trouble me... or amuse me."

Vaeronth's presence flared hot in her skull. *It should terrify him.*

She could feel Vaeronth's power swell inside of her, feel the heat her eyes glowed with, felt her dragonmarks and runes come to life on her skin in answer to Thalen's musings.

And for a moment, the entire room was silent. The guards. The other chosen. Even the king turned slightly, watching her now not as a curiosity, but as something far rarer than they had realized.

A threat.

At last, the king's voice rang out once more.

"The fourth trial approaches. Perhaps it will be the last. Perhaps not." He smiled. "Hope, after all, is the most dangerous thing you can give a dying world."

His voice cooled to iron.

"You are dismissed. Prepare. Rest. If you can."

He vanished into shadow.

And Eliryn stayed kneeling, breathing slow and tight, her heart a war drum inside her ribs.

She realized it only then, that Thalen wasn't taking an interest in her because she was a female or because she was a dragonrider.

He was focused on her because he knew about the prophecy.

Chapter 22: Ash Between Footsteps

"Loss does not take your breath. It waits for you to in-hale—and then it steals it." —Unknown

The doors to the Hall of Judgment groaned shut, sealing the firelit chamber and the king's voice in memory alone. The echo of his words still rang in Eliryn's chest like the residual hum of struck metal.

She walked in silence behind the guards, head high, pulse ticking loud in her throat. Her hands remained steady at her sides—but only barely. There'd been no chance to speak to Garic, no glance shared across the golden floor. Only the king's voice, the too-smooth commentary, and the weight of invisible knives.

As soon as they passed beyond the throne wing's marble columns and into the quieter passageways that led back toward the lesser halls, Eliryn glanced sideways.

Silas was beside her again.

He didn't speak right away. He didn't have to. His presence was an anchor. Familiar. Solid.

She stepped closer to him and said, low and fast, "That wasn't just a formality, was it?"

Silas's jaw worked for a second before he answered. "No. It didn't feel like one either."

They turned down a narrower hall where sunlight failed to reach. The torches here burned weaker, casting jagged shadows against soot-stained stone. Her eyes strained—but the hallway blurred at the edges. The dimness pressed against her vision like fog made physical.

She blinked hard. Again. No improvement.

"Eliryn?" Silas noticed her falter. His hand hovered near her arm, uncertain.

"I can't—" Her voice cracked. "I've lost it. My sight. I—I think it's gone."

They stopped walking. Her breathing spiked, shallow and fast.

Silas turned toward her, steadying her gently by the arms. "It's okay. Hey—it's all right. I'm right here."

She shook her head, panic clawing its way up her throat. "I can't see, Silas. I can't—"

Something is wrong.

Vaeronth's voice surged through her mind like thunder cracking stone.

"I know," she gasped aloud. "I know something's wrong—I can't see, I—"

No. Not your eyes. Not just that. Something near.

His presence burned hot in her mind. Alert. Agitated. *DANGER.*

She gripped Silas's forearms tighter. "Vaeronth says something's wrong."

Silas leaned closer, confused but trying to steady her. "We're all right. We're alone."

"No—" Her voice broke. "He says that danger is near."

Something brushed the edge of Vaeronth's senses—a wrongness too slick to grasp. A ripple of malice in the dark.

Too close. MOVE. NOW.

And then—

Silas' hands tore from her grip.

Not just withdrawn—ripped away.

"Silas?" Eliryn's voice cracked. The emptiness hit her like a blow. "Silas?!"

The air shifted. A grunt. The rasp of metal. Flesh. The unmistakable, brutal percussion of a body being struck.

"No—wait—Silas—!"

Stay calm. Eliryn. I can't see through magic and panic—everything's distorted.

Vaeronth's voice roared in her mind, trying to reach her through chaos.

Get to the wall. MOVE. MOVE!

"I don't know what's happening!" she screamed, her hands lashing through air, reaching, finding nothing.

Behind her were the sounds of combat. Desperate. Wet.

And then—

A sound that didn't belong in daylight. A wet tearing noise, thick and final.

"Silas!" she screamed again, the word breaking apart in her throat.

Her knees buckled. The air stank of blood now—heavy iron and something else, something colder. Final.

MOVE! Vaeronth thundered.

Eliryn shoved herself to the right, her shoulder slamming into stone. Her palms scraped raw as she clawed her way along the wall, her mind spinning, her body trembling violently.

She could hear it. The shift of fabric soaked through. The rasp of metal through something soft.

Then: silence.

A stillness so complete it rang louder than screams.

She fumbled along the wall, tears streaking her cheeks, breathing ragged.

Please... Silas... please...

Then—

To your left. Five paces. He's breathing. A heavy pause. *...But not for long.*

Eliryn dropped to her knees. The stone tore at her skin, but she barely felt it. She crawled blindly, shaking.

"Silas?" Her voice was a raw, broken thing.

A breath. Ragged. Wet.

She followed the sound.

Her hands found him by touch alone. Cloth, drenched and heavy. Flesh, trembling violently beneath her palms.

Then—the wound.

She choked on a sob as her hands slid over it. Too deep. Too much blood. She pressed down instinctively. Her hands slipped, unable to find purchase.

"No, no, no, no—" she whispered, words spilling uncontrolled.

His body seized under her touch. She could hear it—the wet rattle of blood in his throat. His lungs were drowning in it.

She bent over him, tears falling freely now. "I'm here, Silas. Please. Stay with me."

And then—his hand moved.

A brush along her side. So faint she thought she imagined it.

But it was real.

A goodbye.

Her breath broke apart. "Please, don't—"

One more breath. Shallow. Fragile.

Then none.

Silence.

"Silas?" She whispered his name again, unable to comprehend it. "Silas?"

There was no answer. Only the steady drip of blood pooling beneath them.

"Vaeronth..." Her voice was hollow. Fractured.

I'm here. The dragon's voice trembled, coiled tight with helpless rage.

He's gone, Eliryn.

She broke.

Her body folded over Silas's, forehead pressed to his, tears soaking into his hair as she whispered his name again and again. Her sleeves were soaked. Her knees ached where she knelt in his blood.

And she stayed there.

Long after the breath had left him.

Long after his skin began to cool beneath her hands.

She stayed.

Because it was all she had left to give.

Because she couldn't make herself let go.

Interlude 9: Malric

"Obedience is not the absence of love. Sometimes, it's the weapon love becomes." —High Marshal Elyen, Letters from the Border War

Malric stood in the shadows of the colonnade.

She didn't know he was there.

But that didn't stop him from watching.

Her shape moved ahead, lean and deliberate, shoulders squared against the weight of the king's words still echoing in the halls behind them. Her hair caught the flickering torchlight like molten copper, loose strands shifting with every step.

His father's voice pulsed in his mind: *remove her tether.*

She leaned toward Silas.

Malric's fingers flexed.

The command wasn't what drove him forward. He told himself that. Over and over.

This wasn't obedience.

It was *need*.

Silas didn't deserve to be the one beside her.

He moved with them, unseen. Like a blade waiting for a reason.

Then—

"I can't... see."

Her voice cracked.

Malric froze.

He felt it, physically, like a dagger between his ribs. He knew her voice now, could track every fracture in it.

She hadn't told him her eyes were that bad.

He hadn't noticed it.

Silas turned to catch her, steadying her by the arms. His touch lingered, too careful. Too familiar.

Something in Malric burned black.

And he moved.

Not for the king.

For himself.

The knife was already in his hand before he realized it.

Silas turned just as Malric struck.

It should have been clean.

It wasn't.

Silas fought.

Malric didn't mind.

His heart was too loud. His vision tunneled.

He wanted it to hurt.

The knife bit again. Again. Not precise now. Not clean.

But effective.

Blood soaked Malric's hand. His blade.

Silas fell.

Finally.

Malric's breath came harsh, ragged, echoing in the narrow corridor.

He should leave.

He didn't.

He turned—just as she called Silas's name again.

Her voice broke.

And she turned directly toward him.

Blind.

But facing him.

He felt it like a curse, that gaze.

Like she knew.

"Silas?! Please—someone, help me! I don't—I don't know what's happening!"

She stumbled forward.

Malric stepped back.

But not fast enough.

Her hands found Silas's body.

Her scream ripped through him.

He watched her collapse beside the corpse, watched her hands press to wounds that wouldn't heal, watched her sob, her voice dissolving into broken apologies no one would hear.

He should have left.

He couldn't.

Because it wasn't supposed to hurt this much.

It wasn't about killing the guard.

It was seeing her break.

And yet.

It did hurt.

Her grief was supposed to free him.

Instead, it anchored him to the moment.

She sobbed his name like a prayer, again and again.

Not Malric.

Silas.

Malric's hand shook.

And the worst part was: he didn't regret killing him.

He regretted that she mourned him.

He took one last look at her.

Blood on her hands. Knees stained red. Her body shaking, her voice broken.

And still—still—she looked stronger than anything he'd ever touched.

He hated that.

He hated her.

He wanted her.

And when she finally learns what I did, he thought, *I hope she tries to kill me. Because it'll be the only honest thing left between us.*

He didn't remember leaving the corridor.

He barely felt the stone under his boots, or the cold air of the upper halls. Only the blood on his hands felt real.

Silas' blood.

Her grief.

Malric reached his quarters like a man sleepwalking.

He shut the door behind him and stood there, in the silence, in the dark, listening to his own heartbeat hammer against his ribs.

Then, methodically, he stripped off the blood-soaked gloves. Peeled his sleeves back. His arms were streaked in red. His throat felt tight.

At the basin, he washed.

Slow. Careful. Mechanical.

But the blood didn't want to leave him.

His knuckles scraped against the basin's edge.

The water swirled pink.

He scrubbed harder.

When he finally looked up, his reflection stared back at him.

Pale. Hollow-eyed. Lips drawn tight.

Not the assassin they'd trained. Not the weapon his father had forged.

Something fractured.

She cried for him.

Not for Malric.

For Silas.

And the worst part was—he understood why.

Silas had touched her gently. Spoken softly. Silas had stood beside her like a shield. Had given her safety.

Malric had only ever given her reasons to fear.

But she wasn't afraid of him.

That's what ruined him most.

She should be afraid now.

He pressed his hands flat to the basin's cold stone, breathing shallow, staring down at the blood-swirled water.

His thoughts kept returning to her.

What she'd looked like on the floor, kneeling in the blood, blind and broken, and still—still—stronger than him.

And all he could think was: I could have been the one to catch her.

He could have knelt beside her. Lied. Said he'd found Silas too late. That he'd tried to save him.

She would've believed him.

She'd have leaned on him.

Trusted him.

Needed him.

And the thought of it hollowed him out.

He dragged a hand through his hair, shaking now. His composure cracking like glass.

He should go to her.

Right now.

Find her. Let her fall into him. Be the comfort Silas would never be again.

She wouldn't even question it.

He was careful. Measured. Trusted.

She'd let him hold her.

His throat closed.

But no.

He couldn't.

Not yet.

His mind spun.

A plan, he needed a plan.

What could he give her?

What could he take away next?

How could he carve away every piece of her safety until he was all that was left?

The worst part wasn't the thought itself.

It was how good it felt.

Malric sat down heavily on the edge of the low stone bed, elbows on his knees, blood drying at his wrists.

He could hear his father's voice in his head. Cold. Triumphant.

But the voice that answered was his own.

She's mine.

She doesn't know it yet.

But she will.

His gaze flicked to the door.

He wondered if she was still crying.

He wondered if she'd say his name when she did.

And that thought—that dangerous, hollow hunger—was the only thing that let him finally close his eyes.

Because now, she was alone.

And sooner or later, he'd be the one she turned to.

He just had to wait.

And he was very, very good at waiting.

The ring pulsed against his finger. Cold. Heavy.

But when Malric looked down at it, he didn't feel chained.

He felt owned.

And he didn't mind. Not anymore.

Because soon, Eliryn would be too.

CHAPTER 23: ALL THAT REMAINS

"In the quiet after violence, everything speaks the truth."
—Proverb, Stormthresh origin

Eliryn sat in silence beside his body.

She hadn't moved. Not even to wipe the blood from her hands. It dried sticky against her skin, matted under her fingernails. Her fingers were splayed wide against the stone, as if bracing. As if balance could still be found.

Silas was gone.

She could still feel where his last breath had shuddered out against her knees. Still felt the weight of him, heavy and slumped, like he'd given up mid-breath. She waited for the tears to come again.

They didn't.

"I should've stopped it," she whispered.

No, Vaeronth's voice came low, uncertain. *Not like this. You couldn't have.*

Her jaw locked. "He died right in front of me."

I know.

"I didn't see anything. I didn't even hear—" Her voice cracked. "Why didn't you warn me?"

Vaeronth hesitated. She felt it. Like stone cracking beneath weight.

I... couldn't.

Eliryn's throat tightened. "You always know. You're supposed to know."

I felt the attack only when it was already in motion. Something dampened me. Blinded me. A magic that shouldn't exist—not anymore. Something coiled through those halls. Older than even I can name.

She shook her head. "That's not good enough."

I know.

His answer was too honest. Too quiet. It didn't make her feel better. It made her want to scream.

"You should've helped."

I couldn't. He repeated.

"You're a dragon!" she snapped. "You could've broken through the walls."

And buried you both, Vaeronth said, his voice rougher now. *I tried, Eliryn. I tried until it burned.*

She wrapped her arms around herself. "Was the blade meant for me?"

I don't know.

Her breath caught.

I felt the danger too late. You were panicking. He was too close to you. His focus... it was on you. He didn't sense it either.

She swallowed hard. "So this is my fault."

No. He was focused on you. He didn't see the threat behind him. But it is not your fault. You didn't cause this.

Her head dropped. The pressure behind her ribs swelled until it hurt. "Then why do I feel like this is my fault?"

Because you cared.

She hated how simple that answer was. Hated how heavy it felt.

"I don't even know who it was," she whispered.

Nor do I. That is what terrifies me.

The silence pressed in.

"So this was another random killing?"

Perhaps. Perhaps not. Vaeronth hesitated. *It could have been for you. Or he could've simply been... in the way.*

The thought hollowed her out.

"He died for nothing."

Not for nothing.

She didn't want his comfort. Not now. Not when her stomach felt scraped raw and her skin was still warm with someone else's blood.

Eliryn.

She ignored him.

Little flame. Listen to me.

"I don't want to move."

You must.

"Why?"

Because whoever did this could still be near. And you can't stop them. Not like this. I can't protect you in here.

"You certainly proved *that*."

I'm sorry.

That made her flinch harder than if he had lashed back at her.

At last, she whispered, "Tell me where to go."

He guided her. Quiet. Focused.

She didn't say goodbye to Silas.

She just left him there.

And as she stumbled forward through the dark, her heart wasn't breaking over a life lost defending her.

It was shattering over the terrifying truth:

Blindness made her worse than weak. It made her useless.

And she hated herself for it.

She hadn't understood—not really—what losing her sight meant. Not until blood had soaked her hands, and Silas's final breath had rattled against her knee. Not until she'd been helpless to save him. Not until her world narrowed to sound and fear and the sound of her own heart screaming.

She was a liability now.

A danger to herself.

And the next time something came for her—she might die before even realizing a threat was near.

She moved forward, hollow and trembling, hand pressed to the wall. Her dragonblood seemed unimportant now, useless with her as its vessel. Her breaths rasped through her throat, too shallow, too fast.

Vaeronth's voice pressed steady through the storm inside her skull.

Fifteen paces. Turn left. Archway ahead.

She clung to him. To the words. To anything that wasn't the silence left behind her.

Then—footsteps.

Light. Deliberate.

She froze.

"Dragonblood?"

Her body jerked.

Whitvale.

She flinched before she even registered him as the owner of the voice.

He stopped short a few paces from her. For once, his voice wasn't oily with amusement. He sounded... startled. "What in the gods' name—?"

"I—" Her voice cracked. She couldn't see him, but she tried to look in the right direction. She tasted blood on the back of her tongue. "I—Silas—someone attacked us."

She heard him step closer. His voice sharpened. "Your guard? Is he dead?"

She nodded helplessly. "He was attacked. I tried to stop the bleeding, but—I couldn't. He's gone."

For the first time since she'd met him, Whitvale didn't say anything clever.

She felt him circling her, hesitant, assessing.

"You're blind," he said softly. Not a question. Not pity, either. Just observation.

She nodded anyways. "I didn't see who it was. I didn't—I don't know who—" Her breath caught, and she took a shaky step back from him. "Why are you even here?"

"I was just walking aimlessly, I wanted time alone to think after our little meeting with King Thalen," Whitvale said. He sounded winded now, or cautious. "I—I didn't expect to see you like this."

Her pulse was a hammer in her throat. She took another step back, nearly slipping in bloody tracks she'd left on the floor.

"Did you know this would happen?" she rasped suddenly.

Whitvale's voice stilled. "What?"

"You're here. So fast. So soon after." Her voice cracked. "Did you know?"

"Gods, no—Dragonblood, of course not."

She couldn't tell if his words were lies or truths and didn't have her eyes to help inform her.

"Then why are you here?" Her breathing spiraled. "Right now. In this hall. So soon after he—after Silas—"

"Because I was walking," Whitvale snapped, his usual polish cracking. "I heard nothing. I have no idea how you could have been attacked that quickly and quietly in the halls so close to the King."

Something shifted.

Eliryn's skin prickled, and Vaeronth's voice surged in her mind—low, grim, certain.

Something is wrong. Be ready.

Then—footsteps. Heavy. Sharp.

Two guards rounded the corner.

Eliryn strained her hearing, helpless. Her hands clenched.

Vaeronth spoke, calm but alert. *Two men. Royal sigils. Left guard: taller, squared jaw. Right guard: young. Nervous.*

She heard their pause.

"That's the dragonrider," the younger guard breathed. He sounded too young for this.

"Gods," the other muttered. Then, louder, "What's happened here?"

"She's injured. Disoriented," Whitvale said tightly.

"I—someone attacked us," she rasped.

Pause. Tight silence. Then—

"What happened?" the older guard demanded.

Eliryn fought to form the words. "I didn't see—I couldn't see. My sight is gone. And Silas—Silas was with me, but someone... someone killed him. I felt him... I felt him die."

The name hit like steel.

"Silas?" One of the guards echoed. "Silas Caelen?"

"Yes. I think..." Her voice was a whisper. "I only knew him as Silas; he's been my guard since the beginning of the trials."

Vaeronth murmured as the silence stretched. *Left guard stiffened. Right is shocked. Voice caught in his throat. They believe you. And I believe they knew Silas.*

"Where?" the older guard snapped.

Eliryn lifted her shaking, blood-caked hand. She tried to point. Failed. Finally, she just gestured helplessly. "Behind me."

"Gods above." The older guard's voice cracked. Then to his partner: "Go. Lock down the North Wing. Alert the Commander. Find who did this."

His partner bolted.

He's scared, Vaeronth told her. *The guard is pulling a rune-disc from his belt. There's a thick blue light emitting from it.*

"Containment protocols activated," he muttered.

Eliryn flinched. "What are you doing?"

"Protecting you," the guard barked. "And everyone else."

Vaeronth snarled in her mind. *He thinks you could be the threat.*

The guard's hand clamped down on her arm.

"Don't—" she gasped.

"I'm not hurting you. We're moving."

"You're dragging me like a prisoner!"

"This is containment. You're covered in blood. You're one of the trial chosen. You're dangerous whether you intend to be or not."

She recoiled instinctively.

Behind her, Whitvale's voice turned sharp. "Watch your tone."

The guard's grip tightened—but hesitated.

Vaeronth murmured. *He's confused who outranks who.*

"I'm blind!" she cried, desperate now. "Where do you think I'll run to?"

Whitvale again, quieter. "She's not resisting."

"She's covered in blood," the guard gritted. "We're securing the scene."

Her breathing cracked. "Where are you taking me?"

"To a secure room. You and him both." A pause, then grimly: "Until we know for certain who's dead. And who did it."

The magic suppressing me earlier—it's gone. I see clearly now. Whoever attacked... uses magic that shouldn't exist. Vaeronth rumbled.

She staggered.

What? she breathed.

Later. Walk. Now.

She let herself be pulled. Her feet dragged over stone, every step unfamiliar. Without Vaeronth's whispered guidance, she'd have collapsed.

They're leading you downward, he said quietly. *A stairwell. Narrow. Guard tower built into the walls. You're heading to a holding floor.*

She tasted iron and fear on her tongue.

Whitvale follows you. He's silent. Thinking.

A door opened. Metal hinges. She was ushered roughly inside.

Small stone chamber, Vaeronth confirmed. *Bench. One door. Whitvale paces. Fast. Nervous. He glances at you constantly.*

Her knees gave out. She found the bench by accident.

"What is this?" Her voice broke. "Why are we here?"

Whitvale stopped pacing. "I don't know. Something's happening in the palace. People are tense. And that audience with the king... none of it makes sense."

Eliryn curled into herself.

"Why did you defend me out there?"

"Because you looked like you were about to collapse."

"And?"

"And I don't think you killed your guard."

"I—Silas..." Her throat closed.

Vaeronth's voice turned softer. *I hear others. Approaching.*

The door opened. She stiffened.

"Eliryn?" A new voice. Warm. Familiar.

"Garic." Her breath cracked, tears she didn't know she had threatening now. "Thank the gods."

This wasn't a time to be concerned with using names amongst mixed company.

She reached blindly, and his hands found hers, steady as stone. She gripped him like the edge of a cliff.

Vaeronth described him instantly. *His face is grim. But his eyes—he's afraid for you.*

Garic crouched, gripping her arms gently.

"You're hurt."

"I'm blind." She finally broke. "And Silas is dead."

"What?"

She told him everything—rushed, raw, stumbling through the words. The chill of the stone corridor. The sudden silence. The way his hands were there—and then gone. The blood. The breath. The way she'd held him and begged him not to leave her.

Her voice came in broken shards, scraped from somewhere deep.

Across the room, Whitvale didn't move. He stood against the far wall like a statue, but Eliryn could feel him watching. Cool. Quiet. Unflinching.

When she finished, the silence held.

Garic's voice broke it like flint on stone. "And no one saw who did it?"

"No." Her voice was hoarse.

Garic's voice was steel now. "Whitvale. You were nearby."

"I found her minutes after," Whitvale said, evenly. "She was already soaked in blood."

"You saw no one?"

"No." His answer didn't waver. "Just her."

Garic stepped closer. Eliryn felt the air shift, his stance widen. "Then someone sent those other guards. Someone trying to sweep this clean."

Eliryn's voice was low, but cut through the chamber like glass. "We'd just split from you. From the others. That hall should've been safe. Should've had eyes." Her hands shook. "And whoever killed Silas... never even touched me. Never even tried."

The silence after that was suffocating.

"I don't understand," she whispered. "He wasn't a threat. He was—he was kind. He was *good*. Why would someone want *him* dead?"

A long pause.

Then—Vaeronth, his voice coiling around her thoughts like smoke: *Because kindness is dangerous in places built on fear.*

Eliryn bowed her head, pressing her blood-stained hands to her eyes—useless now. She could feel the truth of it sinking into her bones like rot.

Kindness wasn't just weakness here.

It was defiance.

And someone had cut it down.

No one spoke. Not Garic. Not Whitvale. Not the guard stationed outside the door.

But inside her, something shifted.

She'd thought she knew how dangerous this place could be.

She'd been wrong.

Silas hadn't died for her.

He'd died *with her* beside him. And the thought hollowed her worse than grief.

Her hands curled into fists in her lap.

Someone had sent that blade.

And she would make sure it found its way back.

Chapter 24: In the Shadow of Loss

"When the blade hangs above your head, even your enemies start to look like friends." —Tales of the Last Trials

The door had been sealed for what felt like hours.

Eliryn sat against the cold stone wall, knees drawn in, hands clasped tight to stop their shaking. She could still feel Silas's blood on her skin. The scent of it had soaked into her sleeves.

Garic sat beside her, a steady presence. He hadn't tried to speak again—just offered silence and a firm grip when her breath had started to quicken, when the panic clawed up the back of her throat. His hand on hers had been grounding. Not enough. But it helped.

Across the room, Whitvale paced like a caged wolf. His usual easy grace was gone, replaced by short, agitated strides and the occasional curse muttered under his breath. He hadn't sat once.

You should not sit silent while grief devours you, Vaeronth murmured in her mind. His presence was a low hum now, simmering. *Let me burn for you.*

"I need you calm," she whispered inwardly. "I need me calm."

The only sound in the chamber was the soft tap of Whitvale's boots on stone and the occasional shift of Garic's clothing as he adjusted beside her.

Then—new footsteps.

Boots. Crisp. Measured. Multiple pairs.

The lock on the door turned with a heavy click.

Eliryn sat up straighter, forcing stillness into herself. Her heart pounded so loud she was sure they could hear it.

The door swung open, and a figure stepped through; one she recognized by voice alone, long before anyone spoke his name.

"Good afternoon, chosen." The steward's voice was smooth as oiled steel. "You'll forgive the wait."

Whitvale stopped pacing. "What the hell is going on?"

The steward stepped inside, flanked by two guards. He ignored the question, eyes passing over each of them in turn.

"I bring word from the crown," he said.

Eliryn stiffened. "About Silas?"

The steward paused, as though weighing how much to give. "King Thalen regrets the incident. The matter is being... reviewed."

"That's it?" Garic said, rising now. "He was slaughtered."

"I did not come to debate," the Steward said coolly. "I came to inform. There will be no delay in the trials. You will proceed, as intended."

"You can't just pretend nothing happened," Whitvale snapped.

"I assure you," the steward replied, voice sharp, "nothing is being ignored. But the Flame burns forward, and our sovereign will not have sentiment delay its will."

Eliryn's hands curled into fists on her lap. "And what is the next trial?"

The steward smiled, just barely. "It has yet to be revealed. But you'll be notified soon. Prepare yourselves."

He turned to go, then paused just at the door, voice softening with theatrical gravity.

"King Thalen offers his condolences... and his gratitude for your compliance. You all serve the realm, whether you understand it yet or not."

A long silence held them.

Then Whitvale muttered, "He doesn't even try to sound like a real person anymore."

Eliryn leaned her head back against the wall, pulse thudding. Her vision was nothing but black and ghosts now. Her voice, when it came, was raw.

"I'm so tired of pretending this is anything other than a death sentence."

Garic's voice came beside her. Quiet. Sure.

"We'll get through this."

Neither of them moved as the steward's footsteps faded.

The door had clicked shut, but no key turned. It was not locked.

Still, none of them made an effort to test the handle.

"We should go," Garic said after a moment, though he made no move toward the exit.

"Should we?" Eliryn asked, her voice low but sharper now.

Garic hesitated. "We were dismissed."

"And they didn't say to stay," Whitvale muttered. "But it feels like a test, doesn't it?"

Eliryn tilted her head toward the sound of his voice.

"It's the kind of trick the court plays. Leave the cage door open, see who runs." He rubbed at his jaw, his usual arrogance dulled. "If we leave without escorts, it could be seen as defiance."

Garic gave a humorless snort. "And if we stay too long, it's passivity."

"Exactly." Whitvale leaned back against the wall. "That's the game. And the trials are just one big game."

He's not wrong, Vaeronth murmured. *But you were never made to play their game. You were made to end it.*

"I'd rather wait for guards," she said aloud. "If someone tries to attack again, I'm not interested in meeting them like this."

Neither man disagreed with her statement.

And so, they waited.

Three chosen, seated in a room that was no longer a cell but didn't quite feel like freedom. Time crept forward. The stones beneath them held the kind of silence that knew how to listen.

When someone finally spoke, it wasn't what she expected.

"I'm not going to sabotage anything this time," Whitvale said.

Eliryn's head tilted slightly toward him.

"I know I've been..." he paused, searching, "...playing a part. Trying to win the way I thought you had to. By being clever. And ruthless."

Garic made a low, skeptical sound.

Whitvale ignored it. "But what happened to your guard," he said softly. "To Silas. I don't want that. I don't want to be next."

He looked between them, lips pressed thin. "There's a killer moving through these halls. An uprising pulsing just beneath the throne. I'm done with tricks. No more games." He met her sightless gaze. "We don't have to be friends. But we're all that's left. And I don't want to die alone in a corridor with no one to know it happened."

A heavy pause.

Then Whitvale stepped forward. She felt the air shift in front of her as he extended a hand, palm-up.

"A truce," he said. "For as long as we survive."

Eliryn hesitated. Her heart pounded. Then she reached forward slowly. Her hand found his, warm and steady.

Garic didn't move at first. Then, reluctantly, he stepped forward and added his hand to theirs.

"Fine," he said. "A truce. But no promises I won't throw you into a pit if you start your old nonsense again."

Whitvale gave a weak, almost human laugh. "Understood."

They stood like that, hands linked in a strange triangle. Three strangers bound not by loyalty, but by the same sharp edge of fear.

A few minutes later, a guard returned. "You're dismissed. Wait in your chambers until further notice."

Whitvale left without another word.

Garic remained by Eliryn's side, gently placing a guiding hand on her arm.

As they turned the corner into a quieter hall, he leaned in close.

"Don't trust him," he said, voice barely breath. "That kind of personality shift doesn't happen overnight. He didn't look shocked enough when I got here. Didn't ask enough questions."

Eliryn's stomach twisted. "You think he had something to do with it?"

"I think he's smart enough to make someone else do his work for him," Garic said grimly. "We both know he's capable of sabotage and cruelty. But I can't say for sure."

Eliryn's voice was a whisper. "Then why shake his hand?"

"Because monsters watch for weakness," Garic answered. "And it's easier to kill someone when their back is turned."

They walked on in silence.

The echo of Whitvale's offered truce clung to her like cobwebs.

She wanted to believe it.

But the halls of this castle had long since taught her: whatever came into this place whole didn't leave that way.

Chapter 25: Not to Reign but to Endure

"They say the throne grants power. But I say: it only reveals who has already paid the cost of bearing it."
—Queen Alindra the Unburned

Eliryn sat on the edge of her bed, unmoving.

The fire in the hearth had burned down to its coals, a soft orange glow throwing long shadows across the stone walls. The castle gave her everything she might physically need—warmth, food, quiet—but none of it touched the raw, hollow ache in her chest.

She hadn't slept.

She couldn't.

Every breath felt heavy, her stomach tight and sour. Though a pitcher of water and a fresh loaf of bread had appeared hours ago, she hadn't touched them. The blood under her fingernails still felt tacky. The smell of it clung to her skin, to her memory.

Vaeronth remained silent. Not absent—never absent—but quiet, like a thunderstorm forced into stillness.

I am here, he whispered once, earlier.

But tonight, even that felt far away.

A knock came at the door. Light. Measured.

Eliryn's shoulders tensed. Her voice cracked raw: "Who is it?"

"It's Garic."

She hesitated. Then, softer, "Come in."

The door opened carefully. Garic stepped inside, holding a wrapped bundle in his hands. She could smell the warmth of it before he even crossed the room.

"I know the rooms provide what we need," he said, voice hesitant. "But I thought maybe... it'd feel different, coming from a friend."

He placed the bundle gently on the table. Fresh bread. Stewed fruit. A clay cup of broth. Steam curled into the cold air.

She didn't bother with the food.

She looked toward him instead.

"Thank you," she murmured. "That's... unbelievably kind."

Garic pulled the chair near her bed without asking. His presence was careful, not intrusive. Like he knew she might break if pressed too hard.

"You didn't deserve what happened," he said softly, voice thicker than usual. "And Silas... he deserved better too."

"I don't think 'deserving' means anything in this place anymore," Eliryn whispered. "Maybe it never did."

Silence stretched, but it wasn't empty.

Then she spoke again, her voice scraped raw but steady.

"I trust you."

Garic blinked, caught off guard by the weight of those words.

"I trust you," she said again, voice hoarse. "And I need you to know... I don't want the crown. I don't want a throne. I don't want power over anyone. I just... I just want to survive. For my mother. For everyone who didn't."

Her throat clenched. Her hands trembled, though she kept them clasped tight.

"I'll help you win," she said finally, voice low. "If it comes to it. I'll make sure it's you."

Garic said nothing at first. He didn't argue. He didn't deflect.

Instead, he reached for her hand.

When his fingers wrapped around hers, it wasn't a gesture of strategy or comfort.

It was a promise.

"Then we survive," he said quietly. "Together."

The words settled into her like an ember, small but solid.

She nodded once, and the knot in her chest loosened.

Garic held her hand for another quiet moment. Then he rose, steady as stone.

"I'll check on Whitvale," he said, voice gentle now. "Make sure the truce hasn't evaporated."

Eliryn almost smiled. "Good luck."

At the door, he paused.

"You're stronger than you think, Eliryn."

And then he was gone.

Leaving her alone again.

But this time, not quite hollow.

She exhaled slowly and leaned back, letting the tension bleed out of her shoulders.

A single breath passed.

Then—another knock.

She didn't move. She assumed Garic had returned. "Come in."

She didn't see the door open of course. But she felt the faint shift of air, the soft creak of the door hinges. The whisper of boots on stone.

Her breath hitched, remembering how vulnerable she was without her sight.

Vaeronth? Her voice in the bond was frayed, thin as cracked glass.

Someone's here. I think it's Garic. Can you help—

Focus. His voice came like steady hands on her shoulders. *Breathe. Ground yourself. Let me in fully.*

I'm trying—

Let go of the fear. Feel only me. I need clarity to give you my eyes.

She forced air through her lungs, fingers twisting in the blanket. The darkness pressed close but she reached for him, for the pulse of ancient flame curled tight behind her ribs.

She let herself fall.

And then—

Light.

Not hers.

Vaeronth's.

The world slid back into focus, strange and re-fracted, every edge gleaming faintly like wet steel. Shadows heavy, colors too sharp. But she saw.

And she saw *him.*

Not Garic.

Malric.

Her breath caught.

Her whole body tensed.

"Eliryn," he said softly, voice like silk stitched over something sharp. "I heard what happened. I'm... sorry."

She said nothing.

Watched him approach. Watched the too-smooth grief in the angle of his mouth, the practiced way sorrow darkened his eyes.

Vaeronth held her steady.

Watch. Do not trust his words. Trust me.

She watched.

Malric stepped inside. The door sighed shut behind him.

"I can't imagine what you're feeling," he continued, voice wrapped in mourning like a performance. "Silas, wasn't it? He was loyal. I know that much."

She narrowed her gaze, forcing calm.

"You knew he was mine?"

Malric didn't flinch outright. But the breath before his answer dragged too long, giving away his agitation.

"Word spreads. The guards talk. Halls have ears."

"And you knew where my room was?"

Another pause.

Then a loose shrug, deliberate. "You know I've been watching."

She said nothing.

Only tracked him. Every step. Every tilt of his head. His hands, carefully visible. His body, never quite at ease.

Malric sat lightly on the edge of her table. Not too close. Not yet.

"There's talk," he murmured, voice soft as silk unraveling. "Among the guards. Some want out of the crown's shadow. Sabotage. Resistance. Whatever it takes."

A glance toward her, compassion tilting his tone.

"Maybe Silas stood in their way. Maybe that made him a target."

She lowered her gaze, her hands pale against the blanket. Blood still stained her nails. She heard herself whisper:

"I keep seeing him in my mind. Reaching for me. Like he still wanted to protect me, even after..."

Her throat closed.

"And the blood..." Her voice cracked. "It was everywhere. It was like when my mother passed. One moment they're alive. The next... gone. And all that's left is the blood."

Malric moved.

Slow. Careful. A shadow in silk.

He knelt before her.

Too close.

Be still, Vaeronth breathed.

And she was.

Through the shimmer of dragon sight, she saw the shift. The crack beneath the mask. A twitch at the corner of Malric's mouth. The faint glimmer behind his lashes.

Calculation.

"I know loss," he said softly. "I know what it hollows out of you. What it makes."

Her throat burned, her vision swimming even through Vaeronth's sight.

It can't be him, she told herself.

He wouldn't come now. Not after Silas. Not like this.

No killer would sit beside her while she broke. No assassin would kneel, touch her, speak softly, unless—

Unless he cared.

Unless all those small glances, those stolen moments she pretended not to notice... were real.

She wanted to believe it.

Needed to believe it.

It was the only reason he could be here now.

And so, Eliryn let herself break.

Her grief wasn't just for Silas. Not anymore.

It cracked open inside her, uncoiling in violent waves.

She broke for her mother, left broken in a burning cottage.

For herself.

For the girl who used to believe the world could be kind.

Her body folded forward, shaking. The sob that ripped from her chest wasn't delicate—it was raw, ugly, the sound of something unraveling.

Malric caught her easily.

Arms around her.

Hands gentle.

Soothing her with the careful touch of someone who knew precisely when to apply pressure, and when to withdraw.

"I know," he whispered against her hair. "Let it out. It's all right."

She buried her face in his shoulder, sobbing harder.

Because surely, *surely*, he meant it.

Surely, no one pretending could speak so softly. Hold so steadily.

But Vaeronth saw.

And Vaeronth knew.

He watched, unblinking.

Tracking Malric's heartbeat.

Felt the faint magic threaded through his skin—the wrongness pressing against his senses like smoke slipping through cracks in stone.

Magic designed to silence, to mask.

There's power around him, Vaeronth rumbled, his voice like stone grinding in her mind. *He is not what he seems.*

Eliryn couldn't answer.

She couldn't hear him clearly anymore.

Not through the storm inside her.

Not through the arms that held her.

Vaeronth curled tighter, helpless in his vigil, forced to watch the predator hold what little remained of his rider's heart.

And Malric, poised in the perfect quiet of her grief, let his hand drift—once, gently—along her spine.

The way someone would soothe a creature they had already caged.

Interlude 10: Malric

"Mercy is the final kindness a killer offers himself."
—Anonymous Executioner's Notes

She had broken more easily than he expected.

Malric stood in the quiet of her bathing chamber, sleeves rolled neatly past his wrists. Steam coiled around him, lit by the faint glow of the enchanted sconces. The ring on his finger—his tether, his tool—hummed low with power. A quiet, steady thrum. It pressed back against Vaeronth's senses, dulled the beast's reach. It had to. Otherwise, Malric wouldn't be standing here now, watching the girl sway between grief and exhaustion, blind to everything but the lies he wove.

She hadn't resisted when he guided her from the bed. She hadn't questioned when he'd stripped her down to her shift with slow, deliberate motions, murmuring soft apologies that never reached his eyes. He'd removed her blood-crusted tunic, the trousers stiff with dried sweat, set them aside like ritual offerings. She stood, pale and pliant, bare feet trembling on the stone.

He told himself this was strategy.

He guided her into the bath. Warm water, laced with herbs she wouldn't smell past the blood in her nose. Her skin shivered as it touched the water, and still she said nothing. She trusted him. Even now. Especially now.

It thrilled him.

He crouched at the edge of the bath, sleeves damp from easing her down, and watched her body float, slack and exhausted. Her shift clung to her skin. She looked breakable. She looked like she was *his*.

He reached for a brush the room provided.

Slow, steady strokes. His fingers worked through the knots in her hair, unwinding blood and salt from copper strands. He spoke softly, the way one soothes a fevered animal.

"It's all right now," he whispered, knowing she'd believe it.

He watched her mouth twitch faintly at his words. He kept brushing.

Each moment here was a borrowed luxury. Her dragon's magic prowled the edges of the ring's suppression, but Malric trusted its power. His father had made sure it was forged with the most dangerous and powerful element the world didn't know existed.

The ring hid him. Cloaked his scent. Silenced his guilt.

Her dragon felt the wrongness, yes. But he was dulled. Muffled. Like a beast chained just out of reach.

Malric smiled faintly to himself.

Silas had been the only threat. Not because he was strong. But because Eliryn had let him matter. Had let him close. That couldn't stand. If anyone would break her open, it would be Malric. That right belonged to him now.

He finished brushing her hair.

Her breathing had slowed. He thought she might be drifting near sleep.

Gently, he reached into the water, fingers brushing her wrist, checking the weak pulse. Steady, but slow. Exhausted.

She trusted him to touch her here.

She trusted the voice that killed her guard. The hands that gutted her protector. The lie that wore the shape of comfort.

Malric dipped a cloth into the water and slowly, methodically, began to wash the blood from her skin.

He cleaned her as carefully as he'd stalked her.

When he spoke again, it was soft as silk and colder than steel.

"Sleep, Eliryn."

She obeyed.

But he wasn't finished.

Once she drifted, slack in the water, he drew her out with clinical precision. Her skin was warm, soft as wet silk. He wrapped her in the thickest towel he could find, swaddling her like a child, binding her limbs gently but firmly. She stirred only once, but his voice quieted her immediately.

"I've got you," he whispered. "You're safe now. You're *mine*."

She didn't hear the last word. Not consciously.

He carried her back to the bed. Slowly. Reverently.

There, he laid her down, keeping her bound in the towel, letting the warmth sink into her skin. He crouched beside her. His breath came slow, measured. He watched the faint tremble of her lashes, the soft parting of her lips as she tried and failed to fight sleep.

She was pliant. Fragile. *Perfect*.

And as he watched her, Malric realized something new.

When Thalen had first ordered her death, it had felt impossible. Like killing sunlight. Like severing a future not yet written. She'd been too bright. Too vital.

But now?

Now it would be a mercy.

Not out of compassion.

But as a gift.

He could end her softly. Gently. He could make her final moments tender. Private. He could kill her in kindness. A final mercy, wrapped in whispered words, by the hands she'd already let hold her.

The thought curled through his mind like a tendril of smoke.

He could make her death a gift. For her. For himself.

She deserved that much.

Didn't she?

He brushed her damp hair back from her face, fingers lingering too long against her cheek. Her skin was warm, flushed from the bath. He leaned closer, breathing her in. She smelled like river herbs and grief.

She was intoxicating.

He stroked her jaw, speaking softly.

"You don't have to fight anymore," he murmured. "I'll carry this weight for you."

Her breathing steadied in sleep.

And he knew: *the deeper she trusted him, the sweeter her ending would be.*

It wasn't madness. Not really. He'd hidden that darkness from her. From himself.

But now, seeing her so soft... so willing...

He wanted to destroy her.

Not out of cruelty.

But because it was the only way to keep her for himself.

He sat beside her for a long time, listening to the ring hum against his pulse.

Planning.

Waiting.

And when she woke, she would find him there.

Exactly where she needed him to be.

Chapter 26: The Hall of Scribes

"What is written endures; what is hidden destroys."
—Scribe Liraeth, Keeper of the Silent Hall

Eliryn woke slowly.

She felt the warmth first—the heavy weight of blankets draped over her body, the residual heat of a bath she didn't remember entering or leaving. Her hair was dry now, brushed smooth and neat over her shoulders. Her mind was fogged, fragile as spun glass.

Then came the pressure of a hand against her cheek. Gentle. Careful. Reverent.

"Eliryn," a voice murmured, soft as silk. "You're safe."

She turned her face slightly into the warmth, craving the comfort instinctively. And when she opened her eyes—blind, unfocused, lost in the swirling darkness—she knew who it was without needing to see.

Malric.

His fingers trailed from her cheek to her hairline, tucking a strand behind her ear. She felt the brush of his lips press against the center of her palm. Not rushed. Not forced. But slow. Devotional.

"I'll return soon," he whispered. "Rest."

She didn't answer. Couldn't. Her throat closed around the words. She felt him shift beside her, the faint creak of the mattress as his weight lifted. The air stirred when he stood. And when the door clicked shut behind him, the sound echoed like the slamming of a cell.

Then, at last, Vaeronth surged forward.

His presence roared into her mind like fire igniting dry kindling. Not gentle. Not soothing. Furious. Protective. Terrified.

You are wrong to trust him.

Eliryn's body tensed, but she did not speak.

He silenced me. Bound me. His magic coiled around your mind and mine. He is not what you believe.

Her lips parted, her voice rasping in denial. "No... no. He wouldn't."

He did.

"He was trying to help. Maybe his magic... maybe he didn't know it blocked you out."

Vaeronth's fury cracked against the inside of her skull. *I sense an old dragon on him, something that should be impossible. And he reeks of death. Something is very wrong with the magic he carries; something is very wrong with him.*

"No." Her breath hitched, tears stinging her useless eyes. "He held me. He—he spoke to me like he understood loss. He cares."

He watched you shatter and called it comfort.

"I don't believe you."

Silence.

Then Vaeronth's voice came lower. Quieter.

You don't want to believe me but you should.

Her hands trembled where they lay atop the blankets. She clutched the edges of the fabric, trying to ground herself, but the warmth that had felt like safety now felt like a cage. She remembered the kiss pressed to her palm—the gentle sweep of his thumb across her skin, the brush of his lips.

Malric couldn't be a monster.

Could he?

Vaeronth lingered in her thoughts like the scent of smoke after a fire.

Open your eyes to him, Eliryn. Before it is too late.

She curled onto her side, pulling the blankets tighter around her body, burying herself in the lie that had felt like safety. Tears burned down her cheeks as heavy emotions claimed her once again.

And outside her door, unseen and waiting, the predator watched.

Eliryn sat in the quiet that followed.

The fire had sunk lower now, the coals little more than faint embers, barely lighting the room. Still, she hadn't moved from where he'd left her.

Her fingers brushed the edge of the clay cup Garic had brought, now cool to the touch. She hadn't eaten. She didn't think she could. But it had mattered that he'd come. That someone had reminded her she wasn't entirely alone in this place built to hollow people out.

The ache inside her hadn't softened, but it had been given shape. Something she could survive with. Something she could fight through.

Screw the prophecy. I don't want a throne. I don't want to reign. I just need to endure.

She would help Garic win, if it came to that. She would stand by him, shield him if she could, and survive in honor of all the pieces of her life that had been taken away. The dragons and the riders. Her mother. Silas.

Whitvale might have played at sticking up for her, but that didn't mean he hadn't been involved. He was clever. Masked. Shifting in and out of his own skin like a snake through grass. She wanted to believe in his truce, but Garic's warning that he couldn't be trusted echoed in her mind.

And Malric...

Her chest tightened at the thought of him.

He had been a mystery from the moment they met, sharp edges wrapped in dangerous charm. She remembered the weight in his voice when he told her he'd been made into a weapon. That he had killed before.

But Malric killing Silas?

The king would have needed a reason. Silas had protected her, yes, but what threat could she possibly be to the king of this broken place? And if it was about her, then why was she left untouched? She had been completely vulnerable in that moment, so if it had been about her, that would have been the best moment to strike.

Vaeronth's presence brushed the edges of her mind: heavy, protective, simmering with a restraint that felt like tension moments from explosion. *Prepare yourself.*

The knock came moments later.

She didn't move.

"Dragonrider," called a voice beyond the door. Male. Too polished to be Garic. Too formal to be Malric.

Another knock.

"The fourth trial begins now."

She forced herself upright, every muscle screaming exhaustion. Her legs barely supported her weight.

And then the room shifted as she borrowed her dragon's sight.

The hearth flared softly. New clothing had been laid at the edge of the bed: black leggings reinforced with fine leather, a dark tunic tailored for movement but edged in delicate silver threading at the cuffs. Beside them—boots. Black as a raven's wing, smooth as riverstone. When she brushed her fingers along them, the leather flexed like skin, like they'd been made for her bones alone.

Practical. Strong.

Like her.

"I see the room still believes in me," she murmured aloud, voice rough with disuse.

Vaeronth stirred. *I never stopped believing in you.*

Her throat tightened. "I know."

She let the guards wait.

Not out of arrogance, but because she refused to meet a new trial wearing a towel and some furs.

She dressed slowly, methodically. She braided her damp hair back from her face with shaking fingers, wove the tail into a knot low at her nape. Slipped the tunic over her head. Laced the boots up her calves.

Each piece felt like a reclamation.

When she was finished, she stood for a long moment, head bowed, fists clenched at her sides.

"I am not broken," she whispered.

Not yet. Her mind answered back.

Finally, she crossed to the door.

The hallway outside her door was already filled with footsteps, soft-soled, clipped with purpose. Two guards stood at attention, flanking a young page with a scroll clutched tight in his pale hands. He bowed when she appeared, though his eyes widened slightly when they settled on her face. On the faint, unfocused way her gaze drifted past him.

"Dragonrider," he announced formally. "You are summoned to the Hall of Scribes for the fourth trial."

She nodded once, then paused. The words scraped at her throat, but she forced them out anyway.

"You'll need to guide me," she said evenly. "I've... lost my sight."

The page blinked, clearly startled. One of the guards shifted behind him, uneasy in the silence.

Eliryn tilted her chin. "If you're waiting for me to apologize for the inconvenience, you'll be standing here a while."

The boy flushed and scrambled to offer his arm. "Of course. I'll... see you there safely."

She accepted his arm like a queen accepting tribute, though her fingers trembled as they curled around the crook of his elbow.

"I don't need pity," she added, voice quieter now. "Just decent directions."

Behind her, Vaeronth stirred in her mind—steady, certain.

You are not diminished. Your eyes are not the only way to see.

She almost believed him.

Her other hand brushed the stone wall lightly as they walked, her touch ghosting along the worn grooves, counting the corridor's pulse through texture and air. One guard led, one followed. Their steps echoed like war drums.

Silence wrapped around them, but she could feel everything. The temperature shift before each doorway. The soft press of torchlight against her skin. The pulse of people they passed—warm bodies, cold intentions.

She wasn't afraid.

She'd lost too much to waste herself on fear at this point.

When the page finally slowed, his voice lost its formal edge.

"We've arrived. The Hall of Scribes. It's large... vaulted. There are columns along both sides. Stone benches in three rows. The panel is seated at the far end. Hearth's unlit."

Eliryn nodded, lips thin.

This was where truths lived. And where lives ended.

"I'll guide you to your seat," the page added, hesitant.

She let him.

When her fingers brushed the bench, she felt the presence beside her before anything else: Garic. His soul hummed steady through Vaeronth's awareness, a low and grounded rhythm. Whitvale's presence prickled sharper, restless as a drawn knife. But Garic... Garic was calm. Ready.

Her throat tightened. She sat, spine straight.

The page lingered, then retreated.

She could feel the weight of eyes on her. Judges. Guards. Spectators. She could feel her dragonmarks glowing softly, like they were waiting, and she could feel eyes on her watching the runes come to life.

Her hands flexed in her lap.

Vaeronth... She called out in her mind.

I am here.

Her voice cracked in their bond.

I need you. I... I'm not enough anymore.

There was a pause, heavy as stone. Then his voice came—slow and molten as a hearth long gone cold.

You will always be enough. But I can help show you.

Her eyes stung. She pressed her lips together, forcing herself to believe him.

Clear your mind, he whispered.

She obeyed.

And the world shifted.

It wasn't as sharp as her own vision. Not truly. But she *saw*.

Breath and heat and motion. Threads of presence. Glimmers of pulse and thought. Like watching a tapestry woven from living light.

Three judges sat before her, draped in gold. Tables scattered with scrolls and knives. Hidden watchers behind lattice screens. She felt their attention like static.

To her left: Garic. Solid. Steady.

To her right: Whitvale. Tense. Coiled.

And above them all, pulsing and vast—the silent, oppressive weight of the Flame.

Watching.

Waiting.

For judgment.

Her pulse hammered, but she sat taller.

She remembered Malric's voice. His hands. His tenderness.

She remembered Silas's blood on her skin.

Let them test her. Let them try.

She was Eliryn, the Last Dragonrider.

And she had already survived more than they would ever understand.

CHAPTER 27: THE TRIAL OF KNOWING

"Memory is a blade no forge can temper; it cuts whether wielded or denied." —Elder Scribe Althara

The scrape of a chair. The shift of robes. The faint crackle of parchment.

Then came the voice—measured, deep, a sound used to being obeyed.

"Chosen."

The word echoed through the Hall of Scribes like a verdict.

Eliryn's spine straightened instinctively, her hands curling briefly against her knees. Her unblinking gaze saw nothing now but the ghostly world

Vaeronth offered her—heat and presence and light like threadbare silk. But her mind was sharp. Her posture, regal.

She heard Garic shift beside her. Calm. Ready.

The panel of judges loomed ahead—three figures, draped in gold-edged robes, unmoved by the weight of history pressing around them.

"You have survived what many do not," the first judge said—an older man with a voice like riverstone, smooth but heavy. "The physical trials. The mental minefields. Each other."

Eliryn fought the urge to huff. Barely.

The judge's voice continued, cold and steady. "But blood and strength are not enough to lead. Not enough to guard the balance of kingdoms. And certainly not enough to understand the burden of power."

She heard the quiet rustle of the female judge leaning forward.

"This trial will test your judgment. Your reasoning. Your knowledge of war, of law, of the bones that hold this realm upright."

Eliryn could almost hear the smile that wasn't on her face.

"You may speak freely when called," the third judge said, voice clipped behind a golden circlet. "If you lie... the Flame will know."

Of course it will, she thought, her throat tight. *Everyone's watching. Even the gods.*

A pause thickened the air.

"Eliryn of Lirin's Edge. Garic of Stonefell. Vraxxis of Whitvale."

She felt Whitvale stiffen slightly at the use of his true name, the edge of pride seeping from him like poison.

"You sit not only before us, but before the will of the realm," the oldest judge said. "The trial begins now."

A silence followed—calculated, suffocating.

Then:

"Garic of Stonefell."

She felt Garic's quiet intake of breath beside her, steady as clockwork.

"Tell us the tactical flaw in the Battle of Hollowmere, and what you would have done differently."

Eliryn listened. And quietly, she smiled.

Garic answered clearly with precision and patience. Strategy spun into steady words. She didn't need Vaeronth's sight to sense the interest prickling from the panel.

The judges wrote. And moved on.

"Vraxxis of Whitvale," came next. "Define the Edicts of Succession—Queen Sanna's reforms and their application following civil upheaval."

Eliryn resisted the urge to roll her eyes as Whitvale answered, smooth and swift as oil on glass.

You're clever, she thought. *But you seem too rehearsed.*

And then—

The woman judge's voice rang out.

"Eliryn of Lirin's Edge."

Eliryn felt Garic shift beside her—subtle, but steady. A tether. Whitvale stilled completely.

The judge's tone sharpened.

"List the five governing councils of the early kingdom and explain how they failed the first dragonriders."

Eliryn tilted her chin slightly. She didn't rush. She let the silence stretch. And when she finally spoke, her voice was calm—but unmistakably dry.

"Ah. So now you care about the history of the riders."

The judges shifted, just slightly.

"Because after standing by while the King wiped them out, you're curious. You want answers. Straight from the last reliable source."

Across the bench, she felt Garic stifle a breath. Not shock. Amusement.

Eliryn's mouth curved faintly. "Is that why you're asking? Do you want to know how my kind came to fall? Because it wasn't the governing council's fault."

A pause. One of the judges' robes rustled—unease.

"You are under oath, Eliryn," the woman said curtly.

"And you said I could speak freely." Eliryn's voice dropped, steady as a knife sliding into its sheath. "The

Flame's here to judge me. I'm fairly sure the Flame and I are already on the same page."

From her peripheral awareness, she felt Whitvale's disbelief—sharp, brittle. Like he couldn't decide whether to be scandalized or impressed.

The silence hung heavy.

Then she leaned forward slightly, voice cool, conversational:

"Council of War. Council of Flame. Council of Law. Council of Grain. Council of Faith."

Her tone turned razor-edged.

"They failed because power scares small men. They failed because none of them could agree on whether to worship the dragons, use them, or kill them. And by the time they decided..." She lifted her hands, palms up, her broken gaze fixed squarely ahead.

"...the sovereign had done what he could to turn us all to ash."

Garic, beside her, said nothing. But she felt him watching her now. Closely.

Eliryn tilted her head. "Would you like me to keep going? I've got centuries of mistakes burned into my skin and an ancient dragon as my source."

A silence, thick as stone.

And then—her skin flashed in answer.

The marks along her arms and throat pulsed once, as if breathing beneath her flesh. Lines of sigils and forgotten runes, the remnants of Vaeronth's ancient binding, blazed softly into view: not just ink, not mere scars, but something older. Something living.

Black, golden, and faint crimson threads curled up her arms like language remembered. Sharp. Unmistakable.

She heard the sharp inhale from the panel. Felt Garic's sudden stillness beside her. Even Whitvale, for all his control, shifted, unsettled.

Her power—the last of the riders' legacy—was on full display where it couldn't be ignored.

Vaeronth stirred in her mind, his voice a low thunder.

They see you now.

Eliryn didn't flinch.

"Strange," she said, voice mild, as if nothing had changed. "I would have thought they'd look away from the truth."

The glow deepened briefly, a heartbeat of molten light, then slowly faded back into her skin like embers banked after a storm.

She folded her hands neatly in her lap, her useless eyes still unblinking.

The panel said nothing.

Not for a long, heavy breath.

Then, finally, the woman judge's voice cracked the silence—far less certain now.

"That will suffice."

Eliryn smiled.

Cold.

Knowing.

In her mind, Vaeronth rumbled softly.

Approval. Not of her defiance. But of her truth.

Well said, he whispered.

I wasn't trying to be defiant, she thought. *I just couldn't be anything other than honest.*

That's why it worked.

The next questions moved forward. Garic answered his flawlessly. Whitvale stumbled once—only slightly, but she heard it. And so did the judges.

When her next turn came, Eliryn didn't lash out. She didn't need to. She answered with calm clarity. She could feel the panel recalibrating. She wasn't just a relic to be examined. She was a threat they'd misjudged.

By the time the trial ended, Garic's quiet support remained beside her like a constant. And Whitvale, for all his precision, no longer felt as composed.

When the final ink dried, the judges rose.

None of them looked at her.

Eliryn smiled faintly, bitterly.

Cowards.

Vaeronth's voice was quieter now. Not approval this time. Something more like... pride.

You didn't lie, he said. *Even when they hoped you would.*

Then maybe I'll pass this trial after all.

You already have.

The scrolls were closed.

The trial was over.

None of them had died. Not this time.

But the Flame had seen them.

And it would decide soon enough what was worth keeping.

CHAPTER 28: THE SHATTERED RITE

"There are moments when history bends and it does not bend back." —The Flamekeeper's Annals

Before the next dawn, Eliryn was sent back to her chamber. No explanation. No verdict. Only a single sentence from the steward as he escorted them from The Hall of Scribes:

"The Flame will reveal its Sovereign at first light."

Her room greeted her like a quiet observer. Firelight hummed low in the hearth. The air smelled faintly of juniper and iron.

She stood motionless for a long time, and then tried to settle and nap before whatever came next.

Then: "Vaeronth."

I'm here.

"What if they name Garic?"

Then we will both stand with him in support.

"And if they name Whitvale?"

Then I will offer to burn down the throne itself, should you desire.

She managed the smallest flicker of a smile, though her throat burned.

"And if it's me?"

A pause, then his voice was low, absolute.

Then we get to work.

She swallowed hard, pressing her palm over her sternum, where the faint warmth of his tether pulsed.

"I don't know if I want it."

I know.

Her knees gave out slowly, folding onto the stone bench at the room's center. She could still feel the echo of every question they had hurled at her, every gaze that had weighed her like a stone in the scales.

"I don't want to rule."

And yet you might.

She closed her useless eyes.

"What happens after, Vaeronth? After they choose?"

Silence stretched for a long moment. When he answered, it was with something like reluctant reverence.

If it's you... they will kneel.

The thought made her shiver.

She closed her eyes and didn't remember falling asleep, she only remembered stirring at the drifting waves of magic that seemed to cloud the room.

The room had been busy crafting her something worthy of facing the Flame and the thousands that would bare witness.

At first, she expected it to offer another set of leather leggings. Another battle tunic. But no.

From the wall, where unseen mechanisms lived, a form emerged.

The room did not give her battle leathers.

It did not choose the practical lines of a warrior, nor the simplicity of a rider.

Instead, when Eliryn turned toward the table, her eyes adapting to Vaeronth's vision, the garment waiting for her was nothing less than a declaration.

The gown shimmered dark as garnet in the hearth's low light—a bodice sculpted in deep crimson silk, boned with blacksteel threading and adorned with intricate gold filigree. The detailing curled like living vines over her ribs and collarbone, each twist of metalwork shaped into roses half-unfurled, petals glinting like pressed sunlight. Gold chains looped from her shoulders, draping delicately around her throat before joining at the hollow of her collarbone, the fastening shaped like a dragon's eye.

Beneath, the bodice flowed into a sweeping skirt of sheer black panels layered over blood-red silk, slit high to bare her thighs as she moved, a deliberate echo of both grace and threat. Down the center fell a silk banner embroidered with curling thorns and a stylized dragon, its coils laced in molten thread, as if the creature had been stitched in fire itself.

Her arms were left bare, the gown designed not to conceal but to display: the twisting marks of her dragonbond glowed faintly along her skin, spiraling from wrists to shoulders, luminous against her gold and crimson frame. On her back, where the shift dipped scandalously low, the full spread of her dragon's sigil would be visible—an ancient script of scales and wings etched across muscle and bone, alive with the slow pulse of Vaeronth's magic.

She swallowed.

A queen's dress.

A conqueror's armor.

A dragon's legacy.

Not something worn by choice. Something chosen for her.

She rose from the bed and stepped toward it without further thought. When her fingers brushed the silk, it felt like flame.

And when she dressed, every chain, every clasp, every weight of gold whispered the same truth:

Tonight, the realm would see her.

Not as a girl.

Not even as a rider.

But as power made flesh.

Her dragon marks flared faintly along her skin, shimmering in the candlelight, almost as though the dress itself had called them forward.

When she reached for the boots the room usually offered her, she found none.

"Really?" she muttered.

Vaeronth's voice curled around her mind, low and deliberate. *Barefoot... you look like a god returning. Like prophecy draped in silk and thorns. They will not remember your face, Eliryn. They will remember your silence, and your marks. And the sound of your steps, bare against stone, as you walk toward fate.*

That earned a soft, almost bitter laugh from her. "Well. Practical as ever."

She knelt beside the mirror, combing her fingers through her hair, working it back into warrior's braids with slow, methodical care. Each twist was an act of quiet defiance. Each tie, a prayer. She left the ends loose down her back, the coppery strands streaked with deeper crimson as Vaeronth's light shimmered faintly against them.

She did not braid her hair to look beautiful.

She braided it to be unbreakable.

When the knock came, she was ready.

"Dragonrider."

The voice beyond the door was unfamiliar—a guard's, but not one she recognized.

She crossed the room slowly and opened the door herself.

The man on the other side froze.

She watched him through the dragon-sight, through her stolen awareness, as he took her in. The gold, the crimson, the bare feet, the shining marks that traced up her arms and throat like living flame.

His throat bobbed once as he swallowed.

Then, carefully, deliberately... he bowed.

"My Lady," he said, voice quieter now. "I... have heard the stories of the Dragonriders. Of the firstborn who walked barefoot into war, and left ash behind them. I do not know what the Flame will choose."

He lifted his gaze, his expression fierce and reverent.

"But I hope it's you."

She felt her chest tighten, but she said nothing, only nodded once, sharp as a blade.

He offered his arm.

"I am to escort you to the Rite."

Eliryn took his arm gratefully.

As they walked, the silence between them felt like a kind of respect. Vaeronth's presence was heavy at the edge of her thoughts, but for once, he said nothing. Even he understood this moment was hers.

The square outside the castle gates was more crowded than Eliryn's village ever had been.

From the carved terraces of Stonefell to the wind-raked steppes near Lirin's Edge, people had come. Banners of old families fluttered beside the patchwork cloaks of field laborers. Children perched on shoulders. Merchants stood quiet behind their carts. Even the nobles had left the balconies to stand among the people, eager to see who the Flame would choose. All eyes turned toward the balcony above the flame-forged dais, where history would soon be made as a new victor was crowned.

Eliryn stood just beyond the towering doors, waiting.

She could feel the sun on her skin. The sounds of the crowd like a single, massive breath held in the body of the realm. When she saw Garic and Corwin waiting, when she heard the gathered city breathing as one collective body, the guard released her arm, stepped back, and spoke low.

"Walk well, Dragonrider."

And then she stepped forward.

The crowd did not gasp when she emerged.

They went utterly silent.

Even Vraxxis, ever the serpent, was staring. Garic turned, his eyes wide, his jaw tightening—but whether it was with awe or something else, she couldn't tell.

Eliryn stood alone now at the edge of the flame-forged dais, the sun gleaming off the gold at her throat, the marks along her arms glowing faintly, undeniably alive. Barefoot. Crownless.

And radiant.

High above, where the judges watched, King Thalen stood draped in black and silver, and the Flame itself waited.

Eliryn took her place beside the other Flame chosen, pretending as though no one watched her.

They wait for something they can believe in, Vaeronth said. *Even now.*

Eliryn swallowed. Her fingers curled at her sides. She wasn't sure what she believed in anymore.

The doors opened.

Golden light spilled across the marble, and the guards flanking the entrance stepped back. A herald's voice rang out above the crowd, amplified by spell and steel:

"Behold—the final three."

The chosen stepped forward, Garic moving first. Eliryn followed, pace even despite the weight of every eye upon her. Vaeronth showed her where the edges were, where the stone ended and the wind began. The dais rose before them, a half-circle ringed with flame inlaid into the stone, its fire a constant burn, neither fed nor fading.

King Thalen stood at its center, robed in black and silver, the Flame's light casting sharp shadows across his features. The three judges from the Hall of Scribes stood to one side. The High Flamekeeper stood to the other, her red and gold robes rippling like fire itself.

For a long moment, no one spoke.

The Flamekeeper raised her hands.

The fire in the dais flared, not brighter, not hotter, but taller, as if reaching up to touch the sky. Wind stirred the edges of Eliryn's hair. Behind her closed lids, darkness still reigned, but she could feel it- the air shifting, the moment rising toward something sharp and irreversible.

"You have all come here to witness the will of the Flame," the Flamekeeper intoned, her voice full and deep. "Three remain. Three who endured. And only one shall bear the burden of its choosing."

A breathless silence stretched across the crowd.

Eliryn's heart pounded behind her ribs, unsteady and hard. She could feel Garic's tension next to her like static in the air. Vraxxis stood to her left, arms folded behind his back, utterly still.

They had made peace with the trial's end, but not with this.

"Step forward," the Flamekeeper commanded. "Each of you."

Garic moved first, his boots quiet on the marble. Eliryn followed, guided by Vaeronth's vision; still only a pale, colorless echo of true sight, but enough to not make a fool out of herself. Vraxxis joined them, the three of them now standing evenly spaced in a line before the Flame.

"We invoke now the sacred rite of descent," the Flamekeeper continued. "Through battle, through mind, through loss, and through the fire itself, the chosen shall be marked. Let there be no further intro-duction; let us move into the ceremony."

A long pause followed.

Then the Flame moved.

Not a flare. Not an inferno.

A coiled arch of precision.

A single tendril of fire, too precise to be wild, too alive to be called mere magic. It rose from the dais like a summoned thing, twisting higher, shimmering gold edged in deep crimson.

It drifted toward Garic first.

Eliryn felt him tense beside her as the Flame circled him once, close enough to sear—but not enough to choose.

It moved on.

To Vraxxis.

The Flame lingered there longer, orbiting him slowly, considering him as an option. His spine straightened. His jaw clenched.

But it left him, too.

And then—

She felt it.

Before she saw it.

Heat brushed her collarbones, her bare throat, her chest.

Her whole body tightened in instinctive fear—but it wasn't burning.

The Flame stopped before her, hovering.

Waiting.

Eliryn trembled.

And then it struck.

Not an attack.

An anointing.

The tendril of flame touched her breastbone, directly above her heart.

And her body bowed.

Not from pain.

From *power*.

The force of it rippled through her bones like a low bell tolling inside her. Heat surged down her arms, her spine, her legs—suffusing her blood, saturating her skin. She felt her dragonbond snap taut—like a chain pulled tight across distance—and Vaeronth roared in her mind, not in fear, but in triumph.

Your soul is known.

Her runes burned to life across her skin, glowing along her throat, her shoulders, down her spine. Every mark the gods had left upon her since the day she'd first touched Vaeronth's scales now shimmered with molten gold, as if lit from within.

And her eyes—

Her useless, sightless eyes flared open.

Not seeing as humans did.

But *burning*.

Pupils eclipsed. Irises filled with pure, opalescent light, bright as the core of the sun.

The crowd gasped, some falling to their knees.

Her hair whipped around her as the air itself shifted, pulled toward her like gravity.

Her marks pulsed in time with her heartbeat.

Vaeronth's voice rang steady through her:

You are the Flame's true chosen.

The Flame didn't retreat immediately. It lingered, coiled around her like a lover's hand upon the throat, as though reluctant to let her go.

When it pulled back, it did not choose another.

The Flamekeeper's voice, when it came, sounded subdued. Reverent.

"Eliryn of Lirin's Edge. The Last Dragonrider. The Flame has spoken."

The tendril vanished.

And silence crushed the square.

Eliryn collapsed to her knees, gasping.

Not in weakness.

In awe.

Her skin still shimmered faintly, her runes etched brighter than they'd ever been. Her eyes, now dimming, still held that inner light—like the embers of something divine.

Garic turned toward her, stunned into speechlessness.

Vraxxis whispered, "No."

The Flamekeeper spoke once more, softer now:

"The Flame has named its sovereign."

Eliryn bowed her head.

Not in surrender.

But in the terrible, unspoken understanding:

She was no longer her own.

Eliryn rose and took a step back, unsteady. Her hands trembled.

Vaeronth whispered in her mind.

Be still. Something is coming.

Then—

A horn. Sharp.

Another. Closer now. Urgent.

Shouting broke across the upper balconies. Movement surged at the gates. Somewhere below, a scream cut through the silence like a knife.

"Eliryn!"

Garic's voice. Sharp. Desperate.

"Stay with me!"

She turned, blindly, reaching. Her fingers grazed his for a heartbeat—a single heartbeat—

Then the world shattered.

The crowd broke.

A scream splintered the air.

She spun, too late, reaching for what was already gone. Garic's voice vanished into chaos. Bodies surged past her, slamming into her shoulders, her ribs, her hips.

Then someone struck her from behind.

Hard.

She fell off the platform.

The stone hit her knees first, then her ribs, then her head. Her breath fled her body. The weight of people storming past knocked into her, boots scraping her back, a heel clipping her cheek, another body crashing over her shoulder.

She curled in on herself, arms covering her head.

She forgot she had just been named sovereign.

She forgot she was a dragonrider.

She forgot she had ever been strong.

There was only instinct now—the instinct of survival, the desperate urge to make herself smaller than the chaos battering her.

She felt... helpless.

Vaeronth! Her mind screamed for him, panic clawing. *Vaeronth, I can't—I can't see—I can't think—I need you!*

I am here.

But his voice was thin, strained.

Her terror sharpened.

Why can't I feel you? Why do you feel so far away?

A pause. Weighted.

Something cloaks you.

She shook her head frantically. "No! Not now—"

You must anchor. Eliryn—listen to me—something is clouding our bond. I—cannot see you.

She couldn't breathe.

She pressed her forehead to the cold stone. All her fear from the trials, from the attack, from the endless dark—none of it compared to this. This hollowing emptiness clouding her mind.

A body collided with her, driving her sideways. She choked on a cry as another boot kicked her ribs, whether by accident or design she didn't know.

Then another scream. Closer. The Flame still burned at the dais and she could feel a spark of it inside her—but she could not see.

She couldn't move.

I can't do this, Vaeronth. I can't do this blind.

You are not blind. His voice frayed. *You are a Dragonrider and you will use my eyes.*

But she couldn't remember how to clear her mind and focus enough to do that.

"Eliryn!"

Garic?

She forced her battered body up, scrambling to her knees—reaching, searching for the voice.

Hands closed on her.

Rough. Familiar.

"I've got you."

She gasped. "Garic?"

But the grip was wrong.

Her breath faltered.

"Come on." The voice, controlled. Too controlled.

She froze.

"Move!" the voice barked, dragging her upright. Her ribs flared in pain, her shoulder burned where she'd been kicked. She didn't resist. Couldn't.

"Where are you taking me?" She stumbled, dragged forward.

"To safety."

"Who—?"

A heartbeat.

Then, it clicked.

"Malric."

She sagged.

He was here. Somehow, impossibly, he was here.

The fear loosened in her throat like a knot undone. Malric had found her. Malric was guiding her.

Vaeronth's voice strained like a cracking rope.

No—!

But she didn't hear it.

She let Malric pull her through the corridor, deeper into the castle's belly, steps staggering, mind clouded.

She didn't question that his grip was too tight.

She didn't question why Vaeronth felt so far.

Because in this moment, surrounded by terror, bruised and blind and forgotten even by her own strength—

Malric felt like a lifeline.

And she would gladly follow him into the dark.

His grip faltered, fingers loosening on her wrist but not releasing.

"Malric," her voice sounded heavy even to her own ears. "Do you know what's happening?"

"No," he said, quietly. "This is unprecedented."

A heartbeat passed. She should've asked more. Should've demanded answers. But her limbs were shaking and Vaeronth still couldn't see clearly, his vision fogged like a window after a storm. Magic pressed on them both, a heavy pull that seemed to drain her energy.

And in this moment, alone, hunted, and blind, she didn't have the strength to doubt Malric.

She nodded once, slow. "Then lead me."

Malric didn't speak again.

He just took her hand, gently now, and led her deeper into the belly of the castle.

INTERLUDE 11: VRAXXIS

"Few survive the moment their illusions are burned away." —Anonymous, fragment recovered from the Ashen Library

Vraxxis of Whitvale stood beneath the high spires of the flame-forged dais with his chin lifted, every thread of his robes tailored to catch the wind just so. Still. Poised. Perfect.

He had already won.

Or so he'd been promised.

The Trials had unfolded exactly as King Thalen, his mentor, had said they would. Wilderness, combat, judgment. All designed. The old rules were real, yes, but enforcement was malleable in the right hands.

And Thalen's hands had never trembled.

"The Flame may choose," he'd told Vraxxis months ago, voice quiet as coals. "But fire bends when it knows where to burn. You were made for this."

Vraxxis had believed him. How could he not? Thalen had given him *everything*—access, names, secrets about the trials no other chosen knew. Even whispers of the growing unrest in the lower guard ranks.

The death of Silas had stirred something. Too loyal, too loved. And then there was the little dragonrider, always at his side.

"There are embers rising," Thalen had warned. "Some of the Royal Guard believe my time should end when the Flame names its next heir. They mistake ritual for weakness. They see only opportunity."

Vraxxis had assumed it would amount to nothing. The guard was fractured, but too cautious to move.

The Flamekeeper raised her hands.

Vraxxis inhaled, slow and measured. He closed his eyes, awaiting the touch of the Flame.

The crowd fell still.

And then—

"Eliryn of Lirin's Edge. The Last Dragonrider. The Flame has spoken. It chooses you."

The words rang out like a death knell.

Vraxxis blinked, waiting for the correction. For another name. His name.

None came.

The Flame vanished. The Rite was complete. It was over in what felt like mere seconds.

And *she* stood crowned in fire.

This was not the plan.

Eliryn was meant to fall long before this—quietly, bloody, with her guard at her side. Forgotten by the time the Rite even happened.

A blind girl with no political house, no ambition. A relic.

But now—

The guards surged. Screams sounded and then came the horns.

The court broke open like a wound.

Vraxxis didn't move. Didn't flinch. Not even as chaos erupted around him.

Because he understood now.

This wasn't about the Flame's choice. It was about Thalen.

The faction among the guard—they weren't rebelling against the trials. They were making their move against the throne.

They believed this was the only moment to strike.

When power transferred.

When the old rule could be ended in ceremony *and* blood.

And suddenly... Eliryn didn't seem like such an innocent anymore.

She'd been close with Silas. Too close. Loyal to the end.

Had she known about the unrest? Had she played meek while the knives gathered?

Vraxxis' gaze snapped to her across the chaos, her pathetic form bowed on the ground amongst the throngs of people.

Then a shadow moved. Fast. Clean.

He knew the stride.

Malric.

The king's dagger. His shadow. His hand in the dark.

Malric reached Eliryn just when it looked like she would be trampled. He caught her in his arms like it had been rehearsed.

For one breath, Vraxxis hesitated.

Had Thalen known? Had this been part of his plan after all?

No...

No. If Eliryn had been truly dangerous, Malric wouldn't be catching her, he'd be cutting her down.

Vraxxis' jaw slackened. His breath steadied.

Whatever this rebellion was, whatever Eliryn may or may not have known, Thalen was already handling it. Personally. Precisely.

"You are the only one who understands what the realm truly needs," Thalen had said.

And Vraxxis still believed him.

Let the Flame choose who it liked. Let the guards rage. Let the relic girl play at prophecy.

She had been chosen only seconds ago and already she was walking straight into her demise.

Malric would see it done.

Thalen would see it justified.

Vraxxis turned, his cloak catching the rising smoke, and slipped into the chaos like it had never touched him at all.

A loyal blade.

A future king.

Still very much in control.

Chapter 29: The Weight of Flame

"In times of unrest, a crown is not a symbol of honor but a mark upon the hunted." —Anonymous, Scribe of the Crown

Eliryn moved through the castle like a phantom in someone else's dream.

Malric's hand remained around hers; not tight, not forceful, but impossibly steady. His footsteps were swift but never hurried. As if he knew exactly how much time they had before something worse caught up to them.

She tried to see.

Tried to focus.

Vaeronth's vision was still with her, tethered like a second heartbeat, but it was hazy, streaked with smoke and slashed with shifting shadows. Every now and then, an image would sharpen: the glint of blood on polished stone, the flash of movement down the hall as they passed, a banner torn in half and dragged across the floor.

But mostly it was fog. Panic. The dragon's perception blurred by chaos and magic.

I can't—she thought. *I can't make sense of it.*

Try, Vaeronth whispered, and there was strain in him too. *Breathe. Let me in deeper.*

She sucked in air. The scent of iron and ash scraped her throat.

"I don't know where we are," she murmured aloud. "I don't know what's happening."

"You don't need to," Malric said. His voice was low, almost gentle. "Only that I'll get you somewhere safe."

She wanted to argue. To ask who had sent him, who he truly served, if he was a part of the chaos they had just escaped. But her legs were unsteady, her vision still broken, and every step behind him felt like the only thing keeping her upright. The echo of the crowd was distant now, replaced by the sound of doors slamming shut, armored boots clanging, the hiss of fire where it shouldn't be.

This was not just an uprising.

This was a *purge.*

A memory broke through: the Flame twisting toward her chest, naming her. That impossible heat that hadn't burned, hadn't hurt, but still felt like she was being marked somehow.

Why me?

She stumbled. Malric caught her elbow before she could fall.

"Down here," he said.

She followed him through a narrow servant's corridor, the walls sweating with old steam. There was no light, only what Vaeronth could see, shapes flickering in and out of clarity like reflections on water. The dragon was struggling. The bond fraying under pressure neither of them understood.

We are not alone, Vaeronth growled suddenly. *Behind us.*

Eliryn twisted her head. "Someone's coming."

"We're nearly there," he said. "Don't stop."

She didn't.

But with every step, the weight of the Flame's choosing pressed heavier on her chest. Not pride. Not even awe. Just *dread.*

She definitely didn't want the throne or the responsibility that came with it.

The corridor narrowed.

Their footsteps echoed differently here—duller, swallowed by stone. Eliryn's fingers skimmed the wall to her right, half for balance, half for orientation.

Vaeronth's vision was like glass covered in dew: fractured, shifting, nothing certain.

"Why now?" she asked, breath hitching. "Why would they attack during the Rite?"

Malric didn't answer immediately. His grip on her hand stayed firm, guiding her down the sloping corridor, but his pace slowed.

"There were whispers," he said finally. "Guards moving in ways they shouldn't. Conversations that cut off too quickly. A few names passed between trusted ears. But nothing concrete."

"And no one acted?" Her voice edged toward disbelief.

"Rumors alone aren't enough to accuse the crown's own," he said. "Not without proof. And no one thought they would be bold or mad enough to strike during the Rite itself."

Eliryn swallowed. She could still feel the heat of the sacred Flame against her chest, phantom-like as it lingered. "They timed it to the choosing," she said. "Didn't they."

"Yes," Malric said quietly. "They knew this would be the moment of greatest focus. The court exposed. The heirs gathered. The people watching."

"So it's not just rebellion," she murmured. "It's spectacle."

"They want the realm to see the collapse," he said. "To believe no power, not even the Flame, can keep them safe."

Eliryn stopped moving.

Malric turned back, the corridor narrow enough that his shadow brushed against hers. Her breathing was shallow. She still couldn't see, could barely sense where the ground met her feet. Vaeronth's vision was scattered, like trying to track stars through a broken mirror.

"So why help me?" she asked. "If the throne is crumbling, if the crown is a target, why not let me fall with it?"

He said, softly, almost as if to himself, "I didn't want you to be part of the spectacle."

She blinked. "What?"

He stopped walking. Not abruptly. Just enough to send a ripple of unease through her spine.

"You were always meant to be chosen," he said. "That much of the prophecy was clear."

Eliryn's mouth went dry.

Malric's tone had changed, still smooth, still calm, but no longer protective. Not quite. There was something behind it now. Something heavier.

"I watched you in the trials," he continued. "More than I should have. I admired you. The way you carried yourself even when you were losing your sight. The way you emerged from the first trial, confident in your bond and your dragon... it was like something out of an old song. Then when I saw you out past the orchards, your hair flowing freely... I thought you looked like a myth."

She shifted a step back.

"Malric," she said slowly. "Why are you talking like this?"

"I don't want this to be cruel," he said, almost tender. "Not like it was ordered to be. A death on the dais? Public? I didn't want that for you."

Something cold slid along Eliryn's spine.

"Eliryn."

His voice changed. Softer now. Careful.

"I watched you on that dais."

Her pulse spiked.

"I saw you step forward in that silk—your skin marked like scripture, your dragonmarks glowing and for a moment..."

She dared to whisper: "For a moment?"

"I didn't want to do it."

She faltered. "Do what?"

Malric turned, slowly. The corridor was so narrow she could feel his breath now.

"Kill you."

Her heart cracked in her chest.

"I've known for since the beginning," he said, voice low. Almost tender. "Thalen told me long before the trials began. You're part of the prophecy. The last dragonrider. The one the Flame marked."

"You couldn't know," she rasped.

"I know everything," Malric said softly. "Thalen showed me. Told me what you'd become. That the sheer weight of your power would eventually break you."

She shook her head, body trembling. "I'm not—I'm not dangerous."

"You are," he said simply. "Not yet. But soon."

She tried to step back. His hand slid to her wrist. Not brutal. Just... final.

"I didn't want this," he whispered. "When he gave the order, I tried to resist. But then I watched you. I listened to you."

"Malric," she pleaded.

"And I realized: this would be a mercy."

Tears pricked her eyes.

"I could make it gentle. Not a public execution. Not some stranger's blade. But me. Someone who..." His voice cracked. "Someone who cared."

"You're not making sense."

"I am," he insisted, pleading now. "I didn't fall in love with you, Eliryn. Maybe I could have. But I fell in love with the idea of sparing you."

She froze.

"I watched you on that stage, and I knew I couldn't let you live long enough to break."

His hand cradled her face, thumb stroking her cheek like a lover's caress.

"I can end it before you suffer. Before the Flame tears your mind apart. Before your power bleeds you dry."

Her voice cracked like glass: "You're wrong."

"I'm merciful."

She shook her head, but he leaned in close, forehead almost touching hers.

"You should thank me, Eliryn. No one else would've cared enough to do this quietly."

Vaeronth roared in her mind: *RUN*

But Malric's voice was the one she heard, steady as a dagger poised at her throat.

"I'll make it painless."

And his next words shattered her:

"This is the kindest thing I've ever done."

Because in his mind, he wasn't betraying her.

He was saving her.

Vaeronth...

His voice cut through like steel: *He has a blade. It's drawn. You need to listen to me. You are not safe.*

She heard it now—the sound she'd missed before. Steel sliding against leather. Breath whispering over a blade's edge.

"I can make it quick," Malric murmured, and gods, he almost sounded tender. "If you stay still."

Her breath fractured. "What are you saying?"

"I'm saying," he breathed, "that the Rite was never meant to end with a dragonrider crowned. You were never meant to survive. You're prophecy made flesh, Eliryn. A prophecy that needs to be corrected."

A step back. Then two.

Her hand scraped the stone wall.

Vaeronth! she cried. *Please—*

Focus, he snapped. *You are not blind. Not anymore. Trust me. Hold still—let me show you.*

Eliryn gasped. And then—clarity. A sudden burst of stolen vision as Vaeronth forced his senses through her failing mind. The world came into burning focus: everything painted in blue flame and edged in terror, but clear.

And there he was.

Malric.

Only a pace away.

Blade drawn. Breath steady.

Face carved in grief that felt practiced.

He moved.

So did she.

Not fast enough.

His knife sliced low instead of high. The blade bit deep—through the silk of her dress, through skin, through muscle.

A brutal, wet sound.

Her body folded.

The pain was instant and total. A sharp, burning line just beneath her ribs. She couldn't tell if it was shallow or mortal. Couldn't tell anything past the agony.

Her knees hit the stone. She dropped.

One hand clutched the wound, hot blood spilling between her fingers. Her other hand scrabbled uselessly against the wall behind her.

Her lungs wouldn't work.

She looked up.

Malric just watched her.

Not panicked.

Not remorseful.

Just... waiting.

Her voice cracked like glass. "Why...?"

And that was what broke her.

Not the blade.

The betrayal.

Malric, who had guarded her. Spoken softly to her. Brushed her hair from her face.

Malric, who she'd thought understood what it meant to experience loss and a destiny not entirely his own.

She had trusted him.

Now he watched her bleed.

"I would've made it quick," he said softly. Like he still meant it. "I didn't want you to have to feel it."

Her entire body shuddered.

Her thoughts splintered.

Vaeronth, she begged. *I can't—I can't do this. I can't fight back.*

Do not give up, he growled. *I see him. I see everything. You need to be brave.*

Eliryn clenched her jaw. Swallowed the scream ripping up her throat. Her body burned. Her vision was nothing but smoke and dragon-sight and pain.

But she stood.

Somehow.

Bit by shaking bit.

She forced her body upright, blood sliding down her thigh.

Malric's expression didn't change.

That broke her more.

He stepped forward.

Eliryn ran.

Not with grace.

Not with strategy.

She just ran.

Staggering, pressing her hand tight to her ribs, stumbling into shadows made of blue fire and fear. She didn't look back.

She didn't need to.

She could hear him following.

And every echo of his footsteps behind her whispered the same thing:

Mercy.

Mercy.

Mercy.

Until she realized—he wasn't chasing to kill her.

Not yet.

He was waiting to catch her when she collapsed.

Because in his mind, she was already dead.

CHAPTER 30: NEW HEIGHTS

"All crowns are forged in the hour before collapse, when the hand that grasps them trembles most." —Fragment from the Lost Annals of the Sixth Reign

She was going to die.

Eliryn staggered, one hand clamped against her side where Malric's blade had opened her like a seam. Blood—warm and slick—soaked down her ribs, her thin dress clinging wet to her skin. Every breath felt serrated, her lungs scraping against the wound as she stumbled forward. Her legs buckled, and she collapsed hard to one knee, gasping.

Malric's voice echoed, far too calm for what he'd done.

"I didn't want you to be part of the spectacle."

Her stomach lurched at the words. The betrayal still hadn't anchored. She felt like she was hearing it all underwater—his quiet admiration, the gentle touches, the whispered comfort she'd clung to like sunlight in a locked room. All of it. Lies.

And then—the blade.

A flash of steel. The tearing heat. And now the blood, her blood, hot between her fingers.

Vaeronth's voice slammed through her skull like a thunderclap.

He moves again. Blade still drawn. Get up, Eliryn. Now.

She tried.

The world tilted.

Bootsteps hammered stone—closer, faster. Then—

"Eliryn!"

Garic's voice. Shattered. Terrified.

She turned her head, vision swimming, just as his silhouette burst into the corridor. Through Vaeronth's blurred and flickering sight, she saw his gaze drop to her crumpled form—then snap to Malric stalking toward her. The moment Garic saw the blood on Malric's blade, everything in him changed.

He didn't ask. He didn't hesitate.

"Get away from her!"

Steel rasped free. A sword. Gods, where had he gotten it?

Garic placed himself between her and death, his blade flashing up, his body shielding hers without a moment's thought. His voice cracked—not from fear, but fury.

"You bleed her and expect to walk away?"

Eliryn's throat caught. He was facing down Malric with no armor, no advantage, just raw loyalty and rage.

"Eliryn," Garic snapped, never taking his eyes off Malric. "Go. Now."

Malric shifted, his blade glinting. Calm. Calculated.

And Garic's voice—steady now, resolute—cut through the air like an oath forged in iron.

"Run, Dragonrider."

Her pulse fractured. The words hit her harder than the wound.

Vaeronth surged inside her mind. *Go. He's buying your life with his own.*

"I can't just—"

You can. You must.

The weight of it broke her.

She staggered upright. Her blood smeared the stone as she stumbled forward. She heard metal clash behind her—Malric lunging, Garic's blade parrying. A grunt. A curse. Someone's breath hitched in pain.

She didn't look back.

She ran.

Every step shredded her. The pain in her side roared, hot and jagged, but she ran. Up stairs, around corners, through halls splintered by flame. Smoke burned her lungs. The world reeled and narrowed and blurred.

But she ran.

Then—wind.

She burst through an archway into open air. Smoke curled into the sky, streaked with ash. She swayed, her vision failing. The whole castle sprawled beneath her, writhing in chaos.

Vaeronth's voice tore through her mind like a battle cry.

I'm coming.

Her pendant seared against her skin as his presence surged outward. A shadow passed overhead—a shadow with wings.

And then—

Vaeronth landed.

He crashed down with the fury of a storm, wings slamming against the air, scales blazing black and gold. He was rage made flesh, fire given breath. His claws cracked the stone as he crouched low, his great eyes locking on hers.

Climb.

She didn't think.

She stumbled forward, collapsed against his foreleg, dragging herself upward by instinct more than strength. His scaled shoulder rose beneath her, warm and solid.

Hold on.

She wrapped her arms around the nearest ridge of his spine as he launched into the sky.

The ground fell away.

The castle—the screams, the blood, the betrayal—all dropped from her as Vaeronth's wings devoured the wind. The air howled past. Her fingers trembled. Blood smeared his scales. Her blood.

She was slipping.

Her strength—the fire inside her—ebbing with every heartbeat.

"Garic..." she rasped. "Why... Malric... why..."

Vaeronth's voice answered, steady as stone.

You will not die here. Not like this.

Tears burned her eyes.

"Vaeronth..."

You are Flame-chosen. Dragonbonded. MINE. I will not let you fall.

She pressed her face to his scales, her skin feverish, her breath thin. The clouds spun around her. The cold seeped in.

"Not yet..." she pleaded with herself.

Below them, the kingdom fractured into chaos. Smoke spiraled from the castle towers. Shadows moved like ants. She felt the weight of the Flame's choosing heavy in her chest—a burden she didn't ask for. A crown she'd never wanted. A prophecy fulfilled in the most horrific way.

And all she could think was: *I don't know how to survive this.*

She didn't know how far they had flown. Minutes. Miles. A lifetime. Behind them, the castle was a blot of stone and shadow. She could still see the flames rising from one tower. She could still feel Garic's command ringing in her chest.

Run, Dragonrider.

Was he still fighting? Was he alive? She didn't know. And the not-knowing crushed something deep inside her.

"He'll live," she murmured, like a spell cast into the sky. "He has to."

Vaeronth said nothing. He flew steady, wings slicing through cloud and silence.

Below them, the realm spread out; fractured, beautiful, unknown.

The Flame had chosen her.

But what if the crown fell?

What if her blood marked not the beginning of her reign, but the end of an era?

Eliryn closed her eyes. Her fingers curled weakly against Vaeronth's side.

I will not let you fall, the dragon said. *This isn't the end.*

And in that moment, with the sky around her and the world unraveling beneath, Eliryn did not feel victorious.

She felt like a question the gods hadn't finished answering.

Chapter 31: The Sky Remembers

"Even the wounded can rise above the ruins, if only to see what the earth forgets." —Dragonrider Chronicles

The sky opened around them, vast and silent.

Vaeronth flew higher than the clouds now, wings cleaving through the last bands of molten gold as if he could outrun the horizon itself. The wind roared past Eliryn's ears, but it couldn't drown the sound of her own breathing—ragged, thin, and wet with blood.

She lay flat against him, pressed low along the ridged sweep of his spine, her trembling fingers curled tight into the warm seams between his scales.

Do not sleep, Vaeronth warned softly, a pulse of fire low in her mind. His voice sounded strained now, almost afraid. *I will carry you, but you must not sleep.*

"I'm not," she rasped, though her words felt like lies even to herself. Every muscle in her body ached. Her side burned where Malric's blade had struck, her blood still a slow, sticky warmth along her ribs. Her limbs felt far away now. Numb. Like her body was no longer hers.

She should have died back there.

By Malric's hand.

Instead, she was here.

Flying.

Her lashes fluttered, memory bleeding through her exhaustion: her mother's voice, her mother's steady hands braiding her hair on that final morning. Lavender oil. A calmness that Eliryn hadn't understood until it was too late.

If she could see me now...

"She would never believe this," Eliryn whispered, her voice thread-thin.

No, Vaeronth agreed. *But she would be proud.*

Eliryn's hands shook harder. She pressed them more firmly against her wound. But the pain only sharpened.

Beneath her, Vaeronth's body tensed. His power burned hot against her skin, but even his strength felt like it was waning. She could feel the distance he was forcing into his mind—the fear he was hiding. She was dying, and he knew it.

And yet he carried her anyway.

She thought of Malric, and bile rose in her throat. His voice haunted her more than his blade.

"I didn't want to hurt you. This is the kindest thing I've ever done."

She had believed him. Trusted him. And when her guard was down, when her heart was bare, he'd tried to carve her open like a ritual sacrifice.

Garic had saved her.

Not prophecy. Not destiny. Not even her dragon.

Garic.

It should have been him, she thought, her pulse flickering weakly. It should've been Garic the Flame chose. He would have led without flinching. He would have survived without breaking.

The Flame chose wrong.

Vaeronth's answer came, soft as embers:

The Flame sees what mortals deny. You are not weak, Eliryn.

She said nothing. She didn't believe him. Couldn't.

Below them, the world blurred into forest and fog, the castle and its ruin reduced to a fading bruise against the earth.

And still Vaeronth flew.

Higher. Farther.

Eliryn's blood stained his scales. She could feel her grip slipping.

"I... can't," she whispered at last.

Vaeronth's voice curled around her like a promise.

Then let me carry you. I will not let you fall.

She sagged forward, her cheek pressed to the smooth curve of his shoulder. Her eyes slid shut—not from sleep, but surrender.

And then, through the haze, something flickered.

Her mother's silhouette.

She stood at the edge of the horizon, her form carved from shadow and sunlight, arms crossed, her expression unreadable.

"I'm still here," Eliryn breathed. It was not a vow. Not a plea.

Just a truth.

And as night closed over them, Vaeronth whispered back:

Then so is hope.

PROPHECY MADE HER CHOSEN. VENGEANCE WILL MAKE HER QUEEN.

She fled the citadel on dragonback, blood in her wake
and shadows at her heels.
But the prophecy did not end—it deepened.
Magic long broken calls for restoration,
and creatures long forgotten rise from silence to demand their due.
The gods are watching. The crown is waiting.
And Eliryn and Vaeronth stand where ruin and rebirth
entwine—
· heralds of a rising magic,
and the war it was destined to unleash.

Coming Winter 2025:
THE SILENT VOW
Book Two of *The Sightless Prophecy Trilogy*
Find updates, teasers, and release info at:
@blacktoppublishing and **@sightlessprophecy**

ABOUT THE AUTHOR:

Jaimie L. Vermette grew up tucked against the edge of the Canadian border, where winter rewrote the world for months at a time and books were the only kind of warmth that lingered.

After earning multiple degrees she doesn't use and working in fields far from fiction, she finally decided to chase the dream she'd shelved for far too long.

The Shattered Rite is her debut novel and the first in *The Sightless Prophecy* trilogy—a dark, intimate fantasy of slow-burning obsession, quiet resistance, and the cost of survival.

She writes for the overthinkers, the ones who feel like they're a little too much... and for anyone who's ever fallen so deep into a fictional world, real life felt like the side quest.

And if you know her in real life... no you don't.